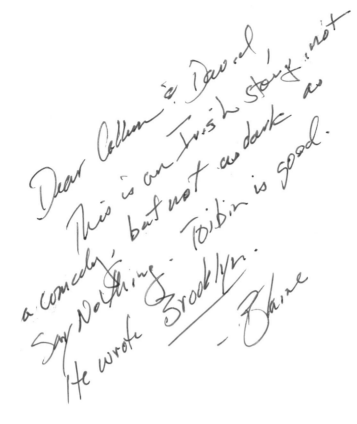

Dear Colleen & David,

This is an Irish story; not a comedy, but not as dark as Say Nothing. Tóibín is good. He wrote _Brooklyn_.

— Blaine

THE HEATHER BLAZING

ALSO BY COLM TÓIBÍN

The South

THE
HEATHER
BLAZING

COLM TÓIBÍN

VIKING

VIKING
Published by the Penguin Group
Penguin Books USA Inc.,
375 Hudson Street, New York, New York 10014, U.S.A.
Penguin Books Ltd, 27 Wrights Lane, London W8 5TZ, England
Penguin Books Australia Ltd, Ringwood, Victoria, Australia
Penguin Books Canada Ltd, 10 Alcorn Avenue, Toronto, Ontario, Canada M4V 3B2
Penguin Books (N.Z.) Ltd, 182-190 Wairau Road, Auckland 10, New Zealand

Penguin Books Ltd, Registered Offices: Harmondsworth, Middlesex, England

First American Edition
Published in 1993 by Viking Penguin, a division of Penguin Books USA Inc.

1 3 5 7 9 10 8 6 4 2

Acknowledgment is made to the Arts Council/An Chomhairle Ealaion for a bursary to assist in
the writing of this book, and to the Tyrone Guthrie Centre at Annaghmakerrig in Ireland,
where some of it was written.

LIBRARY OF CONGRESS CATALOGING IN PUBLICATION DATA
Tóibín, Colm
The heather blazing/Colm Tóibín
p. cm.
ISBN 0-670-84789-5
I. Title
PR6070.O455H4 1993
823'.914—dc20
92-50350

Printed in the United States of America

For Brendan, Nuala, Bairbre
and Niall

PART ONE

CHAPTER ONE

E AMON REDMOND stood at the window looking down at the river which was deep brown after days of rain. He watched the colour, the mixture of mud and water, and the small currents and pockets of movement within the flow. It was a Friday morning at the end of July; the traffic was heavy on the quays. Later, when the court had finished its sitting he would come back and look out once more at the watery grey light over the houses across the river and wait for the stillness, when the cars and lorries had disappeared and Dublin was quiet.

He relished that walk through the Four Courts when the building was almost closed and everyone had gone and his car was the last in the judges' car park, that walk along the top corridor and down the centre stairway; old stone, old wood, old echoes. He loved the privacy of it; his solitary presence in the vast public building whose function was over and done with for the day.

Years back he would stop for a moment, as he had been instructed to do, and examine his car before he opened the door. Even though the car park was guarded, it would be easy to pack explosives underneath; often as he turned the ignition he was conscious that in one second the whole car could go, a ball of flame. He laughed to himself at the phrase as he stood at the window. A ball of flame. Now things were safer; things were calm in the south.

He went over to his desk and sifted through his papers to make sure that everything was in order for the court. He noticed, as he flicked through the pages of his judgment, that the handwriting, especially when he wrote something quickly, had become exactly the same as his father's, a set of round squiggles, indecipherable to most others.

He gathered the papers together when his tipstaff told him that it was time.

'I'm ready when you are,' he said as though the tipstaff were the one in charge. He put on his robe and his wig, pushing back some wisps of hair before walking out into the broad light of the corridor.

He had learned over the years not to look at anyone as he walked from his rooms to the court, not to offer greetings to a colleague, or nod at a barrister. He kept his eyes fixed on a point in the distance. He walked slowly, with determination. Downstairs, the Round Hall was full, like an old-fashioned marketplace. The corridors were busy as he walked towards the ante-chamber to his court.

This was the last day of term, he would have to deal with urgent business before getting down to read the judgment he had been working on for several months. He looked again through the pages, which had been cleanly typed by a court secretary and then covered by emendations. All the references to previous judgments were underlined, with the dates they had appeared in the Irish Reports in parentheses. This judgment, too, would appear in the Irish Reports and would be cited when the rights of the citizen to state services were being discussed in the future, such as the right to attend a hospital, the right to attend a school, or, in this case, the right to full-time and comprehensive psychiatric care.

He waited in the ante-room. It was still not time. He felt excited at the prospect of getting away. Soon, he would be twenty-five years on the bench and he remembered this last day's waiting more vividly than the humdrum days or the significant or difficult cases, this waiting on the last day of term, knowing that Carmel had everything packed and ready to go.

They spent each summer recess on the coast, close to where they had been born, where they were known. He had been brought there as a baby during the first summer after his mother died. He had spent each subsequent summer there as a child with his father. He thought about it now in the minutes before the court sitting.

There was a hush when he came into the courtroom and sat down on the bench. He put his papers in order. The court was full, and it was clear from the number of barristers in the front rows that there was a queue for injunctions and early hearings. He felt a sharp pain in the back of his head and a buzzing sound came into his ears. He closed his eyes until it passed, holding the pages of the typescript between his finger and thumb. The heating in the court had been turned up too high; already the atmosphere was stuffy. He looked around, waiting for everyone to settle. There were too many people standing at the back, some of them blocking the door. He instructed the clerk to tell them to come forward.

One barrister in the front row was already on his feet.

'My lord,' he said, 'I wish to ask this court to dispose of a matter which is of the utmost urgency . . .'

'Is it of such urgency that it cannot wait?' he asked him. There was a snort of laughter from the barristers at the front.

'Yes, my lord.'

He listened for a while to the complex story of a company being wound up and its assets distributed. After a time he interrupted to ask if the man would be satisfied with an injunction freezing the assets until the first vacation sitting. He then noticed a barrister from the other side seeking his attention.

'There's no need for you to address the court, you can spare your client much expense if you tell me that you will agree to have the assets frozen.'

The barrister, whom he recognized as one of the old

Fine Gael establishment, continued to speak, explaining his client's case.

'I must interrupt you to ask if you have been listening to me. Have you been listening to me?'

'Yes, my lord.'

'Then there is no need for you to explain the case to me. We simply want to know if you will accept the court freezing your client's assets, until the court resumes.'

'My lord, I wish to say—'

'Wish or no wish, will you accept it or not?'

'Yes, my lord, on condition that we can have an early hearing.'

'The conditions are for me to impose. Do you understand? I decide on the conditions.'

'We would be grateful for an early hearing, my lord.'

'I shall look forward to seeing you as soon as possible,' he said. 'In fact, I don't know if I can wait.' Again, there was laughter from the front benches.

He listened to several other barristers before reading his judgment; he came to an agreement with each one about early hearings. The barristers left as soon as their business was settled. He began to read.

He cited the facts of the case: the handicapped child who needed constant care and would need such care, in the view of the doctors, for the rest of his life. As far as doctors could judge, his lifespan would be normal. The father was employed and the mother was a housewife with six other children. He tried to set the case out clearly, factually, coldly. He summarized the arguments which the lawyers for the family had made, and then he came to the case for the hospital which wanted to release the child. He had taken notes during the long hearing, but he had tried also to listen carefully to each side and write a summary of the deliberations when he adjourned the court each day.

He began now to summarize the legal precedent governing the state's duties and the individual's rights. There was still a group of barristers standing at the door, adding, he thought when he looked up from his judgment, to the clammy atmosphere of the court. He cleared his throat for a moment and then continued. He cited a number of American cases which had come up in the course of the hearing. He went on to explain that there was nothing in the Constitution which either stated or implied that the citizen had an inalienable right to free hospital treatment. The state's functions and responsibilities had to cease at a certain point; the state had freedoms and rights as well as the citizen.

As he read he became even more certain of the rightness of his judgment, and began to see as well that it might be important in the future as a lucid and direct analysis of the limits to the duties of the state. It had taken him several months, the long afternoons of the spring and early summer in his chambers and then later in his study in Ranelagh, thinking through the implications of articles in the Constitution, the meaning of phrases and the significance which earlier judgments had given to these phrases. He looked through judgments of the American Supreme Court and the House of Lords. He wrote it all down, slowly and logically, working each paragraph over and over, erasing, re-checking and re-writing. Carmel told him that he needed a computer and his son Donal told him the same, but he worked on his judgment in the same way as he had always worked. He would find that a single sentence by necessity expanded into a page of careful analysis; then sometimes a page would have to be re-written and its contents would form the basis for several pages, or give rise to further thought, further erasures and consultation. Or, in the light of early morning, when he read over his work, the argument would seem abstruse, the points made would appear irrelevant, the style too awkward or too dense. He would take the page and throw it in a ball across his office. He would smile then, for that was what his father had always done

7

with paper when he was writing, absent-mindedly rolling a sheet into a crumpled ball and throwing it across the room. Years ago in the morning, when he came down and drew back the curtains, he would find these small balls of paper all over the room.

He realized as he wrote the judgment what it meant: the hospital would be able to discharge the child, and the parents would be left with the responsibility of looking after a handicapped son. He added the proviso to his judgment that the Health Board should ensure, in every possible way, that the child's welfare be secured once he was discharged from the hospital. He noted the state's account of the social services which the parents would have available to them, and he said that his judgment was conditional upon those services remaining at the parents' disposal.

When he finished the judgment he saw that counsel for the state and for the hospital were already on their feet, looking for costs. He consulted with counsel for the plaintiff who said that he wanted the court to make no order regarding costs. He caught the mother's eye, he remembered her giving evidence. She would have little chance if she appealed to the Supreme Court, he felt. He decided to put a stay on costs, and he told the lawyers that he would consider the matter in the new term. One of the lawyers for the hospital said that his client would rather have the matter decided now.

'I think you mean that your client would rather have the matter decided in his favour now but, as I've said, I'll decide in the new term.'

WHEN he was back in his chambers he telephoned Carmel.

'I have everything ready,' she said.

'It will take me a while. I'll see you as soon as I can,' he replied.

He put the receiver down and went again to the window. He watched the small, soft delineations between layers of cloud over the opposite buildings, the strange, pale glow through the film of mist and haze. Suddenly, he had no desire to go. He wanted to stand at the window and clear his mind of the day, without the pressure of the journey south to Cush on the Wexford coast.

The murky heat of the day would settle now into a warm evening in Cush, the moths flitting against the lightshades, and the beam from the lighthouse at Tuskar Rock, powerful in the dense night, swirling around in the dark.

He went back to his desk and thought about it: the short strand at the bottom of the cliff, the red marl clay, the slow curve of the coastline going south to Ballyconnigar, Bally-valoo, Curracloe, Raven's Point and beyond them to the sloblands and Wexford town.

He stood up and wondered if he had anything more to do; his desk was untidy, but he could leave it like that. He was free to go now; he went over to the bookcases to see if there was anything he should take with him. He idled there, taking down a few books, flicking through them and then putting them back again. He returned to the window and looked at the traffic, which was still heavy on the quays, but he decided he would drive home now, pack up the car and set out.

He drove along Christchurch Place and turned right into Werbergh Street. It had begun to rain, although the day was still bright and warm. He hated days like this, when you could never tell whether the rain would come or not, but this, in the end, was what he remembered most about Cush: watching the sky over the sea, searching for a sign that it would brighten up, sitting there in the long after-noons as shower followed shower.

He had known the house all his life: the Cullens had lived there until the Land Commission gave them a better holding outside Enniscorthy. Himself and his father had gone there as paying guests every summer, and each of the daughters had been what he imagined his mother would have been had she not died when he was born. He remembered each of their faces smiling at him, the wide sweep of their summer dresses as they picked him up, each of them different in their colouring and hairstyle, in the lives they went on to live. In his memory, they remained full of warmth, he could not remember them being serious or cross.

He turned off Sandford Road and pulled up outside the house. He left the keys in the ignition as he went in. The rain had stopped now and the sun was out. He found Carmel sitting in the conservatory at the back of the house with the door open on to the garden. She was wearing a summer dress.

'What's wrong?' he asked. She said nothing, but held his look. Her expression was rigid, frozen.

'Are you all right?' he asked.

'I was asleep,' she said. 'I woke when you rang, and then I was so tired I fell asleep again. It must be the summer weather, it's very heavy.'

'Do you feel all right?'

'I feel tired, that's all. Sometimes I hate packing and moving. I dread it. I don't know why.' She put her hand to her head, as though she was in pain. He went to her and put his arms around her.

'Maybe we could take some of the plants down with us. Will there be room for them?' she asked quietly.

'I'll try and find space for them,' he said.

'Sometimes it looks so bare down there, as though the house wasn't ours at all, as though it belonged to someone else.'

He began to pack the cars with bags and boxes, and then he carried out her flowering plants and her sweet-smelling lilies and placed them carefully and gently in the boot and the space behind the front seats of the car. 'One quick jolt and they'll be ruined,' he said and smiled.

'Oh, drive carefully, please,' she said. It had begun to rain and a wind rustled through the bushes in the garden. He found an umbrella to give her shelter as they went out to the car, closing the door behind them.

He drove away from the house. They did not speak until they were beyond Shankill.

'There's something I have to tell you,' she said. 'I was going to tell you this morning, but you were too preoccupied. Niamh came over yesterday to say that she's pregnant. She thought that we had noticed on Sunday when she came for dinner, but I didn't notice anyway. Did you notice?'

He did not reply. He looked straight ahead as he drove. Niamh was their only daughter.

'It was the last thing I thought of,' Carmel went on. 'She sounded very cool, but I think she was dreading having to tell me. How could she be so foolish! I couldn't sleep last night thinking about it. I rang Donal but he didn't know either. You'd think she would have told her brother.'

Carmel did not speak again until later when they stopped at the traffic lights in Arklow. The atmosphere in the car was tense with their silence.

'I asked her who the father was. I didn't even know she had a boyfriend. She said she didn't want to talk about the father.'

When he had driven through the town she spoke again.

'She went to England to have an abortion, and she couldn't face it. She was in the hospital and everything; she had paid her money. I told her that we'd do what we could for her, I told her that I was pro-life all the way. I felt so sorry for her. Imagine Niamh having an abortion. So she's going to have the baby and she's going to keep it. Eamon, I wrote her a cheque. But it's a terrible thing to happen, isn't it?'

'When's it due?'

'November,' she said. 'I can't think how I didn't notice.'

He turned left at Gorey and took the road south towards Blackwater.

'Well, what do you think?' she asked.

'It doesn't matter what I think.'

'It's so hard to talk to you sometimes,' she said.

HE parked the car in the lane and opened the side gate into the garden, letting Carmel go in ahead of him. He had the key. The house had been aired; there was a fire burning in the living room, which their neighbour had lit for them, but there was still a musty smell. Carmel shivered and went over to sit by the window. Eamon carried in the first of the plants and put them in the glass porch at the front. The damp smell had always been in the house, he thought, no amount of air or heat would ever get rid of it fully. And there was another smell too which he remembered now: a smell of summer dresses, a female smell. The women who had taken care of him here. He could almost smell them now, vague hints of their presence, their strong lives, their voices which had been heard in this house for so many years.

The nettles had come back into the garden, despite the weedkiller which had been put down in the spring. The nettles seemed taller than ever this year. He would get one of the Carrolls to put the front garden right. Then there would be a new smell of cropped grass, fresh and sweet with a hint of dampness.

He carried the suitcases and boxes in from the car. By now, Carmel had placed her plants all over the house and was in the kitchen. He went over and smelled the lilies which she had put in the porch. He set up the record player and placed the two speakers at opposite ends of the room. He plugged it in, put on a record and turned the sound up and listened to the music as he unpacked the cases and cleared out the car.

They were close to the soft edge of the cliff, the damp, marly soil which was eaten away each year. He listened for the sound of the sea, but heard nothing except the rooks in a nearby field and the sound of a tractor in the distance, and coming from the house the swells of the music. He rested against the windowsill and looked at the fading light, the dark clouds of evening over the sea. The grass was wet now with a heavy dew, but the air was still as though the day had been held back for a few moments while night approached. He heard Carmel moving in the front room. She wanted everything in its place, the house filled with their things, as soon as they arrived, and he stood up now and ventured in to help her.

CHAPTER TWO

CHILDHOOD. The voice teaching was still vivid in his mind, but he could remember nothing his father said in those early years. Nor could he remember walking from the primary school across to the secondary school except for the bare, creaking stairway to the classroom where his father taught.

He drew on the blackboard with chalk – he remembered this clearly – until he was old enough to sit at the back and listen, or read, or look out of the window at the Turret Rocks and the Wexford Road. He drew maps of main roads and side roads, using different colour chalk; he drew squiggles and matchstick figures. Behind him, the drama of the classroom went on. Sometimes a cheer, a sound like 'Weee, wooo', followed by laughter went up from the boys in the class, but soon it would die down again and his father would resume. Sometimes he was bored, he couldn't wait for the bell to ring. One day he walked up to the top of the class and asked his father if it would be much longer and the class cheered. His father told him to go down and wait in the yard.

He learned to wait, to be quiet, to sit still. And when the schoolday was over they walked home together, the teacher whose wife had died and his son, to the empty house in the new estate up on the hill. A woman came every day, first Mrs Doyle and later Annie Farrell, and made the dinner in the middle of the day, then left them their tea on the kitchen table. His father had work to do, homework to correct, books to read, articles to write. Eamon went out to play, careful not to sit on the cold cement in case he got a cold, and not to get into fights. He was allowed to bring other boys into the house, but they had to play quietly. Often, when they left to go home and have their tea, he felt relieved. He had the house to himself again and could sit opposite his father and work at his lessons. He wondered at his father's handwriting, the strange, indecipherable script, he stared at each word and tried to tell the letters apart, but it was a mystery to him and he did not understand how anyone could read it.

On Wednesdays after tea they walked down to the offices of *The Enniscorthy Echo* to collect a copy of the paper, fresh from the printing presses. Once, a man tried to explain to him about printing, but it was the voice and the size of the printworks he remembered, the rattling noise of the machines and the small, thin pieces of metal with words written on them back to front.

His father's article appeared on an inside page. Scenes From Enniscorthy's Past by Michael Redmond, BA, B. Comm, the headline said, and sometimes there was a photograph of a face or an old part of the town such as the Duffrey or Templeshannon. Each week when they came home his father would cut the article out and paste it into a scrap book. He brought a cloth in from the kitchen to wipe away the paste which oozed from the sides of the newspaper when it was pressed down against the cardboard of the scrap book.

Eamon must have been eight then, or nine. The war was on. He sat in Father Rossiter's car at the top of the Shannon waiting for his father and the priest to finish talking to a grey-haired woman at the door of her house. Each time they seemed about to walk down the cement path towards the gate they started up again. Talking. He was allowed to go with them into some of the houses, but not others. They were giving out money and food vouchers from the St Vincent de Paul Society. There was a strange smell in some of the houses. He looked around to see if he could find what exactly made these houses so different from his own: so bare, and often cold as well.

Most of the men were in England; they were in the British Army or they were working in factories. In all of the visits he never saw a man in any of the houses. Some of the women were smiling and shy when they spoke, staring into the fire and leaving awkward silences until his father and the priest stood up to leave. Others were outspoken, full of words. 'Tis God's truth now, they would say. I'm not telling you a word of a lie. May God forgive me, Father. They had long stories to tell, and letters to search for and then find and offer to the visitors to read. There was one woman who cried, who broke down in front of them and rocked back and forth in her chair, as children his own age sat helplessly watching her, who were pale-faced and suspicious of the two men and the child who had come to the house to listen to their mother telling her story, her face suddenly red and blotched from crying.

IF they moved the car he would be able to see the town below, follow Rafter Street from the Market Square, along to Court Street and then John Street with its line of trees and then the Back Road, Lymington House, Parkton, Pearse Road and Parnell Avenue. Sometimes, the two men would talk for hours, lighting cigarettes and letting the car fill up with smoke and the smell of sulphur from the matches.

Sometimes they spoke in hushed voices, as though he, the boy in the back of the car, might listen to what they were saying and repeat it elsewhere. He tried to follow the conversation. Agreed, agreed, his father said, agreed. He repeated the word to himself until it lost all its meaning and became just a sound. They were silent in the front of the car. Now, he thought, if he concentrated enough, the priest would start up the engine. But once more nothing happened. Why did he not start it? What were the two men thinking about? They drew on their cigarettes without saying a word; both of them seemed to be thinking about something. He listened as they began to speak. They were talking about a woman, but he could make no sense of their conversation.

'Is Father Rossiter Fianna Fáil?' he asked when they came home.

'Priests can't join parties,' his father said.

Soon afterwards, there were more long silences in the car; Father Rossiter would drive them to the door and the two men would sit there discussing something for a while before falling into a long silence. His father began to go down town in the evenings to meetings and Mrs Doyle came over from Pearse Road to mind him. 'How lucky you are,' she told him, 'just to be here on your own. Think of all the houses which have ten or twelve in the family without enough clothes to wear, or even enough food. You're lucky too that you're living in this nice house and your father's a teacher, because otherwise in a few years,' she said, 'you'd have to go to England to get a job.'

She left the fire set for them every evening, or if it was very cold she would light it and leave the fireguard up against the hearth so that when they came in from school the back room would be warm. Eamon had to take charge of it, because his father sat at the table absorbed in what he was reading or writing. His father never noticed anything, even a spark on the rug which could, Mrs Doyle said, burn the whole place down. His father would let the fire go out. He would stand up and look at the embers and the ash and then point to the rug, laughing to himself. '*Rugadh é in Eireann*,' he would say, as he knelt down to try to get the fire going once more.

He remembered the Woodbines in Mrs Doyle's hand and the smoke in her voice, just as he remembered the long silences in the car, and the radio coming slowly alive with sound, and news of the war, and Mrs Doyle one evening telling him that his father was going to buy the Castle.

He waited until they were walking home from school together.

'Are we going to sell the house,' he asked, 'because I don't want to live anywhere else.'

'We're not going to sell anything,' his father said.

'The Castle is too big for us. Is there electricity in the Castle?'

'What has you going on about the Castle?'

'Mrs Doyle says that you're after buying it. It's too dark and old. No one goes near it.'

'But it's for a museum, it's not to live in,' his father said.

Soon, as he lay curled up on the back seat of Father Rossiter's car, he heard them talking about a museum. But the two men mumbled too much for him to catch any more of what they were saying. He asked them, but they continued talking and he had to ask again.

'It's for old things, historical things, like old books, old letters,' his father said. 'People can come and look at them on display.'

His father wrote an article about the Castle in *The Echo* which Eamon studied carefully. He tried to remember all the names and dates: the Normans, the English, Edmund Spenser, Cromwell, 1649, 1798, 1916. He asked his father questions about it and his father told him that the Castle was the headquarters of the English down all the years.

MR MCCURTIN next door showed him a map of the world. Mrs McCurtin said that he should be in his bed, but he waited up to hear the news on the wireless and he studied each country in Europe and down into Africa to see which was in German hands and which was still held by the Allies.

'He's too young to be telling him about the war,' Mrs McCurtin said. His father and Mr McCurtin drank bottles of stout and waited for the next bulletin, the sounds from the radio came in waves as though they were being carried in by the sea.

There was a big reading room in the Athenaeum with a fire blazing and a big table full of newspapers and magazines. There was a rule about silence and even if you wanted to whisper you had to go outside. One day he heard his father telling a man that they were going to buy the Castle from Dodo Roche.

'Does she live there?' he asked.

'When she was younger,' his father said.

'I thought that Spenser lived there.'

'That was in the fifteen hundreds. You're getting everything wrong.'

'Is Dodo Roche going to give you old things for the museum?'

His father had the big key to the door in the garden wall of the Castle, and other keys to doors and presses on a ring.

'Can I carry the big one?'

'Be careful with it or we'll all be locked out,' his father said.

They walked down to the Castle; it was a cold day and the men waiting at the gates were shivering and stamping their feet with the cold. Mick Byrne, who was in Eamon's class in school, was there too with his uncle. Eamon went up to him and showed him the key before handing it to his father.

'Is Father Rossiter not coming?' he asked.

'No,' his father said. 'He's out on a call.'

It was quiet suddenly when they closed the old heavy gate and stood inside the garden of the Castle. None of them had been here before, except to deliver a message to the side door. Mick Byrne and Eamon exchanged glances as though they were trespassing and could be caught at any moment. When his father turned the key and pushed the front door they could see that it was dark inside. Eamon had expected old furniture and cobwebs; instead he could see nothing. One of the men with his father lit a paraffin lamp, illuminating a huge hallway with a low ceiling. There was a sharp, sour smell.

'There's an awful stink,' Mick Byrne said. No one else spoke. One of the men went across the room and pulled back the shutters on a side window and a pale, dim light came into a corner of the hall. His footsteps echoed as he walked back to join the others who were standing there looking around them, afraid to move.

Eamon stood close to his father. One of the men had opened the shutters of another window and it was now bright enough to see the flagstones.

'This is the old part,' his father said as he moved across and pushed a door which led into a room the same size as the hall, but brighter and with a higher ceiling. It was completely empty.

'This is the part the Roches built,' his father said.

Another door led into a kitchen where there were still tables and chairs as though someone had been living there. The men who had come with his father still looked suspicious and nervous, and they restrained Mick Byrne when he began trying to open drawers and presses.

'We can't go upstairs,' his father said, 'because some of the floor is rotten.'

'There's a lot of work needed all right,' one of the men said.

As the spring came his father and the priest sat in the car more and more and talked to each other, smoking all the time. Mrs Doyle would go out to look through the front window, and come back shaking her head. 'They're still talking. They're going to talk all night. You'd better go to bed before your father comes in and catches you up.'

Most of the time they talked about the Museum but they also talked about the war. They talked about how difficult it would be to get the work done with most of the men in England. Some of them were now starting to take their families over, Father Rossiter said, even with the danger. He hated to see people emigrating, he said, he hated it. A lot of the men were in the Local Defence Force as well, but if they were ready to give up a bit of their time, the ones who knew anything about wiring and plastering, then that would solve the problem.

They began to run a raffle on a Saturday night and a dance on a Sunday night to raise money for the Museum. Eamon went down to McCurtin's and waited for the news so that he could check on his atlas and mark any changes in the areas held by the Allies and the Germans, but after a while he lost interest in the radio; there were too many men talking, and sometimes the sound was too unclear, but Mr McCurtin listened all the time; he knew everything about the war.

ONE evening when the sky was bright he went in the car with his father and Father Rossiter towards Oulart. They had put a notice in *The Echo* asking if anybody had old things in their houses which might be of historical value. People had written to them from all over the county. His father wrote back to each person, putting a tick at the top of each letter he had replied to, and then gathering them in a bundle at the back of his scrap book.

A mile before reaching Oulart they were to turn right, down a lane, Father Rossiter said; these were his instructions. But he was unsure which turn to take. They tried one lane, which became increasingly rutted and overgrown, seeming to lead nowhere, and becoming even narrower as they came to a brightly painted gate. His father got out and opened it, held it as the car went through, then closed it and got back into the car. Gradually the lane began to widen again; they reached a clearing and saw a small farmhouse with a galvanized roof.

'It's hard to imagine,' Father Rossiter said, 'people living so far from the road.'

A sheepdog ran from the house and started to bark at the front wheels of the car. Two old people were now standing at the door; they were both watchful, almost furtive. The woman was wearing a cardigan and had her arms folded.

He waited in the car with his father while Father Rossiter went to speak to the couple at the door. They were still unsure whether they were in the right house.

'Do they have old things?' he asked his father.

'They have pikes from 'Ninety-eight,' his father said. 'That's what they said in the letter anyway.'

'Did they find them?'

'Stop asking questions now,' his father said.

Father Rossiter returned to the car and motioned for them to come into the house. The dog had now stopped barking and wagged his tail as they passed.

'We thought that there was something wrong when we saw the priest,' the woman said when they got inside the small kitchen which had a huge blackened fireplace and a table up against the window.

'We have no tea, you can't get any tea around here at the moment,' she went on. 'Milk is the only thing I can offer you. We have plenty of that, thank God.'

Eamon sat down beside the table, running his finger along the plastic oilcloth with its pattern of flowers. The woman put a mug of milk in front of him. There were strange web-shaped cracks in the mug, which he inspected first before tasting the warm milk.

'They came down by here,' he heard the man saying to his father and Father Rossiter. 'No wonder they left whatever they were carrying, sure weren't they bet? Didn't the English have muskets?'

'He's talking about 1798,' Eamon's father said to him

sternly. 'You should listen to him now and learn something.'

The sheepdog came stealthily into the kitchen and lay in
front of the fire with its eyes fixed on the man as he spoke,
and its head resting on its paws. Suddenly, the man
shouted at it and the dog slithered off back to the yard.

'They were hard times all right,' the woman said. The
man went into a room at the side and came back with a
wooden pole with two curled metal hooks at the top of it.
Father Rossiter and Eamon's father stood up and examined
it eagerly. The hooks looked sharp and dangerous.

'The wood's new. I did it myself,' the man said, 'but I
didn't have to touch the metal.'

'Do you have more of them?' Father Rossiter asked.

'Aye, I've twenty or thirty of them in there,' the man
said.

'What were they for?' Eamon asked.

'For using against the English,' his father said.

'Our grandmother now on our mother's side,' the
woman spoke, 'she was brought up here. It was the time of
the evictions. Sure, they used to own from here out to the
road, the whole way, including the two big barley fields.
She knew about the men of 'Ninety-eight,' the woman
looked into the fire and then back at the two visitors. 'She
would have been too young to remember it, but they told
her about it, or she heard about it, and it was she who
always said that they came down this way and that was
the end of them then. That's all I remember now. There
was a man used to come here and they used to talk about
it.'

The room was filling up with smoke from the fire; Eamon
watched a small piece of soot falling slowly through the air
and landing on the surface of his warm milk. It had a
shape of its own, a curly, black shape. He did not want to
swallow it. He studied it for a while as the others talked

and then put his finger into the milk and fished it out. He dried his finger on his trousers, having checked that no one was looking at him.

'Sure, they're no use to us at all,' the man said. 'We'll be gone soon.'

His father told him to help them collect the metal pike tops and put them in the boot and the back seat of the car. The wall of the room where they were kept was all damp, the plaster had fallen off in places, leaving the bare clay visible. When they had taken all the pieces, they shook hands with the brother and sister, who stood at the door watching them as they got into the car. It was darkening now, and the sky had clouded over. Father Rossiter had to switch on his lights as he drove along the lane back towards the main road.

The following day they brought the pikes down to the Castle, where a few workmen were plastering the entrance hall. They had rigged up a bare bulb in the ceiling so the low room did not appear as dark as it did on his first visit. This time Eamon noticed a small stairway in the corner. He was afraid in the building, its vastness and the extent of its disrepair frightened him, as though each step could lead to a terrible accident. The idea that he would ever be left alone in this building filled him with terror.

The stone stairs were part of the old building, his father said. They led right to the roof, and soon when a few lights were put in they would be able to go up there and view the whole town. In the meantime, the men were starting work on the dungeon. He heard about it first from Mick Byrne at school, but he didn't believe it. They used to lock fellows down there, he said. Who used to lock them? The English, Mick Byrne said.

The smell in the small dungeon, a cavern which had been eked out of the rock under the entrance hall, was even more damp and bitter than the smell upstairs. It smelt of clay, but staler. The workmen brought the electric bulbs down so that it was all bright. Eamon kept close to his father.

The workman in charge was called Eamonn Breen. He said that there were two 'n's in Eamonn.

'I'm called after Eamon de Valera,' Eamon said. 'And he's the Taoiseach.'

'Yes, and he's wrong,' Eamonn Breen said.

'You're not Fianna Fáil,' he said. Eamonn Breen later told his father what had happened and they both laughed.

They no longer went home after school, they went to the Castle to watch the builders. Eamonn Breen had built steps into the dungeon and fixed a light into the ceiling and put distemper on the walls. There was still a terrible smell, a cold, bitter smell. When Marion Stokes brought him down the cold air filled his lungs. She showed him the place where a prisoner had cut a drawing of himself into the stone, but it was faint and could be made out only if you looked carefully: just a head, a body, two legs and two arms with a sword hanging from the waist. The man had to draw it in the dark, Marion Stokes said. He had nothing else to do all day. She showed him the floor.

'It'd be cold here in the winter,' she said. 'You'd die of the cold.'

Eamonn Breen drew a map of 1798 with red arrows showing the way the armies came. The map was to go on the wall of the 1798 Room with all the pikes around it. Eamonn Breen was going to make wooden handles for the pikes. Father Rossiter carried down all of the old vestments from the Manse and old pictures of bishops and souvenirs he had brought home from Salamanca and he said that they could fill another room of the Castle.

His father met a man who said that he had the figure from a ship which went aground near Blackwater Head. It would have to be treated for woodworm, he said. Later, his father explained to him about the figure on a ship, how they always had the carved figure of a woman on the prow;

he pretended that he understood by looking at his father and nodding. His father said that it would be a great thing to have in the Museum.

The summer came; it was almost time to go to Cush. His father travelled to Dublin on the train to get exam papers he was going to mark and he brought them home in a black box.

'We might have to go to Cush in an ass and cart,' he said, 'or on bicycles, because there's no petrol.'

'Why can't Father Rossiter drive us? He can get petrol.'

'He's too busy. I couldn't ask him,' his father said.

His father arranged that Jimmy Power, who delivered vegetables, would drive them in his old van.

'Tell no one,' his father said. 'He's only meant to use his van for business.'

In Blackwater, they stopped at Mrs Davis's pub and the two men had bottles of stout; Eamon had a lemonade. 'Isn't the little fellow great?' Mrs Davis said and grinned at his father and Jimmy Power. She was old and walked slowly, pulling herself along as if it caused her pain.

'The Cullens will be delighted to see you. There was talk that you weren't coming, what with the war and the shortages.' There was silence for a second, and then she continued as though on the same topic: 'Do you think they'll invade, sir?' she asked his father. His father said he didn't think so. Jimmy Power nodded in agreement.

'There's men is ready for them around this way,' she said.

'We've had enough troubles of our own. Let the English and the Germans fight it out among themselves. Aren't they well able for each other?' Jimmy Power said.

'It's going to be a long war,' his father said. Eamon felt the rim of the long-stemmed glass hitting against his teeth. He looked at each of them in the half-light of the bar.

'It was a fierce cold winter,' Mrs Davis said. 'It was fierce cold down here.'

CHAPTER THREE

HE woke to the sound of rain being blown against the window. He could hear the strident advertising jingles on the radio in the living room. Carmel must have slipped out of bed while he was still sleeping. He felt tired as he moved over to her side of the bed in an attempt to get back to sleep. He wished it was an ordinary day with fixed routines. He lay there until he knew that he would get no further sleep.

He drew the curtains and looked out at the dark sky over the sea. He put on his dressing-gown and slippers and walked out into the living room. She was sitting at the deal table facing the window, holding a large coffee cup in her two hands. He suddenly felt relieved to see her.

'You were groaning in your sleep. Are you all right?' she asked.

'Did I keep you awake?'

'No, I was already awake, but you were very disturbed.'

'Is the water on?' he asked her.

'Yes, it is. You go and have a bath and I'll make your breakfast. You look tired.'

'Do I not always look like this?'

'No,' she smiled. 'No, you don't.'

In the bathroom he turned on the hot and cold taps and let the water run full-steam before going to the toilet. He was still trying to remember the dream he had, whatever it was, something which still weighed him down. He could not grasp it. He tested the water until it was right and then, having dropped his night clothes on the floor, he

27

lowered himself into the bath. He lay back and began to breathe evenly, more and more heavily until he had forgotten completely the fleeting source of his discontent. He did not move.

He felt better now when he closed his eyes and concentrated on keeping still, not stirring, not letting anything into his mind: no memories, no judgments, no facts. When a thought came he kept it at bay by thinking about his heart beating and trying to get as close as he could to the source of its beat and its pulse. That was all. He heard nothing: he concentrated on the shapes which appeared in the darkness when he closed his eyes, and tried to make them into everything that there was.

As he dried himself he found that he could smile without any strain. He brushed his teeth and put on his dressing-gown and slippers. In the living room Carmel had turned off the radio and put on the record player. The music was quiet, and the sound was low, but he could hear it clearly as he stood there looking out at the sky. She did not turn around when he came in, but stayed exactly where she had been earlier, facing the window. For a second he wanted to touch her, to put his arms around her, but he held back, and went instead into the bedroom and dressed himself.

It was raining harder when he came out and sat at the table; the room was dark and becoming cold. Carmel brought him toast and a poached egg and left the teapot on the table for the tea to draw. She moved quietly as though not to interrupt something. Neither of them spoke until she poured his tea.

'Will we go into the village?' she asked.

'If you want,' he said and looked at her. He hoped she would not misconstrue what he said. He did not know what to say.

'Thank you for the breakfast.'

'I like doing things when there's a long day like this,' she said.

'I was looking forward to a hot day.'

'I know.'

The music played in the background and they both sat at the table listening as the wind whistled around the house. Again, he felt like touching her, reaching across the table to her, taking her hand, but instead he drank his tea and finished his toast and then cleared the breakfast things away.

'Will we go?' he asked.

'It'll take me a while to get ready,' she said.

'I'm ready whenever you are.'

The road into the village was narrow, with many twists and turns. He had walked it and driven along it many times, and yet still, after all the years, he could come to a short stretch which he did not recognize, could not remember having looked at before. The gradual hills were good for nothing, being too sandy, but the fields nearest the road were useful for pasture and corn. Nothing grew high; there were no tall trees or hedges, everything was flattened by the wind coming in from the sea. There were no big houses, just small farms and small livings made from cattle, milk, wheat and illegal poaching for salmon and trout in the river which flowed into the sea at the strand in Ballyconnigar.

Everybody stopped to talk; that was the rule in Cush, even when there was little to talk about. They loved news, and the word about his daughter having a baby would spread among the smallholdings, would be carefully savoured and gone over and would also be withheld from certain people. Yet they would talk about it only among themselves; such items were kept for their own community. In all the years he had never heard them speak ill of each other or of the visitors who came in the summer, or had come in the years gone by and were remembered. He was still an outsider who came only in the summer; and he was a judge, and they were careful what they said in his presence. He did not know how they spoke when they were among themselves.

In the village he was known as the Judge, and if Carmel went into a shop alone they asked after him. They watched his coming and going with interest and curiosity.

He parked at Jim Bolger's and waited while Carmel went in to order *The Irish Times* for the rest of their stay and some Sunday newspapers. The rain had stopped now but the sky was still dark and threatening. When Carmel returned to the car he started up the engine again and drove down towards the bridge and parked at Etchingham's. They got out of the car and walked into the pub and grocery shop. He sat on the high stool while Carmel looked at the shopping list she had taken from her bag. There was no one behind the counter, and they waited in silence.

'I think I'll pour my own drink,' he said.

'You wouldn't want to be in a hurry around here,' a voice behind them said. There was a man sitting against the wall in the shadows. They had not noticed him.

'Ah, we have all day,' Eamon said to him.

WHEN they returned home they sat in the living room listening to the one o'clock news. The weather forecast predicted more rain. Carmel carried out a box from the spare bedroom with the books she had brought for them to read. Every year she read the literary pages and listened to the books programme on the radio so she could find reading matter for their holidays. He took no part in this, insisting, jokingly, that he trusted her judgement and would read anything she gave him, except books about Irish history or the Kennedys.

She took the books out and placed them on a shelf near the window.

'It's extraordinary about Mike, isn't it?' she said.

'What?' he asked. 'What's extraordinary?'

'Did you not hear what Mrs Etchingham told me? I thought you were listening.'

'No, I wasn't.'

'Jim Bolger told me as well. He couldn't believe I didn't know. The front of his house is gone. It fell in after we were here at Easter. He's staying in one of the caravans in Blackwater.'

'I thought that it would last a bit longer.'

'Mrs Etchingham said that he was nearly killed.'

Mike was his cousin who had retired to a house farther down the lane nearer the cliff. He was still in his fifties. Over the years as the soft marl of the cliff gave way to the wind and the sea the house had become dangerously close to the cliff. Now, it had fallen in. Mike was gruff, distant, independent. He hated being offered a lift into the village, as though it was a comment on his not having a car, but he was popular in the area. His living the winter in Cush gave him a status not enjoyed by those who merely came for the summer.

'Our house is next,' he said, and went over to the shelf of books.

'It'll be years before it happens,' she said.

'I remember when there was as much land in front of Mike's house as there is now in front of ours,' he said. 'I remember a big field that sloped down to the cliff.'

'I find it hard to imagine,' she said.

He selected a book from the pile, a history of convicts in Australia, and took it out to the glass porch where he sat in an armchair facing out towards the sea. The rain was still coming down. He flicked through the pages of the book and scanned the index, noting the references to Irish convicts and checking back to read those passages. Soon, he became engrossed in the book.

After lunch the rain turned to a fine drizzle and after a while that, too, eased. He went back to the porch with his book, checking the weather every so often to see if he could go out. There was now a soft, white line along the horizon and an opaque light coming in from the sea.

Carmel said that she was happy to stay indoors; there were still things to unpack. She seemed rested. He put on his raincoat, took an umbrella from the car and set out along the lane, trying to avoid the potholes full of muddy water. In the field to his left, which led straight down to the cliff, some of the corn looked windswept and beaten down. When he came to the turn in the lane he saw Mike's house. The back wall and the side walls were completely intact, but the entire front of the house was missing. The land around jutted out on both sides. The electricity was still connected. It was as though what remained of the foundations and the fabric of the house was being held on the earth by the electricity wires. It was strange too how the small house appeared to have been singled out by the erosion. It seemed unlucky and hard to understand. He went into the house by the back door and stood on the stone floor of the front room. He inspected the walls, half mud, half stone, like all the old houses around here, including his house. He went to the edge and looked down. The collapse of the cliff here had made a new pass down to the strand. There was no steep drop, as there had been in other years, after the winter created new forms in the cliff's face. Clearly, this year there was no need to build steps down to the strand.

He was not sure now that he could in fact remember the field which ran from Mike's house to the cliff. It had been so gradual, this erosion, a matter of time, lumps of clay, small boulders studded with stones becoming loose and falling away, the sea gnawing at the land. It was all so strange, year after year, the slow disappearance of the one contour to be replaced by another, it was hard to notice that anything had happened until something substantial, like Mike's house, fell down on to the strand.

There had been other such dramas in the past, other ways to mark and remember the way this coast was being eaten into. There was the year that they blew up the old watchtower on the hill above Keating's in Ballyconnigar, afraid that it would topple of its own accord and crush someone on the strand below. They blew a huge hole into the hill. He remembered going up to see the damage they had done; the hole was all thin sand and, winter by winter, the hill itself began to disappear until now there was no sign of it. He was there years ago with Carmel one summer's Sunday. They had come down from Enniscorthy on bicycles; they lay there sunbathing on the hot grass. Not a soul came by. He remembered her bare legs, the smooth, silky skin and the slim, lithe shape of her under the bathing costume, and his own excitement as she lay close in against him and kissed him.

He turned now in this shell of a house and walked into the bedroom which was damp and dark. There was no furniture, but Mike had left a stack of books behind. He looked through them, half tempted to take one as a souvenir. They were old novels, a collection of classics. He picked up the book on the top; it was *Cranford* by Mrs Gaskell, but the pages were mildewed and he put it back down. Some memory stirred in him, as though he was about to remember the dream he had had, and he picked the book up again and held it, staring at the title. When he turned he was shocked by the missing wall, by the bare, raw light from the sea. He felt he was trespassing now, and he began to walk down to the strand.

He walked south towards Ballyconnigar. The drizzle had completely lifted and the afternoon became mild and warm with patches of blue in the sky. Each time a wave rolled inwards it unsettled the small stones at the shoreline, forcing them to knock against each other. They made a clattering, gurgling sound as each wave hit them and then retreated. He listened for it as the waves came in, a sound unlike any other, definite and oddly comforting, like two hollow objects being banged against each other, except that this was more modest, intimate. He moved back and listened, realizing that he could not remember that there had ever before been small stones here on the shoreline.

He felt warm as he walked along; soon he was forced to take off his raincoat and put it over his arm. There was no one on the strand. Some mud boulders had rolled down from the cliff and were standing at the bottom; it would be only a short time before the sea would dissolve them. As he looked up he saw that all the time fine grains of sand were being blown down the cliff-face.

At Ballyconnigar he could see how close Keating's house was to the cliff; even since Easter some of the land had been eaten away. The house was like a monument, its glistening whitewash visible for miles. The old woman was dead now; he wondered if the sons, who must be old men now, were still living there. He had an idea that one of them had got married, but he was not sure. He must ask Carmel; she knew about everybody in the area, and kept in touch with Christmas cards and Mass cards, letters and visits when they came for the summer.

Every year the river at Ballyconnigar changed its course when it reached the soft sand. It channelled through, turning this way or that several times during the winter, but when the spring came it settled on one route and the County Council came and put up a small wooden foot-bridge to facilitate the summer visitors. The river was shallow here, but fast-flowing. Farther back, it was deeper and slower in its pace, perfect at certain points for salmon and brown trout. He had forgotten – again, he smiled to himself, Carmel would know – who owned the fishing rights, but most of the locals poached the river, and there was no shortage of salmon or trout at cheap prices. He had to be careful to let Carmel do the dealing and the buying, making her pretend that the Judge believed that everything was legal and above board. Over the years, there had been raids by bailiffs and several of the local men had been to court and paid fines.

Carmel was sitting on the porch when he got home. She was reading a novel.

'Who's in Keating's house now?' he asked.

'Jack is in there with Rita, but I hear she's not well. I went up to Murphy's so I have all the news.'

'I'd say they were talking about Mike,' he said.

'Mrs Murphy said that he wasn't in any danger at all, that he's stayed in the caravan during bad weather over the past few years. I never knew that. She says that he won't get any compensation.'

'No,' he said. 'I checked up on that years ago.'

AFTER a few days of drizzle the weather improved. They sat out in the front garden in deckchairs as the strong sun appeared at intervals from between the clouds. He took his togs and towel and walked down the lane to the strand. The sea was rough, the water a glinting steely-grey. He moved down the strand, away from a family group who had installed themselves at the bottom of the cliff. He took off his socks and shoes and rolled up his trousers so he could paddle in the water, test the temperature. The water came in over his feet with a shock of cold, the sun had gone in again, and he wondered if he should not just go for a walk and come back along the cliff in time for lunch.

He would have to brave it. After a few days he would get used to the searing cold and once down in the water it would be pure pleasure as long as he kept moving and did not think about the cold. He changed into his togs and looked up at the sky to see if the sun would soon appear, but a few heavy black clouds had blown in over the sea. He shivered as he stood there before walking down to the shoreline with slow determination. He waded in, trying not to be put off by the cold. He put his hand into the water, and wet his face and chest. He jumped to avoid the impact of a large wave, but he was now wet up to the waist. He stood for a moment, hesitant and undecided, and then in a flash he dived down into the water, swimming right out, keeping under the surface as much as possible and then turning on his back and letting himself float with his head tilted into the water and his eyes shut. He swam out beyond the point where the waves broke, where the sea was just a slight swelling and falling. The water became bearable as he swam around, he crawled farther out and stopped to look back at the low cliff at Cush, all yellow marly sand and tufts of grass, rising to the higher cliffs at Ballyconnigar where the sand was paler, like gravel.

He shivered as he dried himself. He could not wait to get his clothes on. He dressed quickly and when he reached the shell of Mike's house, having walked up the cliff, he felt a comforting warmth, a sense of ease. The sky was now overcast and grey. Carmel was in the porch and when he opened the door he noticed that she had been dozing with a book on her lap. She woke and smiled at him.

'This weather makes me sleepy,' she said.

He put bread and cheese and salad on the table and made tea. She yawned as she came into the living room and sat down.

'I forgot to tell you that Madge Kehoe invited us for our dinner. She said that maybe we'd play cards afterwards. I said that we hadn't played cards for years.'

'When?' he asked.

'Next week,' she said. 'They have a Christian Brother staying with them.'

'And they want us to play cards?' he laughed. 'I used to play cards with Madge and her mother years ago. Old Mrs Keating was a great player.'

*

SOME days the rain never lifted. It began as a dense drizzle in the mornings and cleared up for an hour or two in the afternoon before coming down again in heavy showers. He watched from the window for any sign of light over the sea, but the sky remained grey. They kept the fire lit and sat indoors reading.

Carmel showed him a letter from Niamh to say that she was living in their house now and wondering where all the plants had gone. She had been to see a gynaecologist, she said, and he had told her she was in good shape. There was nothing to worry about, she said. The letter was written to Carmel, but she sent her father her regards in the last paragraph. He left the letter on the table beside the window, took an umbrella and went out for a walk.

ON the day they were to go to Madge Kehoe's they drove to the village and bought a bottle of whiskey and a box of chocolates to take with them.

'Do you think that this is too much?' Carmel asked him. 'Maybe I should have got sherry instead of whiskey.'

'Is there anything worse than sherry?' he asked, and smiled.

'Tom and Madge will be delighted to see you. Madge went on about the Judge and how they missed you last summer.'

'I remember Madge well. She's a good few years older than me.'

He drove along a narrow lane towards Ballyvalden and Knocknasillogue. The late afternoon sky had suddenly become bright. He passed a herd of cows which were being prodded along by a boy with a stick.

Madge Kehoe was standing at the door when they arrived, holding two eager dogs by the scruff of the neck. She had grown to look so much like her mother that he was sure for a few moments that the old woman, long dead now, with whom he used to play cards, was still alive and standing at the door. Madge's face was wrinkled and her skin withered in the same way as her mother's. The hair was white, but still thick and curly. But the voice was different, lower and stronger.

'Don't mind the dogs now, just come in,' she said. The dogs continued to yelp and bark as she held them.

There was a fire lit in the front room; a sofa and two armchairs had been placed around the hearth. Tom, Madge's husband, stood up when they came in. He had the air of a man sitting in a room he wasn't used to, wearing clothes that he normally wore only to Sunday Mass.

'You're looking well, both of you,' he said.

'It's terrible weather,' Carmel said.

'We've seen the end of the summers,' Tom said. 'We had a few nice days in June, but there'll be no more summers like we used to have.'

They were sitting down by the fire when Madge appeared with the bottle of whiskey which Carmel had left on the hall stand.

'I found this out in the hall, wrapped in brown paper,' she said. 'And this.' She took the wrapping off the box of chocolates. 'I don't know how they got there,' she laughed. 'Isn't God good to us, all the same?'

'The house is looking lovely, Madge,' Carmel said.

'We'll have to have a drink,' Madge said. 'And maybe we'll get a bit of sunshine. Will you all drink whiskey?'

'I won't, thank you,' Carmel said. 'But I'm sure Tom and Eamon will.'

When they went into the large modern kitchen to eat they found another guest at the table. He was an elderly Christian Brother.

'This now is Brother McDonagh,' Madge said, and she explained how he used to come every year for the month of August in the days when she kept guests for the summer.

'And we had too much work here and I couldn't keep it all up, so I wrote to all the regular guests and told them that I was too busy with the farm, but Brother McDonagh wrote back and he was so disappointed and heartbroken that I couldn't let him down, so I wrote and told him to come, and he still comes every August.'

'I love the sea air,' the Brother said.

Madge began to put the food on the table, and they sat down to eat together as a damp August evening settled in.

'I knew your father well,' the Brother said to him halfway through the meal.

'Yes, that's right,' Madge said. 'I forgot to tell you. Brother McDonagh taught in the Christian Brothers' School in Enniscorthy.'

'That's funny,' Eamon said. 'I don't remember you. It must have been before my time.'

'Yes, it was before you were born. I was in Enniscorthy for a good stretch. I remember your father coming to the school, and I remember your mother, God rest her.'

Madge gathered up the dinner plates and put a tart and a bowl of custard in the middle of the table. Eamon looked across at the Brother.

'I loved Enniscorthy. I was sad to leave. It was a beautiful place. There were some great walks. And it was steeped in history.'

There was silence then, interrupted only by Madge serving the dessert. Eamon felt that if he lifted his glass he would not be able to hold it steady, that his hand would shake. Maybe, later, he would be able to talk to the Brother alone and ask him: what were they like? What was his mother like? They began to talk again, about the weather and the crops and Mike's house, but he could not stop thinking about the old man opposite him, and he could not stop wanting to know something, some detail, anything about his father and his mother. He wondered how he could make a question sound casual, how he could ask about them without showing how anxious he was.

'What did you teach, Brother?' he asked.

'I taught History and Geography,' the Brother said. 'Your father taught everything; he was a great teacher,' he continued.

'Oh, he was. We all remember him,' Madge said. 'He was a nice man.' She smiled at Eamon and Carmel. 'All the Redmonds were nice.'

CHAPTER FOUR

H E stood in his suit in the hall while his father searched
for the red sashes. He must have been seven then, or
eight. His father had found the pins which lay on the
kitchen table, and now he frantically rummaged through
the drawers and wardrobes in the two bedrooms in search
of the red sashes.

'They must be somewhere,' he said.

Eamon opened the back door and threw out crumbs
from that morning's breakfast on to the concrete of the
yard. He put the plates in the sink.

'Have you touched the sashes?' his father shouted. 'Have
you been playing with them?'

He knew that there was no need to answer. He wished
that this crisis would come to an end.

'Go into Mrs Cooney next door and ask her if she has
any sashes,' he shouted from the top of the stairs, but
Eamon stayed where he was for a while, listening as his
father pulled out another drawer in the small room. He
opened the front door and closed it behind him to make it
seem that he had gone, but instead he sat on the steps.
There was no one on the street. The sun was high over
Vinegar Hill. Suddenly his father came to the window.

'It's all right,' he said. 'It's all right. You needn't go. I
found them.'

His father put the sash around his shoulder and Eamon
held the two ends together while his father put the pin into
the clasp. They could go now, his father said as he folded

his own sash and put it in his pocket. Later, he said, when he got down town, he would put it on.

Eamon left his father at the bottom of John Street and walked down to the school. He was early, and sat in the shelter until most of his classmates arrived. Already hot in their suits in the afternoon sun, they were put into a line as soon as the Brother blew his whistle. They marched down the Mill Park Road to the bottom of Friary Hill, but were stopped there and told to wait. Friary Hill and Slaney Place were festooned with bunting. At the bottom of Friary Hill there was a huge arch. The Brother in charge had moved back along the line, so it was easier now for the boys to play without anyone noticing. A fellow from the Shannon gave Eamon a kick and put his fists up, daring him to fight, but Eamon stood his ground and ignored him, knowing that the Brother would come back at any moment. Soon, the lines of four had broken up into groups of boys laughing and fighting, but one of the men in sashes came up and told them to conduct themselves or he would have to report them. After a while, the man gave them leave to march towards Slaney Place.

The Brother ran up to the front of the march. He walked backwards as he shouted instructions at the marchers.

'Sing out loud now, so that everyone can hear you. Sing out loud, lads, so that everyone will know that your faith is strong. Louder now. Louder, come on, lads.'

They were stopped again at the bridge while the girls from the Presentation School went by.

> *'Sweet Heart of Jesus We Thee Implore*
> *O Make Us Love Thee More and More.'*

The Brother conducted them as they sang. A few girls smiled as they silently passed. If there was one sound out of any boy, the Brother said, he would get six slaps with the leather here and now in front of everyone. Eamon noticed that his new shoes were starting to stick to the hot

tar of Slaney Place. The Brother said that everyone was to
stand up straight.

They marched across the bridge and then into Templeshannon where they were halted again. The windows of
the shops had statues of the Sacred Heart and the Virgin
Mary on display. Eamon looked at the pale blue cloth and
the mild eyes of the Virgin in one of the shop windows as
they waited at the bottom of the Shannon. His legs were
tired standing; it would be much easier if they could just
walk without being stopped all the time, he thought. As
they moved slowly up the Shannon they passed more
stewards in suits and red sashes, men whom Eamon
recognized from the St Vincent de Paul, or the Museum,
or the Athenaeum. The stewards stood, sternly watching
the procession, their hands behind their backs. They were
the ones who controlled the stopping and starting. He
watched out for his father and his Uncle Tom but he could
not see them. On the steepest part of the hill they were
stopped again as the Women's Confraternity passed by on
the other side.

> *'Star of the Sea, Pray for the Wanderer,*
> *Pray for me.'*

The women wore mantillas and carried Rosary beads.
They were followed by the gold canopy under which Father
Rossiter carried the monstrance with the Blessed Sacrament. An altar boy carried the incense but there was no
smell. The smoke was blowing in the other direction. They
bowed their heads as the Blessed Sacrament passed.

His father was standing on the bridge with his hands
behind his back. He looked very serious, and Eamon knew
that he must not wave to him or say anything. Along by
the Post Office he saw his Uncle Tom who put his hand
out and stopped the procession, and held it for a few
minutes before letting it go again.

An altar covered in red cloth had been put up in front of

the fire brigade building. The Market Square was full by the time the marchers from the Christian Brothers arrived and it was hard to find a place to kneel. Soldiers stood to attention at the front of the altar as the final part of the procession moved into the square. Red and yellow bunting was tied at the monument and led to the first-floor windows in the square. People watched out from all the houses, with the exception of the houses which had no one living in the floors above the shop. As Father Rossiter ascended the platform one man in officer's uniform shouted orders out in Irish and the soldiers stood to attention; he shouted out more orders and they lifted their rifles.

Benediction began. The crowd sang 'O Salutaris Hostia' and bowed their heads and struck their breasts three times when Father Rossiter raised the monstrance.

It would not be long now, he knew, as he walked home with his sash carefully folded in his pocket, before they went to Cush. It was June. The summer had already started, and his father's holidays from the secondary school would begin soon. His father would want to go to Dublin then, and so he would be taken out of primary school a week or two before the official time for holidays and sent to Cush.

ONE Friday a few weeks later he came home from school and everything was packed for him.

'Are you ready?' his father asked.

'Why didn't you tell me before?'

'It would make you unsettled.'

'It wouldn't make me unsettled.'

'You'd better be on your best behaviour in Cush. Bill Miller's going to drive you down with all the stuff.'

'And when'll you be down?'

'I'll be down soon enough.'

'Did you pack books for me?'

'Ah, hurry up now. He'll be coming soon.'

They drove out past Donoghue's by the side of Vinegar Hill. The van was old and there was a hole in the floor, which Mr Miller told him to be careful of, and then laughed hoarsely. The clouds were moving fast in the sky as they neared The Ballagh and soon it began to rain. There were no wipers on the van, so they had to drive very slowly.

'Say a prayer now, young fellow, that there's nothing coming,' Bill Miller said.

They drove through Blackwater and then down towards the sea. The day had cleared again but there were brown puddles in the potholes. Mrs Cullen was waiting for them when they came down the lane and parked beyond the marl-hole.

'Your daddy wrote and said you were coming,' she said. Her hair was tied in a bun. She kept her hand over her eyes to shade them. He carried all the boxes from the van and put them into the side room where he and his father slept. He sat at the kitchen table then and had a cup of tea with Mrs Cullen and Bill Miller.

Mrs Cullen believed that he should be outdoors all day. Even if he wanted to read she would make him go down to the strand or sit out in the garden. If it rained she would watch the weather to see if it was clearing up so she could send him out again.

'All the boys your age round here are out picking potatoes,' she said.

He went early one morning with Phil Cullen to pick potatoes. His job was to load them into the sacks. Once his back began to ache he could not wait for the morning to be over. When he thought it was mid-day he found that it was only ten o'clock; it was the first fine day since he had come and he regretted having volunteered for this work. Eventually, Phil found him sitting down resting against a full sack of potatoes.

'He's not too bad when it comes to eating them,' Phil said to one of the other workers.

'If you follow the cliff you'll find your way back home soon enough,' Phil said. 'You can tell her that we finished early.'

'Are you sure?' he asked.

'Go on,' Phil said.

As he walked back towards the Cullens' house, he realized that he missed living in his own house, having his own key and knowing that he could walk into any room he liked without disturbing someone. Suddenly, he wanted to go home. He lay down on the warm grass, looked up at the sky and decided to wait there for a while before going back to the Cullens' house.

MRS KEATING came to the house one night to visit.

'Do you remember his Uncle Stephen?' Mrs Cullen said to her. 'He had brains all right. Sure, so did his father.'

'That's right,' Mrs Keating said. 'All the Redmonds had brains.'

'Isn't he the image of his mother around the eyes?'

'He is, but he's a real Redmond. And how are they all in Enniscorthy?'

'They're very well, thank you,' he said.

'We're waiting for you now,' Mr Cullen said. 'Talk never played a hand of cards. Are you going to play? Isn't that what Mrs Keating came over for?'

'There'll be no fighting or arguing,' Mrs Cullen said. 'You wouldn't believe the way they fight over cards.'

Eamon wondered if they were going to let him play. He had watched them the previous year: he would have difficulty, he knew, with twenty-five or forty-five, but if it was whist or solo he knew how to play, he had worked out the rules.

'So who's going to play, then?' Mrs Keating asked. 'Is young Redmond going to play with us?'

'Some other night,' Mrs Cullen said. 'We'll have to teach him how to play.'

'I know how to play,' he said.

'He knows how to play snap,' Phil Cullen said.

'I know how to play solo,' he said.

One of the Cullen girls came over and put her arms around him.

'Who taught you how to play solo?' she asked.

'I taught myself,' he said.

'Why don't we divide into two schools of four?' Mrs Cullen said. 'I have another pack in the room inside. And you can learn then.'

'One school for solo; one for forty-five,' Mr Cullen said. 'Which do you want to learn?' he asked Eamon.

'I want to learn solo.'

'I thought you said you could play,' Phil said.

'Leave him alone,' Mrs Cullen said.

There were two cards missing from the second pack and Mrs Cullen had to go to the press to look for loose cards. She came back with two from a different pack, took a pencil and wrote their trump and value on them. Mrs Keating, Mrs Cullen, Eamon and Phil Cullen sat at one table. Mr Cullen, Mrs Keating's daughter Madge and two of the Cullen girls sat at another table. They had already started a game of forty-five. It was still bright enough to see the cards and it was only later, when they had played several hands, that one of the girls turned on the oil lamp and hung it from a nail on the wall.

Solo. Eamon tried to remember. There were no partnerships, each player played alone. There were trumps and you bid in turn on the value of your hand. Misere was the most difficult to make: it meant that you had to win no tricks at all. Mrs Cullen said that she would deal the first hand and she would keep the score. She never played cards for money, she said. No one in this house, she said to Mrs Keating, had ever played cards for money. It had ruined a few homes, she added. Mrs Keating nodded in assent.

Eamon did not bid on the first hand. He preferred to sit

back and wait. He knew that Mrs Keating was a good player; he had heard Mrs Cullen say that she was the best player for miles around. She bid a solo and made it easily and then laughed to herself. The game at their table was quiet and thoughtful; the others shouted all the time, their playing was full of threats and promises, each swearing that they had the card which was going to carry the day and shouting with pain and disappointment when they were defeated.

'Quiet there now at the next table,' Mrs Cullen said as another hand of solo was dealt.

When Eamon looked at the next hand he realized that he had a good chance of making a misere: he had the deuce of all four suits; he had the three of hearts, the three of clubs, the four of diamonds and the nine of spades to cover him on the second round. The nine of spades was dangerous but the rest were safe. He thought of the rules again.

'I'll go solo,' Phil said.

'Six spades,' Mrs Keating said quietly without looking up from her hand.

'Misere,' Eamon said.

'The Redmonds were always great at cards,' Mrs Keating said. 'I remember your Uncle Stephen when he was your age.'

'What's the trump?' Phil Cullen asked him.

'There's no trump in misere,' he said.

'Will you leave the child alone?' Mrs Cullen said.

He had to lead, and he led with the two of hearts and sat back to watch the play.

'He knows how to play all right,' Mrs Keating said.

When Mrs Cullen played another heart he dropped his three, he was still safe. The next lead was a spade. He played his two, Phil Cullen won with the eight, and led another round of spades with the six, Mrs Cullen played the five, Eamon had no choice but to play his nine. Mrs Keating waited for a moment as though she could not decide what to play and then gently placed the seven on the table, finishing the contract. Eamon could feel his ears begin to redden. In winning the trick he had lost the game.

'You didn't have enough protection in spades,' Phil Cullen said. 'You'd need something lower than the nine.'

'Don't mind him,' Mrs Keating said. 'You just need to be lucky.'

He could feel his face burning and he was sorry that he had taken the chance. For the rest of the night he felt a strange guilt. In the morning when he woke up he had the sense that he had done something wrong.

'Are you on for a game tonight?' Phil Cullen asked him.

'Can we play again?' he asked.

'As long as there's no fighting, I'll play,' Mrs Cullen said.

His father came to Cush one day with a black box full of examination papers to correct. A special table was put into the bedroom for him to work. At the end of each page he wrote a mark in red.

'Who's winning?' he asked his father as the pile of corrected papers began to mount.

'Leave your father alone,' Mrs Cullen said, 'and go outside in the fresh air.'

In the village his father bought him his own pack of cards, and he hid away from Mrs Cullen, in the girls' bedroom or in his own room, and began to deal imaginary hands of solo to imaginary partners, playing each hand as though he had not seen the others, and trying not to cheat, trying not to allow his knowledge and his memory to stretch beyond each hand. He enjoyed playing his card game on the bed as his father worked. In the evenings now he was ready for them. There were always three others willing to play until it was his bedtime. A few nights Mrs Cullen was enjoying the games so much that she let him stay up late. His father played too; one night he won a

spread misere. Mrs Cullen said it was the first time she
had ever seen anyone succeed at spread misere. Eamon
took chances now without worrying; most of the time he
won, and when he lost he knew that there would be another
game, another opportunity.

One evening he went on the ass and cart with Mrs
Cullen to have tea with Mrs Keating and Madge Keating
and play solo afterwards. Mrs Keating, he felt, was the
only one who really understood the game; the rest of them
could play, his father, Mrs and Mr Cullen, Phil and the
girls, but Mrs Keating was the only one who really loved
the game, who knew what the chances were, who knew the
likelihood of each opponent having certain cards, who
knew the weaknesses of her opponent's playing style, who
knew what luck meant but balanced it with skill. Mrs
Keating loved winning. She looked like a big white cat
when she won. He knew that she liked playing with him,
he felt a kinship with her. Often, when one of the others
won the bid, Eamon and Mrs Keating would close in
together, they would begin to guess what cards the others
had and they would send signs to each other. They
understood the cards as the other two did not.

In the end, however, much depended on luck and
chance. There were few safe hands and fewer foolproof
bids. If it was his bid he would watch Mrs Keating plotting
against him.

'I've got a nice little card for you now,' she would say
and lay it down on the table and look up at him, a deep
cunning in her old eyes.

'You'd need something better than that, Mrs Keating.'

'You're a real Redmond,' Mrs Cullen would say. Often
Mrs Cullen would become forgetful or distracted and Mrs
Keating had no patience with her.

Mrs Keating did not want the night to stop; she made a
rule that they would not put away the cards until someone

played a spread misere, whether they won it or not. It was after one o'clock when they set off for Cush on the ass and cart. There was a full moon over the sea below Keating's and the sky was bright with stars and so they had no difficulty seeing the turn for Cush at the hand-ball alley and making their way along the narrow road home. His mind was full of cards. As he lay in bed he thought of the games they had played and the strategies he had used until he fell asleep.

The black box was now filling up with corrected examination papers. One day Eamon stood at the door watching his father correcting the papers outside at a table under one of the small trees. His father was wearing a straw hat. Suddenly, a gust of wind blew and the rain started and one of the papers blew down the garden. His father ran after it and put his foot on it before it got away even further. He had to gather up all the papers and take them into the house. Some of them were wet: the rain had got mixed with the ink and made the writing blurred.

The weather improved and soon the days were sweltering with heat. He had been in the sea only once since he came, but it had been too cold and he had no urge to go back again. But now his father wanted to go and made him find his togs and take a towel. The papers were nearly finished. They walked down the lane; his father had rolled up his shirt sleeves and was wearing sandals with no socks.

'The thing to do,' he said, 'is to go into the water without thinking about it. Think of something else, and just get down in the water, and then, as long as you keep moving, you'll be warm enough.'

'But it's cold,' Eamon said.

'Not on a day like today. We should be in twice a day.'

They found the gap in the cliff. Steps had been cut into the moist clay, which made some of the descent easier, but for the last stretch there was nothing except banked sand

and they both had to run down. His father took off his sandals and rolled up the bottoms of his trousers to go and check the water. Eamon lay on the warm sand.

'It's roasting,' his father said.

'I know you're joking.'

His father sat down with his arms clasped around his knees and looked out to sea. There were no clouds, just a vague haze on the horizon. The sea was calm and clear.

'I wonder if there are seals,' his father said. 'There were seals last year.'

'Phil said he saw seals.'

'It's a sign of good weather,' his father said.

There were a few people farther down the strand, but otherwise it was empty.

'There are probably a lot of people in Curracloe,' his father said.

'They have a shop there now. It's called the Winning Post.'

'Who told you that?' his father asked.

'Josie Cullen was there.'

They waited in the mid-day heat until his father began to undress. Eamon still lay stretched out with his clothes on. When he sat up he saw that his father was wearing togs. His body was white, except for the black hair on his chest. He paid no attention to him as he walked down towards the sea. Eamon sat and watched as his father stood in the shallow water and then blessed himself before wading in slowly, jumping at first to avoid the waves breaking against him. His father dived into the water and swam out before turning to do the backstroke.

He changed into his togs. He felt sweaty in the heat and noticed when he lay out flat on the sand again that the sand was sticking to his skin. He stood and walked down towards the sea. He knew it would be cold, but with the warm sun on his back it was not as bad as he expected. His father was waving to him and swimming in a dog-paddle stroke towards the shore. Eamon moved out until he, too, had to jump to avoid the waves. He wondered how you could get the courage to dive in: what would those first moments be like? His father was beckoning him to come out farther.

'It's too cold,' he shouted and made as though to shiver.

'Come on,' his father shouted and moved faster towards him.

'Don't splash me,' he said.

His father came and put his cold hands on his back. He squirmed.

'It's easy, come on,' his father said.

He felt wet now and he shivered as he stood up to his thighs in the water.

'I'll give you a piggy-back,' his father said.

'You're too wet,' he said.

'Come on.' His father stood in front of him and stooped. He put his arms around his neck and as his father stood up he let him hold the soles of his feet.

'You're heavy,' his father said, as he waded out slowly. Eamon was above the level of the water, but his father was moving straight out from the shore until he was up to his waist in water.

'Don't throw me in,' he said.

'No, you can jump in,' his father moved farther out into the deep and hoisted him up even higher on his back.

'Let go my neck,' he said, but Eamon held on as a wave broke right over them. He was now completely wet.

'Let go my neck,' his father said again. Eamon waited for a moment and then jumped as best he could into the water. He had forgotten to close his mouth, which was full of brine when he surfaced. He was out of his depth now, but able to keep himself up in the water without his father's help. When his father turned and floated, he floated too, with his head right back in the water, his body relaxed, but enough air in his lungs to keep him from sinking.

His father swam out, while Eamon moved in towards the shore and practised his strokes. When his father emerged they went for a run to dry out in the sun. Eamon brought his towel and put it around him on the way back.

'A swim twice a day from now on,' his father said. 'I'll have the papers finished by Friday. I'll take them to Dublin on Monday.'

'I'll be swimming on my own so. The Cullens are too busy. They don't like swimming.'

'I'll be back on Tuesday,' his father said. He dressed himself and sat down again, his hands once more clasped around his knees as he stared out to sea.

'It's a great country when the weather's like this,' his father said.

Soon, they climbed up the cliff, each helping the other, Eamon taking his father's sandals when he needed both his hands to pull himself up. They were hungry now, and they knew that their dinner would be on the table for them when they got back to the Cullens' house.

CHAPTER FIVE

H E sat drinking coffee, watching from the porch window as the sky became a clearer blue. The swim that day in the past, his arms around his father's neck, the texture of his father's wet skin and the thrill of the water were still with him. Clear and sharp memory of hot days in summer when they came to this house as visitors. Some of it more real and vivid and focused than anything that had happened since. It was not yet ten o'clock and this would be the fourth day in a row of pure sunshine, a miracle after the days of wind and rain. The sky was white and hazy at the edges and the sun hot in the middle of the day with the garden full of bees and grasshoppers. Hardly anything had changed in all the years; the nettles grew high in the rain and sunshine, the pink flower of the wild rose settled against the trellis as it had always done. If he let his mind wander he could see his father's shadow correcting examination papers at the table in the corner of the garden, and the sudden gust of wind and the papers blowing as the rain began and the blotched writing becoming indecipherable. The long evenings in the house in the days before he and Carmel made the windows larger and put on a slate roof. The people moving as shadows; the cards on the table; the slow gestures as Mrs Cullen went over to the wall and lit the lamp; the room lighting up.

He walked into the bedroom and put on his togs and then his dressing-gown and a pair of sandals. He stood at the front door for a few moments and took in the sun. Carmel was in the garden. Once outside, he noticed that the air was brisk; it would take another hour or two for the day to become really warm. He took a towel which had been drying on a bush and walked down towards the cliff, hoping that he would meet no one. Some of the locals were working on a field of hay over the brow of the hill; the fields bordering the cliff had already been cut, and a green-tinged stubble had been left behind.

There was no wind, but there was still a faint dew on the grass. He spread the towel out on the edge of the cliff and sat down. The sea was a light green with patches of a darker green and farther out patches of blue. He watched the waves as they rolled in and quietly broke near the shore.

He made his way down to the strand where it was warmer, more sheltered. He took off his sandals and dressing-gown and walked towards the water, shivering as he put his feet into the cold sea. Maybe he should have waited. He stood there for a while before walking back to where his things lay. It was peaceful; he listened for the sound of the combine-harvester, but it was too distant, or else they had stopped working. He put his hands behind his head and turned his head around from side to side, doing exercises to relieve the tension in his neck. He did it until he was tired and hot. Now, he could try the sea again. He walked down, determined not to stop even to test the water. He waded in, ignoring the splash from an oncoming wave, then stopped and dived, swimming out as fast as he could, letting the shock of cold run through him. He lay back in the water and looked down the coast, noticing how sharp and clear everything now was in the early light. He tried not to think about the cold.

Carmel was still working in the garden when he came back to the house.

'The postman's been,' she said as she stood up, a small shovel still in her hand. 'He's that small friendly man. He hasn't been here for a while. He had a big package for you which I had him leave on the table. He wants to talk to you about becoming permanent. He asked me about it last year too, one day when you weren't here. He says he's done the Irish exam but they still won't make him permanent.'

'Does he think I run the Post Office?' he asked.

'He thinks that you have pull,' she said.

The envelope had a government stamp. It contained the previous year's Law Reports in booklet form. His own judgment on the health case should be in one of them. He checked through to make sure it was there, and came across several other judgments he had made during the year. He went into the bedroom and dressed himself, and then took a deckchair and a small table into the garden and began going through the Law Reports. After a while, as he read, he realized that he wanted to mark certain passages so he went inside and found a biro. He became engrossed in what he read, and he left notes, comments, exclamation marks and question marks in the margin.

It was difficult, particularly in the Supreme Court judgments, but also in some of the High Court rulings, not to see the personal politics coming through even in the most balanced decisions. He enjoyed the signs of this and derived particular pleasure from the more subtle and half-disguised manifestations of it.

He put the reports aside when Carmel came out with tea on a tray. She unfolded another deckchair and sat down beside him.

'I shouldn't be reading these now,' he said. 'I should save them up for when it rains.'

'Was the water warm?' she asked.

'No,' he said. 'It was an ordeal.' He put his hands behind his head and laughed. 'But I feel good after it.'

'It's funny about the postman. I think he thinks that you can have him made permanent. You should try to help him.'

Carmel read a novel while he lay back and did nothing.
But the lure of the reports was too great and after a while
he found himself curious about some judgments which he
had not followed closely at the time they were made. He
began to look through the booklets again. The morning
slipped away.

He became involved in the intricacies of the law, reading
as avidly as though the pages were full of easy gossip. He
was interested in the workings of his colleagues' minds,
their strategies, the words they chose. A few times he was
disappointed by the arguments which were not followed
through, by the vague assertions and the weak grasp of
case law. There were several judgments which he read after
lunch, written by his younger colleagues on the High
Court, judgments he could not have written himself, since
they were so detailed and all-embracing in their knowledge
of technical matters such as patents, copyright and the
intricacies of tort and property rights. He was more
interested, however, in broader questions, in the cases
which could raise much larger issues than the mere right
and wrong of the arguments presented to the court.

During the afternoon the sun disappeared behind the
house and the front garden was left in shadow. He fell
asleep for a while and when he woke up he saw that Carmel
must have folded away her deckchair and gone inside. He
still felt the excitement of the Law Reports, and regretted
that he had read so much in one sitting and not left more
for the days to come. He folded his deckchair too and left
it resting against the wall of the house. He found Carmel
in the kitchen.

'I'm thinking of going into the town,' he said. 'I'll drop
in on Aunt Margaret, but I won't be too long.' He went
out through the house to the car which was parked in the
lane.

The land looked good in the warm light of the summer
evening. The hedges were thick with growth and the trees

were in full leaf. As he drove towards the Ballagh he
noticed the gradual appearance of bigger fields, better land,
beech and oak trees. He noticed, too, the presence of big
old solid houses surrounded by stone walls. A few miles
later, however, the land deteriorated once more: there were
no crops grown here, none of the wheat or barley which
the better land yielded, only cattle and sheep. There were
no big houses either, just small vested cottages at the side
of the road.

It was the first time he had driven into the town this
summer. But as he drove into Templeshannon he felt that
he had always been here; the sudden clarity of his recog-
nition made the rest of the world strange and unfamiliar.
There had been changes: Bennett's Hotel was gone and
Roche's Malting had several big tin lungs beside the old
stone warehouses. He passed the Post Office and turned up
Friary Hill, surprised for the moment at how narrow it
was, how small the houses were.

He stopped outside his grandfather's old house where
his father had been born. His Aunt Margaret still lived
here. She was in her eighties now – eighty-five maybe,
eighty-six, he wasn't sure – but her mind was still perfect,
or so Carmel told him. Carmel was in constant touch with
Margaret.

He could see her sitting with her back to the bay window
as he opened the garden gate. She was reading a newspaper, holding the print close up to her face. When he tried
the doorbell there was no response. He did not want to tap
the window in case it frightened her. He banged the
knocker for a while and then he heard her coming. She
opened the door, peered at him and then took off her
glasses and looked again.

'Come in, come in, come in,' she said.

She led him into the bright front room and fussed for a
moment over the cushions on a chair. He noticed a bandage
around her leg.

'It's lovely to see you now,' she said. 'Carmel has been in a few times. She said that you would be in one of these days, but I thought you might wait until the weather got bad again.'

'It's lovely, isn't it, the weather, and the house and the garden look lovely as well,' he said.

'It's nice in the summer,' she said.

She smiled at him as though he was a small boy, arriving with his father to see her, proud of some new piece of knowledge he had acquired or some new achievement. She was always gentle, eager to please and prepared to disguise her own keen intelligence and sharp memory if these were to interfere with the general harmony. She had never married, never known the control a wife and mother exercises, the unsimple compromises a man and a woman make with each other. She had worked in an office all of her life, grateful for a secure job, having lived through times when there were few secure jobs to be had.

She went down to the kitchen now and came back with a bottle of whiskey on a tray with a glass and a jug of water. He noticed that she was unsteady on her feet. She left the tray down on the coffee table in front of him.

For him there had always been something childlike and sweet about her. She had come through, unscathed, into old age. She was free of them all now. She had told Carmel that she was happy not to have anyone to look after, even though she missed them, especially her brother Tom, with whom she had shared this house after their parents' death.

'You know yourself how much whiskey you want,' she said. 'There's no point in me pouring it for you.'

'Will you not have one yourself?' he asked.

'Maybe I will,' she said and laughed. 'You know I normally don't.' She went down to the kitchen again and returned with an empty glass and a bottle of lemonade.

'You'll go home and tell Carmel now that I've taken to the drink,' she laughed again.

'Carmel would be delighted to hear that you're taking a drink,' he said. She poured the whiskey and added some lemonade.

'Let me see if I've any news for you now,' she said. 'You couldn't come all this way without some news.'

Slowly, as he sipped his whiskey, she went through all his relatives one by one, distant cousins in North Wexford who were always asking for him, other cousins in America, old family friends in Cork. She talked about the Bridge Club, remembering if he had ever met any of the people she was telling him about, or if she had told him of them before.

'I've a lot to tell you now,' she said. 'It's so long since I've seen you. I hear everything about you from Carmel.'

There was a great deal he wanted to know, of which he possessed only snatches now, things which would disappear with her death. At times he felt that he had been there, close by, when his grandfather was evicted, and that he had known his father's Uncle Michael, the old Fenian, who was too sick to be interned after 1916. Or that he had been in the bedroom, the room above where they were now, when his grandfather came back to the house on Easter Monday 1916 and had sat watching him as he pulled up the floorboards under which he had hidden a number of rifles. Or that he had witnessed his grandfather being taken from the house at the end of the Easter Rising. These were things which lived with him, but he could only imagine them.

Some of these events were so close, they had been recounted and gone over so much. He realized that he would never fully know what went on, there were too many details left out. Margaret would volunteer memories or incidents, but if she was asked too much her eyes would soften and the look on her face become vague.

'I'm not looking forward to the winter,' she said, and she started to explain how her house had been under a sort of siege the previous winter. When she turned on the light in the kitchen at the back of the house, she said, somebody would throw a stone through the window from the sloping field behind. Young lads from the town, she said, waited there for hours. One of the stones had hit her on the leg and terrified her. So she couldn't use the kitchen after dark, she kept an electric kettle in the living room and made tea there.

'Did you not ring the Guards?' he asked.

'I rang the Guards, I rang Corrigan who owns the field, I even rang the Manse, and they were all full of sympathy. Father Doyle came down to see me, but no one did anything. I meant to tell Carmel about it, but I couldn't bring myself to say anything. It's very hard. No one would believe me when I said that they must have waited for two or three hours every night with stones. Waiting for me. I could feel them out there. I hope they find something else to do this winter. It's the last thing you expect that your own would turn on you.'

She stopped and looked into the distance. The silence lasted between them for a few moments as he wondered what he could do to help her. He even found himself wondering if what she said was true.

'I'll go and see the Guards about that,' he said.

'We used to do it ourselves, you know,' she continued. 'But we thought it was harmless. Knocking on doors and running away, that's what it was then, that's how we used to torment the neighbours. You'd give the door a big bang and then go and hide. There was a man up the Irish Street, a Mr Metcalfe, a Protestant man, he used to go mad at us, he'd chase us up to the Market Square. I suppose that sort of thing is old-fashioned now. Your father used to love it, and Tom.'

She offered him a second glass of whiskey, but he told her that he was driving.

'You'd better not then,' she said, 'although they'd never stop you.'

'Do you ever think of them,' he asked, looking up at her, 'my father and Tom?'

'Think of them?' she asked. 'I do all right, I do.' Her tone was factual and melancholy. He let the silence continue between them, sorry now that he had asked the question, that he had not let her talk of her own accord. She was thinking, a troubled look appeared on her face. He wished that he could ask her another question.

'Are you playing any golf at all?' she asked him.

'I grew tired of it,' he said, 'and tired of the club.'

'They're terrible snobs, all those golf people,' she said.

'I was no good anyway. I don't even play bridge any more,' he said.

'Carmel told me that,' she said. 'I love the bridge myself. It keeps you very alert.'

'You must come down some day now before we go back, I could come in and collect you in the morning,' he said.

'It would be nice now, but don't worry about it, because I know you're on your holidays.'

'You could have your lunch with us.' He heard himself saying the word 'lunch' and felt uncertain about it. She would always call it 'dinner'.

'Lunch is the word in Dublin now,' he said. 'Do they still call it dinner here?'

'Luncheon,' she said in an English accent, 'that's what Mrs Allen in the Bridge Club calls it. But it's all the same really, isn't it, it's all food.' She laughed. 'Luncheon,' she said again. 'Funny, all the words they have.'

He took the whiskey bottle and offered her some.

'I don't know why I'm offering you the whiskey,' he said.

'Oh, I won't have any more. I won't be able to sleep if I have any more.'

There was silence again in which he felt close to her and happy sitting there talking to her.

'Madge Kehoe invited us over and we had a great evening,' he said.

'She's very nice. I haven't seen her for years. I got a Mass card from her when your Uncle Tom died, and a letter. It was your father who knew the Kehoes and the Keatings; they've always been very nice. Her mother was nice as well, old Mrs Keating.'

'It's changed a lot down there, the erosion,' he said. 'The old house is nearly at the cliff.'

'That's been going on for years, for years since that terrible storm. It was before you were born.'

'And was there no erosion before that?'

'So they used to say. I remember your father saying that. He loved it down there, your father.'

They talked until darkness fell. She sent him out to the kitchen to get an electric fire. The summer was over now, she said, even though the days were good. It was beginning to be cold at night. As he turned on the light in the kitchen, he realized that this was the target for the stones, but they came only in the winter, she had told him.

'I'll go and talk to the Guards,' he said when he came back, 'about those fellows up in the field. They should be able to stop that. Or I'll talk to John Browne. Did you ever contact him?'

'He has a clinic alright in Murphy Floods on a Saturday. They say that he's very obliging.'

'He could sort it out for you.'

'There's another of them as well who has a clinic,' she said absentmindedly.

'I'll talk to the Guards anyway,' he said.

'They'd listen to you,' she said, and smiled at him warmly.

He carried the tray with the empty glasses and the bottle of whiskey down to the kitchen before he left.

'It was lovely to see you now,' she said. 'It was a great surprise.'

CHAPTER SIX

'WHISHT, whisht.' His grandmother put her hand up to stop them talking and then inclined her head towards the door, waiting for a sound. And when they listened and discovered that there was no sound, the men around the fire went on talking until it was time for news on the wireless, when she would order silence again.

'Tom will want to know the news when he comes in.'

The chimney smoked in the dark back room. 'Who's my pet?' she asked him, and they all looked at him. He did not reply.

'Who loves you the best?' she asked him, and went as though to tickle him. Her grey hair was tied back in a bun.

'You do,' he said.

They always quizzed him about school: how many slaps he got, how he was at spelling, how he was getting on at his Irish. Irish was important if you wanted to get a good Leaving Cert and a good job, his grandmother said.

'Your Uncle Stephen and your Daddy were great at Irish. Your Daddy got a university scholarship.'

In November when it became dark at half past four his Uncle Stephen came home from the Sanatorium on the Wexford Road and lay in bed in the front room downstairs. Eamon was allowed to sit with him as long as he did not go too close.

'Do you like reading?' Stephen asked him.

'Some books,' he said and he played with a toy car

around the table and the floor, while Stephen sat up in bed reading. There was a fire burning in the grate.

'When you're older you'll love books,' Stephen said. 'There are great books.' He was wearing a pullover over his pyjama-top.

As the light faded Stephen lay back with his head on the pillow and his eyes closed. Eamon thought that he was asleep until he began to cough. At first it was a weak wheeze which came in waves with his breath, and then it seemed that he could no longer breathe, and then Eamon could hear him struggling for air as the real coughing began. It sounded as if he was going to be sick. Eamon waited by the window watching him. 'Get newspaper quick,' his grandmother said to him as she came rushing in. 'It's in the bottom of the press in the kitchen.'

He ran out of the room and down to the kitchen where he found an old newspaper and brought it back to the front room. His grandmother was holding Stephen in her arms and saying 'you'll be all right' to him over and over. He thought that his Uncle Stephen was crying. He went back out into the hall and stood there listening to them. After a while he went down and sat in the kitchen. When his grandmother appeared he saw that the newspaper she had in her hand was bright with blood.

On Christmas morning he awoke early, before the first thin strip of grey dawn appeared over Vinegar Hill, and went downstairs and turned on the light in the back room. The room was still warm from the fire. He found his present from Santa Claus on the table and set about unwrapping it. It was what he had wanted: a fort in separate pieces and some soldiers. There were also several bars of chocolate.

He went back upstairs, his teeth chattering with the cold, and dressed himself. By the time his father appeared he had assembled the fort on the dining-room table. He showed his father how he had pieced it together.

It was a clear day with edges of frost on the pathway down towards the Back Road. They walked to nine o'clock Mass, meeting those coming home from eight o'clock Mass and greeting them with 'Happy Christmas' and 'Many Happy Returns'. At the bottom of Pearse Road a woman asked him what he got from Santa and he told her that he got a fort and soldiers.

They walked up the aisle of the cathedral to Our Lady's side altar, but there was no room there and they had to kneel on the ground until a woman moved over and made space for them, but there still wasn't space for Eamon on the seat and he had to sit on the foot-rest.

The preparations for the consecration began to the constant sound of coughing and shuffling, soon replaced by a reverent silence once the bells rang. He watched his father out of the corner of his eye as he opened the missal at the place where the black-edged Mass card for his mother was kept. He watched his father's lips move as he prayed, the missal still open, and his mother's smiling face, familiar he had looked at it so many times, centred in the card and below it the date of her death – 16 August 1934 – and her age, twenty-eight. He turned away as his father closed the missal, having finished whatever prayer it was he had been saying.

They went home after Mass and had breakfast. Then his father gathered all the presents they were to take to his grandmother's house: books for his grandfather and Uncle Stephen, a scarf for his Aunt Margaret and a cardigan for his grandmother. He found some wrapping paper and sellotape and set about writing cards for each of them.

'These are from you now,' his father said, 'and you're to hand them to everybody.'

His father put the presents in a shopping basket and gave it to Eamon to carry. They walked down John Street and Court Street towards the Market Square. His father stopped to talk several times. Eamon held his hand and tried to tug at him to make him hurry up, but one man in a brown coat who was on his way to have his Christmas dinner, he said, with his sister in St John's Villas, started to tell his father a long story which Eamon could not follow. He put the basket down on the ground and waited.

In Irish Street there was a different number of steps leading up to each house. He climbed each set and then jumped off while his father stood and watched.

'You'll break your ankle on this street some day,' he said.

There was a candle with holly in the window of his grandmother's house. His grandfather was watching out for them and came to open the door. He had a pint bottle of stout in his hand.

'Come in out of the cold,' he said.

Eamon put the basket in the hall.

'We met Johnny Corrigan,' his father said, 'and he kept us standing for ages.'

His grandmother was in the kitchen with his Aunt Margaret and his Auntie Molly who was married to his Uncle Patrick. Two of his cousins were in the back room in cowboy suits. They all stood round as Eamon distributed the presents. Stephen sat by the fire, huddled in against the wall with his legs crossed. He opened his parcel slowly and smiled when he saw the book. He reached behind him and handed Eamon another parcel with a book inside. Eamon had a box of sweets for his cousins.

The men were told to go into the front room once Uncle Tom and Uncle Patrick came back from Mass and the children were sent out to play so that the women could set the table and get everything ready for the dinner. Eamon brought his cousins up to Irish Street and they jumped off the steps until Aunt Molly came to look for them.

Stephen was still sitting by the fire, a glass of Guinness

in his hand. Eamon's grandfather was also drinking Guinness, but the other men were drinking ale. There was a smell of cooking all over the house and the windows in the room were covered in condensation from the heat. Aunt Margaret carried in a tray full of bowls of soup and all the men sat down. Aunt Margaret had paper hats for Eamon and his cousins and she put a bottle of orange in front of each of them. His grandmother said grace and they began to eat.

'Thanks be to God,' his grandmother said, 'for Christmas.'

She brought in the turkey on a huge plate with utensils for carving. The other women carried the vegetables, while Eamon's grandfather opened more bottles of Guinness and ale.

'Isn't it great,' his grandfather said, 'that we're all here and that we've plenty to eat.'

'There was a terrible crowd at nine o'clock Mass,' Eamon's father said.

'At six o'clock Mass,' his grandmother said, 'there were the same people as last year, bar poor Mr Doran who died. Women with work to do, and a few holy men.'

By now everyone had a plate of turkey and vegetables, and there was silence for a while as they ate.

'I always think of it at Christmas what we went through after the Rising in the town,' his grandmother said to his Aunt Molly. 'You'd be too young to remember it, Molly. Easter, nineteen and sixteen. It was before Stephen was born. They interned half the town in Frongoch, left us with nothing. They arrested Tom and Daddy here in this very room.'

'Was it a jail?' Eamon asked.

'And then we thought we were going to have Christmas here without them. It was a very bitter time. And then they suddenly let the whole lot of them out the day before

Christmas, and we went over to meet them on the train.
I'll never forget it. I always think of it at Christmas.'

'Was it a jail?' Eamon asked again.

'Eat up your dinner,' his father said.

After the trifle and the plum pudding the men went to
Benediction in the Cathedral.

'Come straight home, now,' his grandmother said. 'No
going into pubs.'

'It's the power of religion,' Stephen said and laughed.
He was sitting by the fire again.

'Were there iron bars in Frongoch?' Eamon asked when
the others had left and the women were washing up in the
kitchen.

'I don't know. I wasn't there.'

'But was it a jail?'

'No, it was more like an internment camp, a big
dormitory.'

'Was it near here?'

'It was in Wales.'

IT was dark when the men came back. Stephen was sitting
beside the fire reading, the women were still in the kitchen
and Eamon was playing cards with his cousins. When they
came in, his grandfather went over to the fire, and held his
hands towards the flames.

'It's cold,' he said as the other men came into the room
with their coats still on. 'Close that door now or you'll let
the heat out.'

'Were you in the pub?' Stephen asked.

'We were. There was a big crowd there. There was even
one of the Guards there.'

His grandmother and his two aunts came in.

'Was there a big crowd at Benediction?' she asked.

'O Salutaris Hostia,' Stephen said.

'I can smell the drink,' she said. 'That'll be the end of

the family in this country, men going out to drink on a Christmas Day. This town'll be ruined by drink.'

'I hope you haven't been touching it while we were out,' his grandfather said.

'I poured it down the sink, every bottle of it, while you were out, didn't I, Margaret?'

'Ah, you didn't,' his grandfather said.

'I did so. You needn't go down. You won't find anything except empty bottles. You've had enough drink, all of you, to do you for the whole New Year.'

'We'll have a cup of tea then,' his grandfather said, 'while we decide what to do.'

His grandmother went down to the kitchen and came back a few minutes later carrying a tray with a bottle of sherry, bottles of ale and stout and some glasses.

'You can drink at home on a Christmas Day,' she said.

'The family that drinks together,' Stephen laughed.

'So you didn't pour them down the sink,' his grandfather said.

'I didn't have the heart,' she said. 'Would you prefer tea, anyone?'

They all settled around the fire, the women with glasses of sherry, the men with beer, the three boys with glasses of lemonade. Eamon watched as his father tipped his glass to the side and poured the beer in slowly, letting it slide softly down the edge of the glass.

'Let us drink,' Stephen said, 'to the conversion of all Russia.' He laughed.

'Drink to me only with thine eyes,' Aunt Margaret said.

'My father sang that song,' his grandmother said. 'It was his favourite song. I'd love to hear it again.'

'I'd love to hear "I Dreamt That I Dwelt In Marble Halls",' Aunt Molly said.

'Fill up my glass,' his grandfather said, 'and I'll do it.'

He cleared his throat as the others watched him. Eamon moved over and sat on the ground near his father. His

grandfather's voice was softer and weaker than he remembered. After the first verse he stopped, and Eamon's
grandmother took over, smiling at his grandfather as she
did so. Her voice was much stronger, but she kept it low to
match her husband's, and when she finished her verse, he
started up again. For the last verse they joined together:

> *'I also dreamt which charmed me most*
> *That you loved me still the same*
> *That you loved me, loved me, still the same.'*

He left the high notes to her, let her voice soar away
from his, and she left space for him to join in again when
the song was coming to an end. They all clapped when it
was over. Eamon noticed that there were tears in his
grandmother's eyes.

'Tom will sing,' his grandmother said. She stood up and
went to the door.

'Be thinking of the words now,' she said as she went out.

'Does anyone know,' his grandfather asked, looking at
Aunt Margaret and Aunt Molly, 'where she hid the bottle
of whiskey?'

'You'd better ask herself,' Aunt Margaret said.

'What are you going to sing, Tom?' Aunt Molly said.

'Maybe one of the boys will sing first,' he said.

His grandmother came in then carrying another tray
with a bottle of whiskey, a jug of water, and smaller glasses.

'Go easy on this now,' she said.

'You're a great woman,' his grandfather said.

Eamon noticed that Stephen was staring into the fire,
not paying attention to what was going on in the room. He
didn't take any whiskey and barely spoke when he was
offered more beer.

'Come on, Tom, your song,' his grandmother said.

'I'll do Boolevogue,' he said.

'Oh, that's lovely, that's lovely, now,' his grandmother
said.

73

He started gently in a quavering tenor voice, looking down at the floor, but after the first two lines he sang with feeling:

> *'At Boolevogue as the sun was setting*
> *O'er the bright May meadows of Shelmalier,*
> *A rebel hand set the heather blazing*
> *And brought the neighbours from far and near.'*

By the last verses he was singing with great passion, the voice no longer quivered. They all watched him, listening intently to the story of the song as though they had never heard it before. Stephen closed his eyes as the song came to an end and hunched his shoulders.

'Singing is lovely at Christmas,' his grandmother said. 'And Tom has a great voice. It's Margaret's turn now,' she said. 'What will you sing, Margaret?'

'Let someone else sing first.'

'Will you sing the Jewel song with me?' his grandmother asked her.

'Wait till I think if I know all the words.' She thought for a moment. 'Come on out into the front room and see if we know it,' she said.

'Put more coal on the fire, when we're out,' his grandmother said.

In the next room they could hear the two soprano voices, starting, stopping again and re-starting.

'They're great when they sing together,' his grandfather said.

The two women appeared at the door.

'We have to stand up,' Aunt Margaret said. 'There's no point in singing this sitting down. It's very hard now, so if we stop, you'll just have to put up with us. Are you ready?'

Eamon turned around and watched them as they held their breath so they could each begin at the same time. They started the song, listening carefully to each other's voices, trying to harmonize on the high notes and then quickly hand over to each other. His grandmother's face was red with the heat of the room, but she smiled as she sang, and made theatrical gestures as the song came to an end.

'That was great,' his grandfather said. 'You sang that at the Athenaeum concert, I don't know how long ago. I don't know how we'll follow that.'

'You're a great audience,' his grandmother said and smiled as she sat down.

When the night was over Eamon and his father walked up together through the still, empty streets of the town. He could see the stars of frost on the pavement under the street lights on Court Street. He kept his hands in the pockets of his coat to keep them warm.

His grandfather died in January; Eamon remembered how his father came into his bedroom and pulled back the curtains and told him. He turned away and tried to go back to sleep. His father told him that he should get dressed, but he curled up in bed once his father had left the room, and closed his eyes.

Mrs Doyle was working in the kitchen when he came downstairs. She told him that his grandfather had fallen down dead just as he was going in the door of his own house. His heart, she said, it was his heart.

'Did he get a pain?'

'He was very peaceful.'

When he went down to his grandfather's house with his father he saw that the curtains on the front windows were drawn and there were black ribbons with a note bordered in black.

'Do you think he should go up?' his father asked his Aunt Margaret.

'I don't know. Does he want to?'

'Go up now and say a prayer,' she said to him. 'Kneel down and bless yourself first.'

There were people in the house whom he did not know, and others came to the door, their faces solemn and watchful. He walked up the first small flight of stairs and waited there. He could hear them saying the Rosary in the front bedroom, their voices murmuring together in a sing-song of prayer, and then the moment of silence before the return of the single voice: 'Hail Mary, full of grace, the Lord is with thee.'

He moved up a few more steps towards the room, he could now see the candlelight flickering on the wallpaper, he could smell the softening wax. He crept up closer until he was near the top of the stairs. The Rosary came to an end and they began reciting the Hail Holy Queen.

'Did your Mammy say you could come up?' a woman asked him as she came up the stairs. 'Did you ask your Mammy?'

He looked at her hard, unfriendly face. He did not know her. He could feel his own face breaking apart, but he did not cry and instead kept his eyes fixed on the woman and said nothing.

'Which of them are you?' she asked.

'I'm Eamon,' he said.

'And did your Daddy say that you could come up?'

He did not reply, but turned away from her.

'You're very bold,' she said and walked past him up the stairs.

In the back room downstairs the people were whispering; there were bottles of stout on the table and some of the women had small glasses of sherry in their hands.

'That's the last of them gone,' a man said. 'That's the last of the Fenians.'

Stephen was in the kitchen with Tom.

'Do you want a bottle of orange?' he asked Eamon. When his grandmother found Stephen in the kitchen she made him move into the back room out of the draught.

'You'll get your death in here,' she said. She was wearing black; even her stockings were black.

'He went very fast,' someone said to her as she passed into the hall.

'You'll have to be very good to your mother now,' the woman whom Eamon had met on the stairs said to Tom.

'Aye, aye,' Tom said.

Eamon went up the stairs again and sat on the top step. There was no noise coming from the front bedroom now except the whispering of prayers. He said his own prayers then, but stayed outside, all the time trying to imagine what it would be like to see his grandfather when he was dead.

THERE was a mist over the graveyard which became sleet as they said the prayers over the coffin. Eamon's feet were freezing, his toes were aching with the cold. He held his Aunt Margaret's hand and stood behind his father whose frame blocked Eamon's view of the grave. When he found a chink in the crowd, the coffin was already in the ground. A man was holding an umbrella over the priest. His Uncle Tom and his Uncle Patrick were holding his grandmother on each side. Stephen was standing in front of Eamon, beside his father. He was shaking with the cold. As he put his hands behind his back Eamon saw how thin his fingers were, how frail his hands.

As soon as they came home, Stephen went to bed and they lit a fire for him in the room upstairs. Eamon wondered who would use the front room now; who would sleep in the bed. Would they use the same mattress on which the dead man had been laid out? He knew that he could not ask. His grandmother was in the kitchen crying; his father and his uncles went down to her and he heard one of them telling her that she would be all right, but that only made her crying worse.

'I won't be all right,' he heard her saying, as she motioned them away.

THEY walked up through the town again; the sleet had lifted, but it was freezing cold.

'You'd better go straight to bed. I'll make you a hot water bottle,' his father said.

'Am I going to school tomorrow?' he asked.

'We'll see in the morning.'

The house was cold, he could see his breath when they turned on the light in the hall. It seemed strange, as though they had been away for a long time. He tried to remember when they had last been there, and realized that he had slept there the previous night, and left only that morning to go to the funeral.

'It's the coldest night of the year,' his father said as he put a match to the fire.

Eamon fell asleep as soon as his father put the light out in his bedroom. He knew when he was woken again that it was not yet morning; aware that he had been asleep for only a short while. He was tired and the bed was warm. When he put his hands up from under the blankets he could feel the cold.

'You're going to have to get up again,' his father said. 'Put on an extra jumper and vest.' When he turned on the light, Eamon noticed that his father was still wearing pyjamas.

'Why do I have to get up?'

'Your Uncle Stephen's after taking a turn.'

He looked at his father, and wondered if he could not put back the time an hour, maybe two hours, to when he had just fallen asleep.

'Tom's waiting for us downstairs. We'd better hurry up.'

'Where are we going?'

'We're going back down to the house. You can sleep down there.'

It occurred to him that they might put him to sleep in the bed in the front room upstairs where his grandfather had been laid out, and he did not want to sleep there, so he knew that he would have to try and stay awake. He looked down the stairs from the landing and saw that there was another man with his uncle; they were both standing in the hall with their hands in their coat pockets. He took his shoes into his father's bedroom and sat on the bed putting them on. His father was almost ready.

'Did you put an extra pullover on?'

'Look, it's under this one.'

There was ice on the path as they walked down towards the Back Road.

'Watch you don't slip,' his father said. The other two men did not speak. Eamon wondered if he was still asleep, if he could be dreaming, but he knew that this cold was real and the darkness actual.

'Did the doctor come before you left?' his father asked Tom.

'Yes, I had to go and wake him. As soon as he came down and saw Stephen he told me to go for the priest. I had a terrible time trying to wake the Manse, but Father Quaid said he would go down immediately, and then we came over here.'

'It's bad so, is it?' his father asked.

'The doctor says he won't last the night.'

They walked in silence along the ice-covered pavements of John Street, Court Street, Rafter Street and the Market Square. When they arrived at the house the Rosary was being said in the back room. The people were kneeling down and did not look up when his father and uncle came in and knelt down too and bowed their heads in concentrated prayer. Eamon counted twelve of them now and himself; most of them were neighbours. When the Glorious Mysteries were over they started again, this time the Sorrowful Mysteries. When Eamon went to the toilet he met his Aunt Margaret who said that they were going to say the Rosary all night.

'Your Uncle Stephen will be in heaven before the morning,' she said.

He thought of Stephen's soul floating out of him, seeping out of his body up through the house and into the sky. His father came into the kitchen. 'We're going to go upstairs now. We've made a bed for you in the back room so you can say a prayer and have a little sleep.'

Eamon went in and lay on the cushions they had put down for him. He left his clothes on but took off his shoes. They continued to say the Rosary in the room and he woke a few times as the prayers rose and fell, but soon he was fast asleep. He did not wake again until the dawn had broken. Someone had put more blankets on him; the room was empty now. He remained still for a while, afraid to move; he felt hot and sweaty and he wanted to go to the toilet, but still he was afraid.

Suddenly, he heard the bed being moved in the room above and as he lay there he knew that Stephen was dead. He turned and tried to sleep again, but he could not, and he wondered if someone would come. Eventually, his Aunt Margaret and his Uncle Tom came into the room, they were looking for something and did not notice that he was awake. They moved quietly about, whispering to each other, trying not to disturb him. Soon they closed the door and he was alone in the room again.

He did not know what they did to someone who was dead. Did they take all their clothes off? What did they wear when they were buried? An image of his mother came to him from his father's Mass card, but he kept it away from his mind; he tried to think instead about his dead uncle. He waited there until his father came into the room.

'Stephen's gone to heaven,' he said as soon as he saw that Eamon was awake.

Eamon turned away, he did not want his father watching him across the room. He shut his eyes. His father came over and touched him on the shoulder. He wanted to turn towards his father, but he kept his eyes shut and his fists clenched.

'Eamon, you'll have to get up, you can go to sleep later on.'

The house was quiet now, all the neighbours had gone. He went into the kitchen and looked at the clock, it was half past seven. The house was freezing. He went to the front door and saw two nuns coming up the path, walking towards him. He found his Aunt Margaret and told her and she went out to meet them and took them upstairs.

After a while his grandmother came down from the room in which Stephen had died. Her hair was loose around her shoulders, but when she saw him she put it back in place behind her head with her two hands. She was wearing a black coat.

'Poor Eamon,' she said. 'Poor Eamon.'

He put his face against her and his arms around her, but she moved away quickly and went and sat on her own in the back room until the others came and sat with her.

'No one is to touch me,' she said. 'No one is to come near me any more.' They sat in silence, all of them, until one of the nuns came and asked where the blessed candles were kept.

PART TWO

CHAPTER SEVEN

HE woke during the night and went downstairs to his study. He had been dreaming, but now the dream had escaped him. He went into the kitchen and took some cold water from a plastic bottle in the fridge. He sat at the kitchen table for a while and then went back into the study. It was a warm night.

He sat at his desk and looked down at the judgment he had written in longhand on foolscap pages. It was ready to be delivered. He wondered for a moment if he should have it typed, but he was worried about it being leaked. No one knew about it; even as he sat down to write it himself he did not know what he would say, what he would decide. There was so little to go on, no real precedent, no one obviously guilty. Neither of the protagonists in the case had broken the law. And that was all he knew: the law, its letter, its traditions, its ambiguities, its codes. Here, however, he was being asked to decide on something more fundamental and now he realized that he had failed and he felt afraid.

He took a biro from a drawer and began to make squiggles on a pad of paper. What was there beyond the law? 'Law'; he wrote the word. There was natural justice. He wrote the two words down and put a question mark after them. And beyond that again there was the notion of right and wrong, the two principles which governed everything and came from God. 'Right' and 'wrong'; he wrote the two words down and then put brackets around them and the word 'God' in capitals beside them.

Somehow here in the middle of the night with the moths

and midges drawn to the window, the idea of God seemed more clearly absurd to him than ever before; the idea of a being whose mind put order on the universe, who watched over things, and whose presence gave the world a morality which was not based on self-interest, seemed beyond belief. He wondered how people put their faith in such a thing, and yet he understood that the courts and the law ultimately depended for their power on such an idea. He crossed out the word 'God'. He felt powerless and strange as he went back to read random passages of his judgment. He decided to go to bed and sleep some more: maybe he would be more relaxed about his judgment in the morning.

Carmel did not stir in the bed when he came into the bedroom, but he knew that she had woken. When he got into bed he put his arms around her. She kissed him gently on the neck and then turned away from him, letting him snuggle against her. She fell back asleep, and he lay there for a while holding her until he grew drowsy and fell asleep as well.

He was wakened by the alarm clock and reached across her to turn it off. They both lay there without moving or speaking, as though still asleep.

'Are you in court today?' she finally asked, almost whispering.

'Yes,' he said.

'Do you have a full day?'

'There's a lot of work to get through.'

Another last day of term; another year gone by. He hoped that all the urgent applications for injunctions would go elsewhere. He knew that the press would be in his court today. This case was newsworthy. He hated the journalists' faces looking up at him, eager for something instant which they could grasp and simplify. He snoozed for a while and when he woke he found that Carmel had left the bed. He moved over to her side and lay in her heat until he knew that it was time to get up.

It was a fine morning. Thin wisps of white cloud hung in the sky like smoke, and the sun was already strong. He realized as he tested the water in the shower that he would like to get into his car now and drive with Carmel to Cush and never set foot in the court again.

She was still in her dressing-gown when he came downstairs. She poured tea for him.

'I think everything is ready now,' she said. 'Are you looking forward to getting away?'

'Yes, I am. I was just thinking that I'd be delighted never to set foot in the court again.'

'You'll feel differently at the end of the summer.'

He went into his study again and sat at the desk. He thought that he should read the judgment over again before going into the court, but he could not face it. He felt unsure about it, but as he left the house and drove into the city the uncertainty became deep unease. It was not yet nine o'clock when he arrived at the Four Courts, and he was not due to deliver his judgment until eleven, or maybe later, depending on what injunctions were being sought.

The line of reasoning in his judgment was clear, he thought. It had not been written in a hurry; evening after evening he had sat in his study and drafted it, working out the possibilities, checking the evidence and going over the facts. Even so, he was still not sure.

He stood at the window of his chambers and looked out at the river which was low now because of the tide and because of the good summer. He watched a boy moving between lorries and cars on a horse, riding bareback with confidence. When the lights changed to green, the boy and his horse joined the flow of traffic towards Capel Street.

He had taken the judgment from his briefcase and placed it on the table. He went over and looked at it again. The case had happened in one of the border towns. A lot of people must live on the edge there, he thought, with strange upheavals, odd comings and goings. But this had nothing to do with the case, as far as he knew. The case was simple: a sixteen-year-old girl attending a convent school had become pregnant and been expelled. She was due to have the baby over the summer and wished to return to the school for her final year, but the school had made it clear that she would not be re-admitted. The girl and her mother sought a court order instructing the school to take her back.

The girl was clever, according to the school reports which had been produced in evidence. Her becoming pregnant had been a great trauma and she had confided in nobody until it became obvious. Both the girl and her mother had given evidence. The mother seemed surprisingly young, but had been very confident in the witness box as she told of her visits to the school to talk to the principal and her long discussions with her daughter about her pregnancy and her future. She seemed sincere and deeply upset about her daughter's expulsion.

It would have been easier for everyone, she said, if her daughter had had an abortion. But because they decided to have the child and bring it up in the town, her daughter was being made to suffer. She would have to go to the Vocational School or travel every day to another town. She was being victimized, stigmatized, her mother said. She told the court that the principal had been more interested in keeping the pregnancy a secret than in her daughter's welfare or the welfare of the unborn child.

The daughter was a smaller, softer version of her mother, but just as articulate and just as sure that an injustice had been done to her. She liked the school, she said, she had a good relationship with all of her teachers, she expected to go to university after her final year. She told the court about her worry when she thought she might be pregnant, how she hoped she would have a miscarriage and wondered if she could get away and have an abortion without anyone discovering. When her mother found out, she said, she told her that all the family would support her. Her father had been upset for a few days but he said nothing bad to her.

The principal was new, she said, she had replaced a nun who had run the school for years. She was young and everybody liked her. So she was not afraid when she was called into the office. But she was very surprised, the girl told the court, when she was informed that she could not come back that term. It was a few days later that the principal told her mother that she would not be allowed back to the school the following year. She was shocked by this and hurt, the girl said. She didn't want to go out and began to feel ashamed and depressed.

She told counsel for the school that she knew what she had done was wrong. And she agreed that it was a bad example for younger girls, especially in a Catholic school. She had told everyone she was sorry, she said. No one wanted to expel the boy, she said, although some people knew who he was. She felt being expelled from the school stigmatized her.

He had spent three days listening to the case. The principal could only have been in her late twenties. She, too, was calm, assured and articulate. She was employed to run a Catholic school, she said. It was an educational establishment, but with a very specific ethos. She was prepared to forgive anybody a transgression, she said, and it was for God, not her, to judge, but she had to protect the school's ethos. There were, she told the court, great pressures on the girls in a changing world, but some things were still not acceptable to her as principal, to her board of management or to the majority of the parents. She had the right to decide if a girl should be expelled and she had decided to exercise that right.

Parents who had children in the school spoke for both sides. Some said that the girl should be forgiven and treated as a normal student in her final year. Others said that a teenage pregnancy should not be looked upon as normal or acceptable, and allowing the girl to return to school would have an abiding effect on her fellow students.

Eamon was aware as the case went on that the costs were rising and if the girl and her family lost it would be a great financial blow to them. He was disturbed by the case, which was widely reported on radio, television and in the newspapers. He remembered how calm the young girl had been, how vulnerable. He realized that this was one of the few cases he had heard where both sides were clearly telling the truth and were not afraid of the truth. All the witnesses were sincere, no one wished to hide anything.

He listened carefully to the counsel's submissions about various articles of the Constitution, but there was no argument about facts or truth, guilt or innocence. In the end he was not the legal arbiter, because there were so few legal issues at stake. Most of the issues raised in the case were moral: the right of an ethos to prevail over the right of an individual. Basically, he was being asked to decide how life should be conducted in a small town. He smiled to himself at the thought and shook his head.

As he worked on the judgment, he realized more than ever that he had no strong moral views, that he had ceased to believe in anything. But he was careful in writing the judgment not to make this clear. The judgment was the only one which he could have given: it was cogent, well argued and, above all, plausible.

He went to the window again and stood there looking out. How hard it was to be sure! It was not simply the case, and the questions it raised about society and morality, it was the world in which these things happened which left him uneasy, a world in which opposite values lived so close to each other. Which could claim a right to be protected?

He went over to his bookshelves and took down the sacred text: *Bunreacht na hEireann*, the Irish Constitution. This contained the governing principles to which the law was subject. The preamble was clear about the Christian nature of the state, it specifically referred to the Holy Trinity. He thought about it again, how the school had a duty to defend Christian principles, and indeed a right to do so, under its own articles of association and also under the general guidance of the Constitution.

Surely these rights and duties were greater than any rights a single individual, whose presence in the school might undermine the school's ethos and principles, could lay claim to?

His tipstaff came with tea. He began to think again. He wrote down three words in a note-pad: charity, mercy, forgiveness. These words had no legal status, they belonged firmly to the language of religion, but they had a greater bearing on the case than any set of legal terms. Opposite them he wrote three other words: transgression, sin, scandal. He sighed.

One other matter began to preoccupy him. The family, according to the Constitution, was the basic unit in society. He read the words in the Constitution: 'a moral institution possessing inalienable rights, antecedent and superior to all positive law'. What was a family? The Constitution did not define a family, and at the time it was written in 1937 the term was perfectly understood: a man, his wife and their children. But the Constitution was written in the present tense, it was not his job to decide what certain terms – he wrote 'certain terms' in his note-pad, underlined it and wrote 'uncertain terms' below that – such as 'the family' had meant in the past. It was his job to define and redefine these terms now. Could not a girl and her child be a family? And if they were, did the girl have rights arising from her becoming a mother, thus creating a family, greater than the rights of any institution?

He thought about it for a while and the consternation it would cause among his colleagues, a broadening of the concept of the family. The girl would have to win then, and the school lose. The idea seemed suddenly plausible, but it would need a great deal of thought and research. It had not been raised as a possibility by counsel for the girl and her mother. Lawyers, he thought, knew that he was not the sort of judge who would entertain such far-fetched notions in his court.

If he were another person he could write the judgment, but as eleven o'clock grew near he knew that the verdict he had written out on his foolscap pages was the one he would deliver, and it would be viewed by his colleagues as eminently sensible and well reasoned. But he was still unhappy about the case because he had been asked to interpret more than the law, and he was not equipped to be a moral arbiter. He was not certain about right and wrong, and he realized that this was something he would have to keep hidden from the court.

The downstairs corridors of the Four Courts were like some vast marketplace. He had to push his way through the passage leading to the side door of his court.

'The courtroom is packed, my lord,' his tipstaff said.

'Are we ready then?' he asked.

He tried to act as businesslike as possible when he came into the courtroom and everybody stood up. He sat down, arranged his papers in front of him, put on his reading-glasses, and consulted with the clerk, learning that there were several barristers seeking injunctions. He tried to deal with them promptly, realizing that, if he hurried, he could be finished by one o'clock, which meant that he could be in Cush by four, or half past four, and if the weather was warm enough he could have a swim. He told the clerk that he was ready to begin the judgment. He surveyed the court for a moment: the press benches were full as he had expected, and the public benches were also full. He knew that this judgment would be news. It would be carried on the radio and there would probably be editorials in the newspapers. He would certainly be attacked in *The Irish*

Times. As he settled down to read the judgment, sure now of his conclusions, he thought about how ill-informed and ignorant the comment would be, and how little of the processes of law the writers would understand.

He did not intend his judgment to be dramatic, but he wished to set out the facts first, clearly and exactly. The argument at times, he knew, was close and dense and it would be difficult for most people in the court to follow, but a great deal of it was clear. After half an hour, when he had set out the facts and paused for a drink of water, he was aware that no one in the court knew which side he was about to come down on. He could feel the tension; and the few times he looked up he could see them watching him carefully. He caught the mother's eye only once: she had the resigned look, he felt, of someone who knew that she was going to lose. People would have warned her that he was not a judge who would rule in her favour. He avoided eye contact with the girl.

As he read on and came near the passage which would make the result clear he found that he was enjoying the tension and noticed that he had begun to speak more distinctly, but he stopped himself and went back to the rigorous monotone which he had adopted at the beginning.

A murmur started in the court as soon as it became clear that he had decided in favour of the school; from the bench it sounded like the murmur in a film, and he felt that he should bang the desk with a gavel and shout 'Order in the court', but he continued as though there had not been a sound.

When he had finished, counsel for the school was on his feet immediately, his face flushed with victory. He was looking for costs. There was no choice, he could delay it until the new term, but it would be pointless and he wanted to have done with the case. The costs would be high, he listened to the submission from the other side. When he looked over he saw that the mother and father were holding each other, and both were looking up at him as though afraid.

'Costs follow the event and I see no reason why it should be different on this occasion,' he said. The mother began to cry. Although he had awarded costs against her, he thought she would probably not have to pay all of them. He wondered as he gathered up his papers if she would appeal, but he thought not; he had based a great deal of his judgment on matters of fact rather than law, and the Supreme Court could not dispute many of his findings. She would not have much chance of winning an appeal, he felt.

Back in his chambers he went to the telephone immediately.

'I'm ready now,' he said as soon as Carmel answered.

'We're going to pick up Niamh in Rathmines. She's decided to come down with us today. She's taking the carrycot and all the things so we'll need to collect her,' Carmel said.

'I thought she wasn't coming,' he said.

'She's finding it very hard,' Carmel said, as though he had complained about her coming.

'I'll be there in half an hour,' he said. He sat down at his desk and put his head in his hands. He could feel the sweat pouring down his back and his heart beating fast. He tried to control his breathing, to breathe calmly through his nose. He tried to relax. He remembered Niamh best when she was fourteen or fifteen, when she was still growing; even then she was tall for her age and interested in sports; hockey, tennis, swimming. They had pushed her too hard, Carmel said, forced her to study when she did not want to. She had studied social science when she failed to get the points for entry to study medicine. She had become a statistician, working on opinion polls and surveys of social change. She had become independent and distant from them until she was pregnant, when she and Carmel became closer, but he did not believe that she had felt any affection for him since she was in her early teens.

He sat at his desk as his heart kept pounding. He wondered if he was going to have a heart attack, and he waited for a dart of pain, or a sudden tightness, but none came and slowly the heartbeat eased.

Niamh was standing at the door of a small house down a side street in Rathmines. She waved when he beeped the horn and shouted that she would not be long.

'I thought she was living in a flat,' he said.

'Yes,' Carmel said, 'but there are three flats in the house and she knows the other people, they're all friends. They're very good to her, they babysit and help out.'

Niamh came out of the front door with the baby. He noticed that she had lost weight and let her hair grow longer. She smiled at them.

'I hope there's loads of space in the boot because I have to take the computer as well as the baby, and that's not forgetting the go-car and the cot.' She handed the baby to Carmel. Eamon went into the hall, brought out the cot and put it in the boot.

'The computer will have to go on the back seat,' he said. 'Are you sure you need it?'

She went past him without answering. He carried a suitcase and put it into the boot. He stood there then looking at the baby who looked back at him sullenly and curiously, fixing on him as something new and strange. Suddenly, the baby began to cry, and continued to roar as they arranged the go-car on the roof-rack and set off through Ranelagh and Donnybrook. 'He's very big,' he said after a while when the child had quietened down. 'He's much bigger than I expected him to be.' He looked behind at the child who began to cry again.

'It's better maybe if you don't look at him when he's like that,' Niamh said.

He knew as they drove past Bray that if they turned on the radio they would get the three o'clock news which would probably report on the judgment. Carmel would want to know about it, she would want to discuss his reasons for ruling in favour of the school, she would go away and think about it and want to discuss it further. With Niamh in the house it would be worse. He realized that he would prefer if they never found out about it. It would be difficult to explain.

'Who else is living in the house with you?' he asked Niamh. There had been silence in the car for some time. Both women told him to keep his voice down.

'The baby's asleep,' Niamh said.

At Arklow he took a detour to avoid the traffic in the town. It was close to four o'clock, and it was only now that he became relaxed enough to enjoy the good weather, the clear light over the fields and the heat which he knew would persist for at least two more hours, despite the clouds banked on the horizon. When they passed Gorey, the baby woke and began to make gurgling sounds.

'You should teach him "The Croppy Boy",' he said and laughed to himself as they passed a sign for Oulart. Niamh said that she would have to change his nappy, so they stopped the car and got out. He walked up and down taking in the heat as the two women busied themselves around the child, who had begun to cry again.

When they reached Blackwater Carmel said that she wanted to stop to get some groceries and to order *The Irish Times* for the duration of their stay. The baby was asleep again and he and Niamh sat in the seat without speaking. He closed his eyes and opened them again: in all the years there had been hardly any changes in the view from here up the hill. Each building was a separate entity, put up at a different time. Each roof was different, ran at a different angle, was made of different material: slate, tile, galvanized. He felt that he could be any age watching this scene, and experienced a sudden illusion that nothing in him had changed since he first saw these buildings.

THEY drove towards the sea at Ballyconnigar and then turned at the hand-ball alley to Cush. There were potholes on the narrow road and he had to drive carefully to avoid them.

'What's for dinner?' he asked.

'I'm not making any more dinners,' Carmel said and laughed.

'I hope you can cook, Niamh,' he said.

'Niamh is an excellent cook,' Carmel said.

'It's time men pulled their weight,' Niamh said drily.

There was always that moment when he saw the sea clearly, when it took up the whole horizon, its blue and green colours frail in the afternoon light. The road was downhill from then on. He drove along the sandy road, saluting a few people as he passed.

'I want to unload really quickly,' he said, as he stopped the car beside the house, 'because I want to go for a swim before the sun goes in.'

'I'd love to go for a swim too,' Niamh said.

'I'll take the baby if you both empty the car,' Carmel said.

Niamh had gone to change, and he stood waiting for her. There was a sweet, moist smell from the high grass in front of the house. He was tired and felt the burden of the day in his back muscles and his eyes. Suddenly he looked up and his eye caught the rusty red paint on the galvanized iron of the gate. He liked the colour, and it seemed familiar as he stood there and took in the scene: the rutted lane, the tufts of grass clinging to the sandy soil of the ditch, and the sound of a tractor in the distance. He stood there for a moment fixing on nothing in particular, letting each thing in the landscape seep towards him, as he tried to rid himself of everything that had happened that day.

Down on the strand they could see as far as Curracloe.
Niamh wore only a light dress over her swimming-suit, so
she was already in the water while he was still undressing.
When he took off his shoes he felt an instant release as
though a weight had been lifted from him. Most of the
strand was in shadow. He left his clothes on a boulder of
dried marl and walked towards the sunlight on the fore-
shore, stepping gingerly over the small, sharp stones which
studded the sand.

The water was cold; Niamh waved to him from way out.
He watched her long, thin arms reach up from the water
as she swam parallel to the shore. He was tempted, as
usual, to turn back, but he waded in farther, jumping to
avoid a wave, and then he dived in and swam hard out,
glidi⸴ g over each swell as it came. He turned and put his
head back, letting it rest on the cold, blue water, and
opening his eyes to stare up at the sky. He breathed in
deeply and floated on the waves, relaxed now and quiet.
He curled back towards the water after a while, and swam
farther out, each movement half instinct, half choice.

He cast his eye down the coast and noticed as he turned
that a family was moving slowly up the strand towards the
gap, carrying rugs and babies, struggling as they reached
the cliff. He watched Niamh wading out and drying herself.
She waved to him. No one else would come until the
morning, except maybe a tractor using the strand as a
short cut. He was tired now; the swimming would be easier
the next day and the day after that. He changed to a dog
paddle which consumed less energy than the breast stroke.
A cloud passed over the sun and left him in shadow so that
he could feel a cold edge to the wind on his face. He turned
again and floated, keeping his eyes closed for as long as he
could, not knowing whether the water was taking him in or
out. For a few seconds he forgot himself, sustained by the
rise and fall of the waves and the knowledge that it would
carry him as long as he relaxed and remained at peace.

As soon as he arrived back at the house he knew that Carmel and Niamh had been listening to the six-thirty news.

'Well, you were busy this morning,' Niamh said.

'Was it on the news?' he asked, as if it was a routine matter.

'Do you think I should be expelled as well?' she asked.

'Your father's on his holidays, Niamh,' Carmel said.

'That's not what you said before he came in. My father thinks that unmarried mothers shouldn't be allowed to go to school,' she laughed bitterly.

'What exactly is biting you?' he asked.

'That poor girl. How could it be right to expel her and never let her back?'

'Read the judgment and find out,' he said.

'Did you bring it with you?' she asked.

'Of course I didn't.'

'I think it's a disgrace, that's what I think,' Niamh said. 'It's an outrage.'

'But you would think that, wouldn't you?'

'I know about it. I know what it's like to be a woman in this country, and I know what it's like to have a child here.'

'And I suppose you're a legal expert as well.'

They had supper in silence, which was broken only by the whimpering of the baby. He faced the window and noticed the first throbbing rays of the lighthouse glinting in the distance. He wanted to ask Carmel what she had said about him and his judgment before he came in, but he realized that he could gain nothing by doing so.

'Do you want more tea?' Carmel asked him.

'Yes, please,' he said. He tried to make his voice sound neutral, as though he was not annoyed with them. He was too tired now to want any further argument. He sat at the table as they cleared away the dishes.

'We're going to take Michael for a walk,' Carmel said to him. 'Are you staying here?'

'Yes,' he said.

'Are you all right?' she put her hand on his shoulder.

'I'm tired,' he said. 'I'm glad to be here.'

He stood up and walked into their bedroom, and rummaged through the suitcases until he found a book. He lay down on the bed, but as soon as he opened the book he knew that he was too tired to read. He knew that he would sleep. He took off his jacket and his shoes and rested on his side, facing away from the window.

She woke him when she turned on the bedside lamp. He felt heavy and tired as he turned towards her.

'It's all quiet now,' she said. 'You were fast asleep.'

'Is it late?'

'It's after ten. You were on the news again. Not you, but there was a report about you.'

'Nothing that they haven't said before.'

'The Irish Council for Civil Liberties – Niamh says that Donal is a member – have issued a statement.'

'Our son and our daughter,' he said and laughed.

'They're fine people, both of them,' Carmel said.

'I suppose I'm the one who's wrong?'

'No, you're all right too,' she stood over him and smiled. 'After a few days here you'll be fine, but I don't understand your judgment. It seems wrong to me.'

She lay down beside him, not bothering to take off her shoes.

'I'm tired too,' she said, as she turned towards him and put her arms around him. 'I don't know why I'm so tired.'

CHAPTER EIGHT

THE shock of the alarm clock in the early morning. It was winter. He snuggled up in the warm bed, trying to stay awake and lie on until the last minute. His father was a light sleeper, the alarm would have woken him in the front room and he would stay awake until he heard some sound. Eamon dreaded the creak of his father's footsteps on the bare boards of the front room; he knew that if he did not get out of bed his father would come to rouse him. One more minute: he lay still in the warmth of the bed and waited. The tip of his nose was cold and the bed more comfortable than he had ever imagined. He felt sorry that he did not appreciate it more at night. Then suddenly he braced himself, he jumped out into the freezing air, and walked shivering across the floor to turn on the light.

When he was dressed he felt less sleepy. He went out into the back yard and took the bicycle out of the shed and wheeled it around to the front of the house. There was a vague light over Vinegar Hill and the Turret Rocks. The ground was damp and as he rode down the hill he knew that he would have to watch for ice.

He passed Parkton and Lymington House and the bottom of Pearse Road. He felt afraid as he rode past the dark trees at O'Flaherty's, and the big old house lurking behind. He shivered with relief when he crossed New Street and started to freewheel down Spout Lane to the cathedral.

Bill Devereux, the sacristan, was already in the vestry, unwrapping a bundle of candles.

'It's not too bad, now, this morning,' he said.

'It's freezing, Mr Devereux,' Eamon said.

'Not if you're wearing warm clothes.'

Eamon searched through the soutanes to find one which fitted him. Each time when he finished serving Mass he put the soutane he had used in a place which he tried to mark and remember, but it was never there when he returned.

'If you don't hurry up, I'll have to light the candles myself,' Bill Devereux said. 'There are new lilies on the altar and you're to be careful with them.'

He was ready. The long pole had a cone below it to extinguish the candles when the Mass was over. He went out on to the altar and looked down at the vast shadowy church, dimly lit now for first Mass on Sunday. He reached up to the high candles on the altar. He had to use his two hands to angle the lighted taper against the wick of the candle, and he had to watch and wait to make sure that it was burning. When four on one side were lit, he walked back down the steps, genuflected, checked that they were still burning and then lit four on the other side. As he genuflected on his way back to the sacristy he noticed the lilies. They seemed carved from wax themselves, hand-made, so pure in their colour and shape.

'I didn't do any damage to the lilies,' he said when he came to the sacristy.

'You're very serious this morning,' Bill Devereux laughed.

There was a red carpet in the room where the priest was dressing. Eamon waited as Father Howlin placed the green and gilded chasuble over his head. He had learned the word for each thing: the amice, the alb, the girdle, the stole, the maniple and the chasuble. Usually, when Father Howlin was dressing he did not speak, but turned and indicated with a nod that he was ready to go. Then they walked out on to the altar and the Mass began.

'*Introibo ad altare Dei*,' the priest began in Latin, and
Eamon called out the reply which he knew by heart without
having to look at the response card on the altar steps in
front of him. He liked the Latin sounds, just as he found
comfort in the smell of the candles, the shape of the chalice,
the squat curve of the ciborium and the small red curtains
inside the doors of the tabernacle. When he had begun to
serve Mass first, he had been so interested in each thing
that he had often forgotten to call out the response, but
usually there was another server there. This morning,
however, he was alone so he had to concentrate.

He went around to the side steps to pour the wine and
the water, and came back to ring the bells by his side to
alert the people to the imminence of the consecration. He
watched for the raising of the host and rang the bells before
bowing his head. And then at the raising of the chalice, he
rang the bells again to break the hush in the vast cathedral.

When Mass was over he came back to the sacristy to
find that two other servers had arrived. Bill Devereux
motioned Eamon to come with him to ring the twenty to
eight bell, while the others put out the candles and
prepared the altar for eight o'clock Mass. Eamon kept his
soutane on. They walked past Calvary and crossed to Our
Lady's altar. Bill Devereux opened the small side door with
a huge metal key and they walked up the winding stairway
until they came to the stem of the spire. From there, they
looked down into the body of the church where a few
people had already gathered for the next Mass.

'Some people come to two Masses,' Bill Devereux said.
'You'll probably come back with your father.'

'I'd say so, all right.'

'We'll make a saint of you yet.'

He pulled back the bolt and opened the door which led
on to the ramp, which in turn led to the spire. It was a
clear day now, but there were still patches of mist over the
river.

'We'd better hurry up, or we'll be ringing the twenty-to bell at a quarter to. Do you know what that is?'

'What is?' Eamon asked.

'Ringing the twenty-to bell at a quarter to.'

'No.'

'I thought that you knew everything. It's an Irish Bull. Did you ever hear that before?'

'No.'

'Well, go home and tell your father that nine o'clock Mass next Sunday will be at ten o'clock and ask him what he thinks of that. Will you do that?'

'Yes, I will.'

Bill Devereux took the rope in his hand and pulled it firmly, holding it hard and not letting go until he had to; there was no sound, his face was taut with concentration. He pulled again, this time harder, holding on once more for as long as he could, and now the first ring came, booming down to them, loud enough to fill the air.

'You do it,' he handed the rope to Eamon. 'You should be strong enough.'

Eamon held the rope, he could feel the great weight of the bell, he tried to pull evenly without jerking the rope.

'That'll wake the whole town up now,' Bill Devereux said. 'Men, women and children.'

When they went back to the ramp the day had become brighter. They stood there looking over the rooftops towards the river and the vast red-brick mental hospital beyond it.

'That's a grand day now,' Bill Devereux said, and waited there, rubbing his hands together to keep them warm. Eamon stood beside him, freezing.

'Look down there towards the river,' Bill Devereux said. 'Look down now.' He held Eamon, who was shivering with the cold, by the shoulders. He pointed. There was a creamy mist like white, thick smoke, hanging over the river.

'I've never seen it like that before. Do you know that? In

all the years. It's never been as white as that.' He shook his head. 'You'd think you would have seen everything.'

WHEN he had changed out of his soutane, Eamon put on his coat and went out the side door to get his bicycle. He freewheeled down Cathedral Street into the Market Square. As eight o'clock rang out he passed a few late-comers rushing up towards the cathedral. He stopped in the Market Square and bought a newspaper for his father. In Court Street a street lamp was still burning, and there were lights on in the front windows of some of the houses in John Street. He went to Corrigan's for the milk. His father had given him the money to pay the week's bill. When he knocked on the door, Mr Corrigan came out in a collarless shirt and looked at him.

'You're too early altogether. What has you up at this hour?'

'I was serving Mass.'

'The cows aren't milked yet. You'll have to come back. Unless you want yesterday's.'

'No.'

'Come back then around nine or half nine.'

He wheeled his bicycle up the hill. He noticed that the curtains in his father's room were still drawn. He would be asleep now, but Eamon's coming in, no matter how quiet, would wake him. He put his bicycle into the shed and went into the house through the back door which he had left unlocked. There was a smell of gas in the kitchen, he checked the cooker and the grill; his father sometimes did not remember to turn off the gas. But everything was turned off. He went into the back room and drew the curtains, listening for some sound from upstairs, but there was nothing. He tiptoed up to the toilet, still listening for a sound from his father's bedroom.

Downstairs, he spread a piece of butter as thinly as he could across a thick slice of bread. He put jam on the bread. Later, he would have the sausages which his father had got for him the previous day, but his father would have nothing because he was fasting for communion. He could only drink water. Eamon wondered what Mass his father would go to. It was probably too late for nine, and his father did not like ten o'clock Mass because there were too many children. So it would be eleven. He did not understand how he managed to fast that long. Maybe today he would miss communion.

He set to lighting the fire, rolling a piece of newspaper into a tight knot and then placing some lighting twigs, which he got from the shed, around it. He observed it carefully while it lit, before adding more sticks and some turf and a few pieces of coal.

His books were on the table where he had left them the previous night. His English composition was already written, and his maths. His father taught History and Irish. There was never anything to learn in history, Eamon forgot nothing that his father said. He knew the Plantations: Laois in 1555, Munster 1575, Ulster 1598 and later in the reign of James I. Henry VIII came to the throne in 1509, he divorced Katherine of Aragon in 1533. Elizabeth came to the throne in 1558 and she died in 1603, the same year as the Treaty of Mellifont. Sometimes his father examined them in dates: Eamon had to be careful not to show that he knew more than anybody else in the class. The others got things mixed up, they had the Flight of the Earls before the Battle of Kinsale, which, as his father said, made no sense.

Some things were not so easy. Unseens in Latin he found difficult. He hated guessing, but Mr Mooney told them not to leave gaps, they would get no marks for gaps, so he was forced to guess. He worked hard at his vocabulary, and now that he was in his second year, Mr Mooney asked him a question only when nobody else knew the answer. He sat at the table in the back room in the quiet morning with the

fire crackling in the background and started to work at his
Irish, writing down all the words he did not know on one
side of the page and their English equivalents on the other,
trying to remember each Irish word, how it changed in the
genitive if it was a noun, and how to form the past if it was
a verb.

After some time he heard his father and he went upstairs
to him.

'I'm going down to get the milk,' he said.

'I heard you getting up,' his father said. He was sitting
on the bed still wearing the top of his pyjamas. 'I'd say it
was very cold. We should get you a pair of gloves.'

'I won't be serving Mass for much longer.'

When Eamon came back his father was sitting by the
fire reading the paper.

'Have you had your breakfast?'

'No.'

'Have it now then, because I won't have anything. I'm
fasting for communion.'

Eamon melted the lard in the frying pan and fried the
sausages. He did not have tea, as he knew that it was
rationed, and he left it for his father. He cut a slice of bread
and poured a mug of milk. The milk was still warm. He
carried the food into the back room and cleared a space for
it on the table.

'Was there much of a crowd at seven Mass?' his father
asked.

'Not many, there were more at eight Mass.'

'Who said Mass?' his father asked, still reading the
paper.

'Father Howlin.'

'A real howlin' sermon,' his father said.

'There's no sermon at seven o'clock Mass.'

'They don't need it, I suppose. They're very holy all the
people at seven o'clock Mass.'

'Are you going to eleven Mass?' he asked his father.

'I am.'

'I think it'll be Father Doyle,' he said.

'You're the one with the inside information,' his father said. 'Those sausages would make your mouth water,' he continued.

'Do you want one?' Eamon held it up on his fork and laughed.

'Don't tempt me. If the Pope says that you can't eat, then you can't eat. What's good enough for Rome is good enough for me,' he smiled and looked into the fire.

'What's an Irish Bull?'

'What do you want to know that for?'

'Bill Devereux told me to ask you.'

'An Irish Bull? The Easter ceremonies will be held at Christmas, that's an Irish Bull.'

'Nine o'clock Mass will be held at ten o'clock. Is that an Irish Bull?' he asked.

'It would suit Bill Devereux better to be lighting candles and saying his prayers,' his father said. 'Will you tell him I sent him that message?'

They walked along the Back Road together to Mass. Everything looked different now in the clear daylight. It was hard for him to imagine how afraid he had been just a few hours earlier when he had passed the gaunt trees at O'Flaherty's, now that it was bright and he was walking with his father.

The cathedral was crowded. They walked up the men's side in the centre aisle until they saw a man his father knew who moved over and made room for them. Even as the Mass began people moved up the church looking for seats.

They sat down for the sermon. The priest talked about the importance of the home, but Eamon did not listen after that, he looked around him and thought about school and how he would wash the potatoes when he went home and grill the chops, which Mrs Doyle had shown him how to cook. It struck him that he should not have come to a second Mass. Soon, he would stop serving Mass altogether and attend only one Mass with his father on Sundays.

The priest walked from the pulpit back to the main altar, there was the noise of people coughing and shuffling in their seats. At first he thought that his father was going to sneeze – he had the habit of sneezing in confined spaces – and he hoped that he would be able to find a handkerchief in time. But his father was not sitting down any more, he was trying to stand up, and the people in front turned to look as his body jerked forward as though something was pushing him. He let out a moan suddenly as a few men from behind held him and then lifted him out of his seat into the aisle and loosened his tie. They tried to lead him out of the church, but there seemed to be no life in him, and they had to carry him towards the door.

People looked around in alarm and wonder and then turned again to face the altar, glancing behind sometimes to see if it was all over. Eamon left his seat and walked down the church, but the doors were blocked by late-comers, all of them men. He could see no way through. It had happened so quickly. He went back to his seat again. He looked for the man who had made space for them in the pew but he was gone. There was no one around him whom he recognized. He knelt until he heard the bells for the consecration, then he decided he would try and push his way out into the front yard of the cathedral. He stood up and genuflected, as if to make clear that he was leaving. He took his father's missal and walked hesitantly towards the back of the church. Through a gap in the figures kneeling in the doorway he caught a glimpse of his father lying in the foreground of the church, with men standing around him. He turned away. And when he did so he found that he was facing the altar just as the priest raised the host and the bells rang out. He knelt down where he was and waited. After the consecration he returned to his seat. He was shaking. He thought that they would come looking for him and it was best if he stayed where they could find him.

He did not want to go outside. After the Mass he did not join in the rush to leave, but sat there and waited. He saw faces that he recognized but he did not know what to say to them. Eventually, he joined the crowd edging down the main aisle. Outside, he looked around, but he could not see any of the men who had carried his father out. The churchyard was thronged now, and he had to follow the pull of the crowd towards the gates. He waited on the other side of the railings, wondering what he should do. Eventually, when no one approached him, he decided that he should go home. His father would be at home by now: people often fainted in Mass, he had fainted at early Mass once himself.

He knew, however, as he approached the house that his father was not there. He let himself in, put his father's missal in the press, took off his coat and put some coal and slack on the fire. He went into the kitchen and began to wash the potatoes, scrape the carrots and put them into saucepans of water on the gas rings. Several times he went to the window and looked out, but the street was empty. He took the breakfast things from the table in the back room and put them into the sink. It would take twenty-five minutes for the potatoes to boil, he checked the clock in the back room for the time. It would take fifteen minutes for the chops to grill. If his father was not back in ten minutes he would put his own chop on.

When he had eaten he went back to his Latin, took an unseen from the sample exam papers which his father had got for him in Dublin and tried to work on it. He read it first to get a general impression of its meaning, and then he set about translating it line by line, feeling frustrated at the sentences which contained words he did not know. He resisted guessing and simply left them blank.

He went to the front window and looked out once more.

It had started to drizzle, the day had darkened and Vinegar Hill was only faintly visible. There was nobody on the street. It was cold. He went upstairs and took a blanket from the bed. He lay down on the sofa in the front room with the blanket wrapped around him. He turned his face away from the window and soon he fell asleep.

It was dark when he woke again. He heard the sound of a key in the door, and heard the light in the hall being turned on. It would be easy, he thought immediately, to have his father's pork chop cooked in fifteen minutes and he could put the left-over potatoes and carrots into a colander and heat them up over a saucepan of boiling water.

'There's nobody here,' he heard a voice saying. He was not sure who it was.

'I'm here,' he shouted out.

The light was suddenly switched on in the front room, and when he turned towards the door it blinded him and he had to shield his eyes.

'You shouldn't be here on your own,' his Uncle Tom said. 'We've been looking for you all over the place.'

'I couldn't find anybody.'

'You should have waited around.'

Another man stood there, a man who lived in Court Street and was in the St Vincent de Paul with his father.

'Your father's after having a turn,' his uncle said. 'He's been taken down to Wexford. It looks as if they're going to move him to Dublin.'

Eamon said nothing. He tried to weigh up what he had been told. He wanted the two men to go.

'Do you want a cup of tea?' he asked.

'No, we're all right now,' his uncle said.

He stood up from the sofa and drew the curtains.

'I'd better check the fire inside,' he said and walked past them into the back room.

'We rang your Aunt Kitty in Tullow,' his uncle said.

'You'd be better up there until your father is well again. You can't be here on your own, and there's no one to look after you down below in our house.'

'How long am I going for?'

'You'd better pack your things for a while. Have you got a suitcase or a hold-all?'

He noticed that the other man was looking around the room, taking it all in.

'What hospital is he going to in Dublin?' he asked his uncle.

'We don't know yet. It'll probably be Vincent's. But there'll be time enough for that now.' He made a motion as though to hurry him on.

'What am I going to do about school?' he asked.

'You'd better take your books with you, and enough clothes.'

'Enough clothes for what?'

'You'd better hurry up now, your Auntie Kitty is going to meet you off the bus.'

Upstairs he went into his father's room, where the bed was still unmade and his father's pyjamas lay on the floor. He picked the pyjamas up and put them on the bed. He found a suitcase under the bed, full of old clothes which he emptied out on to the floor. He took the case into the back room and rummaged through his chest of drawers, putting what he thought he would need into the suitcase. He carried it downstairs and piled books and papers into it as well, going through each school subject and making sure that he had enough books and material. The suitcase would not close, so he took some of the books out and put them into a separate bag. His uncle and the man from Court Street were sitting down on chairs in the back room.

'How long will I be away?' he asked his uncle.

'I don't know. He's gone to Dublin for tests. It depends on what the tests say.'

'I thought you said he was going to Dublin. I thought you said that he is in Wexford now.'

'They decided to move him.'

'Have you told the Brothers that he won't be in school tomorrow?'

'We'll go down and do that after we've dropped you at the bus.'

They walked through the town, the two men taking turns to carry the suitcase, and Eamon carrying the bag with his books. They waited at the bottom of Slaney Street until the bus came. His uncle bought him his ticket and slipped him two shillings.

'Will you see him?' he asked.

'He'll be home before too long,' his uncle said.

The bus nosed slowly along the narrow road to Bunclody. It was smoky and overheated. The windows were covered in condensation. When he cleared a space to look out, Eamon found that he could see nothing except his own reflection and the droplets of rain clinging to the glass.

The rain became heavier as they climbed beyond Bunclody into the mountains. If the bus broke down, he thought, there would be no one around for miles. He pictured all the passengers walking back in the rain in search of a farmhouse with a telephone. The man opposite him who was smoking a pipe leaned over and spat out on to the passageway. The man cleared his throat and spat again, and then sat back in the seat, smoking his pipe.

His aunt and uncle met him at the bus stop in Tullow. His mother's three older sisters lived in America, but Kitty was younger than his mother and had married into a farm in the hilly land above the river near Tullow. He hardly knew her; he had met his cousins, her children, a few times, but, being from a farm, they were different; also, they were younger than he was and they had country accents.

'You've gone very tall,' his aunt said.

They put the suitcase into the boot and set off.

'Who left you to the bus?' she asked.

'My Uncle Tom and another man.'

'Weren't they very good?' she asked.

They talked among themselves in the front of the car. He listened but he barely understood. He had been to their house once before, but this time the journey seemed longer.

'I'd say you'll find it different up here,' his aunt said.

They parked the car at the side of the house and were met by several sheepdogs, which stood around him barking when he got out.

'Don't mind them,' his uncle said. 'Don't mind them at all.'

The children were sitting in the kitchen around a table. There were clothes hanging over the range. There was a girl younger than him, and two boys aged about seven or eight, and then another girl younger again, and a baby in a pram. There was a serving girl working at the sink.

'We'll put the tea on now,' his aunt said, 'and then you'll all want to go to bed early.'

Eamon stood against the wall, his bag still in his hand, and looked at them, looked around the kitchen. He wondered if there was a school nearby he could go to, he wondered where he would sleep. He wanted to explain to his aunt that he studied every night before he went to bed, but she was busy with the baby.

'Sit down and have your tea,' his uncle said to him.

After supper they went to bed. He would have to share a bed with his two cousins who wore their underpants and vests in bed as well as their pyjamas.

'Are you coming to school with us in the morning?' one of them asked.

'I don't know. Is there a secondary school?'

'It's a national school.'

He stayed awake for a while trying to think about what was going to happen, but he could think of nothing except the empty house at home, everything still and untouched in the darkness, all of the rooms quiet, the fire gone out, the milk he collected in the morning, which now seemed so far away, slowly going rancid in the night. He imagined each room, each piece of furniture until slowly he, too, fell asleep.

CHAPTER NINE

THEY moved closer together in the half light of the bedroom. As they started to make love they could hear the baby crying in the living room. Eamon closed his eyes and let his tongue run around Carmel's neck and shoulders as she reached into the slit of his pyjamas and held his penis. The baby stopped crying and they could hear Niamh moving about, talking to the baby as she put him in the pram.

'I'm too old,' she said and kissed him.

'Don't worry, it's okay, it's nice being here like this,' he said.

She began to masturbate him, slowly and rhythmically at first. He stroked her hair and ran his hands along her thighs. When he began to ejaculate she held him and kissed him.

'Holidays,' he said and smiled.

'I hope Niamh didn't hear us,' she whispered.

When they were dressed they went out into the garden. Eamon carried out a table and chairs and they had breakfast with Niamh while the baby slept in the pram in the shade. It was a warm day; a high wind blew clouds across the sky.

Carmel made more tea as Niamh drove into the village to get the newspaper and some groceries.

'I'd say the sea is rough today,' he said.

'Donal's coming today,' Carmel said. 'You'll be able to go for a swim with him.'

'How's he getting here?'

'He has a car. He's had a car for two years. I think he's bringing a girl.'

'He's been causing a lot of trouble over Free Legal Aid.'

'I know.'

'He's not going to get much of a practice if he continues issuing statements.'

'He's actually doing very well. Also, he has a lot of principles.'

'They all start off like that,' Eamon said.

'He's a little like you when you were his age, very earnest, with no sense of humour about himself. It's a Redmond trait.'

'Are they going to stay for long?' he asked.

'No, they're only coming for the day,' she said.

Later, when Niamh returned, Donal and his girlfriend were with her. They had met in the village and driven together back to Cush. Carmel stood up to greet them. As Eamon stood too he noticed how much happier and more animated Carmel seemed now that Donal had arrived. Donal looked thinner each time he saw him, more adult and distant. Today he was wearing a collar and tie. His girlfriend was wearing a summer dress, her hair was cut very short.

'This is very remote, isn't it?' she said. 'It's a real hide-away. You'd never find it if you didn't know it.'

'Donal's father's been coming here since he was a child,' Carmel said.

'Donal told me about the cliff.'

'Has it eroded much this year?' Donal asked him. He made the question sound professional and serious.

'It's much worse at Keating's than here, but there's a big gap this year where Mike's house used to be, so at least it's easy to get up and down to the strand.' It occurred to him as he spoke that they were using up a vital topic of conversation.

'Lunch is in an hour,' Carmel said, as she stood in the

doorway. 'There's chicken and new potatoes, and there's a salad, that's the menu. It will be served when Niamh comes back.'

'Where's Niamh going?' he asked.

'She's going to get your Aunt Margaret,' Carmel said, 'so that we can have four generations of the family together. I'm going to take a photograph.'

'I'll take it, so you can be in it too,' Donal's girlfriend said.

'Someone's going to have to change Michael,' Niamh said. 'Will you do it, Donal? It'll be good training for you.'

'There's no need to start,' Donal said.

'I'll do it,' Donal's girlfriend said.

'You're on your day out, Cathy,' Carmel said as she lifted the child. 'He's used to me. When I bring him out he'll be all clean.'

Donal unfolded several deckchairs and they sat in front of the house, facing the sun.

'Has the weather been good?' Donal asked his father.

'It rains at some stage every day, but it's been warm.'

'What's the sea like?'

'There's been no real scorching day, but it's getting warmer, or maybe I'm just getting used to it.'

Cathy had been out of earshot, wandering in the garden. She came towards them now.

'This is a lovely house,' she said. Her accent was pure south Dublin. She was very confident.

'You don't recognize Cathy?' Donal said to him.

'Recognize her? I've just met her.'

'He wouldn't remember me,' Cathy said.

Eamon noticed that both of them had become hostile. 'I've a very good memory for faces,' he said. 'It's not as good as Carmel's, but I think that I would remember you if I had met you before.'

'Maybe it's a guilty conscience,' Donal said.

Eamon looked at him sharply. 'What do you mean?'

'She appeared before you,' Donal said.

Eamon looked at her again, but he could not remember her face.

'I was the one who looked for costs in the Ryan case. I was the junior at the hearing. I didn't have much to do until the last day,' she said.

'You're in the Law Library?' he asked.

'That's right, but I've appeared before you only once.'

'And you were acting for the girl and her mother, is that right?'

'That's right,' she said politely.

'Did you see what *The Irish Times* said about your judgment?' Donal asked sharply.

'It's a funny day now when a newspaper starts making legal judgments.' He was suddenly angry. 'But I don't think that we can discuss the case, if you don't mind. I'd rather go back to discussing coastal erosion or the temperature of the Irish Sea.'

'I'm sure you would,' Donal said.

'They won't be appealing anyway,' Cathy said. 'They haven't got the funds.'

'Maybe you could donate your fee since you feel so strongly about it.'

'I didn't get paid,' she said.

'I should say that Cathy asked me not to mention the case,' Donal said. 'But I felt that it should be raised, just to clear the air.'

'The air down here is perfectly clear,' Eamon said. 'At least it was before your arrival.'

'I'm sorry that we caused trouble,' Cathy said.

'I'm sorry that Donal has caused it,' Eamon said.

He went inside and told Carmel what had happened.

'Each of you,' she said, 'is as sanctimonious as the other.'

It was so long since he had heard her speak like this that he was taken aback. He stood watching her.

'I'm going for a swim,' he said. 'I'll be back before lunch.'

WHEN he came back he found that they had carried the dining-room table into the garden. Donal was bringing out chairs, while Cathy set the table.

'I'm under instructions to apologize to you,' Donal said.

Eamon smiled and put his hand on Donal's shoulder.

'Is it too windy for Aunt Margaret?' Carmel asked when she came to the door.

'Does Aunt Margaret know about Niamh's child?' Donal asked.

'No, she doesn't,' Carmel said. She shook her head and sighed.

'What are you going to do?' Donal asked.

'I don't know. I'll worry about that in half an hour. If it's too draughty for Aunt Margaret out here then we'll move the table inside.'

'If you put her sitting in the sun,' Donal said.

'And you can all have drinks now,' Carmel said. 'Martini, red or white wine, sherry, gin and tonic. Cathy, what would you like?'

'This is like the Continent,' Donal said. 'Eating out in the open. You'd think that we were in Italy.'

'Wait until Frank Murphy's tractor goes by,' Eamon said. 'Then we'll all know that we're in Cush.'

When Aunt Margaret arrived Carmel brought out a rug in case she needed it to wrap around her shoulders. Niamh carried out a high chair for the baby who immediately began to bang a spoon against the plastic table which was attached to the chair.

'Isn't he the grand little fellow, Aunt Margaret?' Carmel said.

Eamon wondered if Niamh had told his aunt about the baby on the journey from the town, but Aunt Margaret gave no sign. She smiled.

'Isn't it funny, the way he's banging the spoon?' she said.

They all sat down to eat, busied themselves passing the food and pouring more wine. A few times the wind blew up, rustling the leaves in the low hawthorn bush at the edge of the garden, but the sun remained strong.

'Isn't it a beautiful day?' Aunt Margaret said.

'It's definitely the best day so far this summer,' Carmel said.

Niamh tried to spoonfeed the baby, but he was too distracted by the company to eat anything. Carmel went in to prepare the dessert while Donal cleared away the dishes.

'It's good to see him pulling his weight,' Niamh said to Cathy. 'His father never does a tap around the house.' She smiled at her father.

'Doesn't he work all year?' Aunt Margaret asked.

Carmel carried out a tray with rhubarb tart and cream and plates and cups and saucers. Donal came behind her with a pot of coffee. It was agreed that Donal and Cathy would do the washing up. Carmel sat back in her chair, her cup in her two hands and spoke to Aunt Margaret about her trip to Wexford and what she had bought there, and what the shops were like. She was so much more at ease here, Eamon noticed, than in Dublin. When Donal and Cathy came back out, Carmel tried to find a topic which would interest them all. Niamh put the baby on the grass with some toys.

'Would you like to live in the country, Cathy?' Carmel asked.

They discussed the country then, how lonely it could be, but how you would know everyone and you would have better neighbours than in the city.

'I like Dublin,' Carmel said, 'but I'm not from there and I'd be more at home in a small town. In Dublin we know everyone around us, but it's not the same. They're all from different places and they all have their own lives.'

Donal and Cathy got their swimming-togs from the car.

'It's too soon after eating,' Carmel said. 'You'll get a cramp.'

'We're going to go for a walk first,' Donal said. 'We'll walk the food off us. Niamh is going to come with us, if the baby is okay here.'

'The baby's fine here,' Carmel said. 'But you should leave another hour before you go into the water.'

When they had left, Carmel went into the house to make more tea for Aunt Margaret.

'You're in very bad form today,' she said to Eamon when she met him in the kitchen.

'Am I?' he asked. 'I feel okay. I'm just not talking.'

'As long as you're not fed up with all the visitors.'

'I'm sorry if I seem fed up. I'm enjoying all the conversation.'

As soon as Carmel went out again, the baby began to cry. She lifted him up, put his face in close against her own and smiled at him. He continued to cry, ignoring her smiles and trying to push her away.

'He's usually not like this at all,' she said to Aunt Margaret. 'He's usually very happy and content. Aren't you?' She held the baby high in the air and suddenly he smiled at her.

'Now look at him, he's smiling.' He smiled again, a broad smile.

Carmel began to tell Aunt Margaret about the baby and what a shock it was when Niamh told her the news.

'I was in Clarendon Street church that day,' she said. 'I told God that if he had anything special for me to do, I would offer it up. I remembered that later on. I meant it. I did, Margaret. And when I came home wasn't Niamh waiting for me. She was afraid to tell me. At first I didn't know what to say, but anyway I decided that we'd do everything we could to help her. I supported the Amendment, I'm pro-life all the way. So you have to have the courage of your convictions, and do your best. And I'm going to take the baby every day in the autumn, because Niamh is going to work full time and she needs every encouragement.'

He listened to Carmel as she spoke, noticing that she left no room for Aunt Margaret to dissent from what she was saying. He had not known that Niamh was going to work full time. Carmel had never told him that she was going to take the baby every day in the autumn, but maybe, he thought, this was her way of telling him.

Carmel poured him a brandy. He nursed the glass in his hand and sat back in the chair, listening to the two women talking, glad in some vague way that his two children were close by, with each other, maybe in the water now, enjoying the day as well. He closed his eyes and drank in the heat of the fading sun.

After the photograph had been taken, Donal and Cathy drove Aunt Margaret back into the town on their way back to Dublin.

'Keep up the good work,' Donal said to him as they shook hands.

'The Four Courts will never fall again, you can be sure of that,' he said in reply, smiling sourly.

'Good luck anyway,' he said to Cathy. 'I'll know you the next time I see you.'

'But will she know you?' Donal asked.

'Stop, Donal, we've caused enough trouble,' Cathy said.

It occurred to Eamon what a good story their earlier confrontation would make when they got back to Dublin.

CARMEL was cleaning off the table in the garden when he first noticed her holding her head.

'I shouldn't have had that brandy,' she said.

'I'll finish the table,' he said. 'You've been working hard all day. Go and lie down.'

He had expected her to protest; it was unlike her to walk

away so calmly. When she had gone he carried the cups and glasses back into the kitchen and put them on the draining-board. He still thought that she would reappear, but she did not. When he had put the tablecloth into the washbag in the bathroom he tiptoed into the bedroom. The curtains were drawn and she was lying on the bed with her eyes open.

'Can I get you anything?' he asked. 'Do you have a headache?'

'It's not exactly a headache. I don't know what it is. Maybe if I sleep for a while it'll go.'

'Do you want me to lie beside you, Carmel?' he asked.

'Yes, or maybe just leave the door open, so I'll know that you're out there. I feel a terrible lightness in my legs. I don't know what it is.'

'Do you want a doctor?'

'Eamon, I feel awful,' she said.

'Would you like me to get the doctor?'

'No, I'll sleep for a while.'

He left the door open and the light on and sat reading in the living room. The baby was asleep and Niamh had gone to bed. He could see Carmel's shape in the bed through the open door. She seemed to be asleep. He went in and lay beside her, reading with his clothes on. He did not want to sleep but soon he found that he was drowsy so he got into his pyjamas and turned off the light. Carmel did not stir as he got under the blankets and he was careful not to disturb her.

SHE woke in the small hours; he felt her moving and then heard her voice. He turned and held her in the dark, but she seemed to push him away. Her voice was muffled, and he could not understand what she was trying to say. He listened and then sat up and turned on the lamp beside the bed. She had her face in the pillow and was still mumbling something. When she turned towards him he saw a terrible distress in her face; her face seemed distorted as she tried to speak. He felt a cold sweat as he watched her move her hand up to her head and hold it, as though she were in pain.

'Carmel, I'm going into Blackwater to get a doctor. I'll ask Niamh to come and mind you.'

He woke Niamh. He did not know what to say to her.

'Don't wake the baby,' she said.

He went in with her to the bedroom. Carmel was still holding her head with one hand as she lay back, inert, on the bed. Her eyes were open.

'Can you stay with her? I'll be back as soon as I can,' he said.

It was close to dawn when the ambulance came. Eamon had to open the gates so that it could turn.

'She has a good chance if we can get her in quickly,' the doctor said.

'I'll follow in the car.'

'There's no real point, I wouldn't say,' the doctor said.

They wheeled her out on a stretcher. She was still awake, and looked as though she was desperately trying to keep her eyes open. He went and held her hand.

'You're going to be fine,' he said. 'We all love you Carmel.' He saw no response in her eyes. He was not sure that she could hear him.

When they closed the doors of the ambulance he turned again to the doctor.

'I'd love to have gone with her,' he said.

'No, they'll start treating her immediately.'

'Is it a stroke?'

'Looks like that.'

'Is it bad?'

'If they get her to Wexford she has a good chance, but you never know.'

'I think I'll drive in and wait in the hospital. We've no telephone here. It seems odd, but we never thought we'd need one.'

He drove along the narrow roads in a daze, trying to remind himself all the time what had happened, trying to go through the previous day in search of clues. He sat in the cold, square waiting room of Wexford Hospital. He watched through the glass panel as nurses and doctors and orderlies and patients in dressing-gowns and pyjamas moved up and down the corridor. He watched for a familiar face, he looked up each time the door opened in dread of a figure coming towards him with news. He worried about Niamh at home with her child, waiting for word, waiting for the noise of his car returning.

They told him that she was stable, and when he asked them for more news the nurse said that she could not elaborate. At lunchtime he walked into the town; when he came back he asked once more how she was, and if he could see her.

'It would be better if she had no visitors,' the nurse said.

'Do you think that she will pull through?' he asked.

'She's stable,' the nurse said, 'and we have her under observation all the time.'

'But she'll survive, won't she?'

'She's had a very serious stroke.' It sounded like an accusation.

He left the hospital and drove back to Cush. Niamh was feeding the baby when he came in.

'There's no news yet,' he said. 'She's in intensive care.'

He lay on the bed in his clothes until he fell asleep. Niamh woke him when it was time for dinner. He had a shower and a change of clothes. Later, he sat on his own in the porch and watched the beams from the lighthouse criss-crossing the darkness.

They telephoned in the morning and were told that she was still stable and could be visited for a short time. Niamh

left the baby with Mrs Murphy in the house above them
on the lane and they drove to Wexford.

'I brought her a book,' Niamh said. 'I know that she
won't be able to read, but I thought it might be nice for
her to have it beside the bed.'

They sat in the waiting room. The coffee-dispensing
machine had spilled over and a woman was mopping the
floor. Neither of them spoke; Niamh went several times to
ask the nurses if they could see Carmel, but she was told
that they would have to wait. When the matron appeared
he knew by her attitude that someone had found out that
he was a judge. She led them along the corridor towards
Carmel's ward. She told him that the consultant wanted to
see him before he left.

There were only two beds in the darkened room; the
other one was empty. He went in quietly while Niamh
waited outside with the matron. He noticed the heat in the
room and the pale skin of Carmel's arms.

'You're much better, Carmel,' he whispered. He was
afraid to touch her. 'You're going to be great.'

She began to mumble as though in a dream, as though
she was deeply disturbed by something.

'I'm listening, I'm here, Carmel.'

The mumbling continued; he strained to make out what
she was saying. It seemed to be a precise, definite question.
She was asking him something. He listened again. Was I
worse before? Was I with . . . But he could only guess that
these were the words. He stayed still. He concentrated on
her, on being with her, saying nothing, trying not to think.

When he went outside Niamh was waiting to go in. The
matron told him that the consultant was ready now, in
his office on the next floor. When he was finished with
the consultant, she said, he could come back down to her
office.

'Judge Redmond,' the consultant said and stood up from
his desk.

'Is she going to pull through?' Eamon asked him when they had shaken hands.

'That's what I wanted to talk to you about. I'm going to send her to Dublin. She's still in trouble, but she must be very strong. There could be some damage, I'm not sure, but they'll know better up there. I would have had the ambulance earlier, except we're short-staffed, but she'll be going up in the next hour. Incidentally, are you insured for the Blackrock Clinic?'

'No,' Eamon said. 'Should she go there?'

'I'm going to send her to Vincent's for the moment.'

'When you say damage what do you mean?'

'To be honest, there's a fair chance that her speech and her general mobility will be impaired. That's the best I can tell you.'

'And the worst?'

'She's stable for the moment anyway. As I say, she's very strong. Some people are.'

Eamon and Niamh drove in silence back to Cush, collected the baby, packed their things and set off for Dublin.

'Do you want me to drive?' Niamh asked.

'Maybe in a while; do you mind?'

'It's terrible to think of her on this road as well in an ambulance, isn't it?' Niamh said.

'She was doing too much. We should never have let her work so hard,' he said. 'Do you want to come and stay at home?' he asked.

'Thanks, but I think I'll stay in the flat. There's a phone there.'

'You would be very welcome.'

'Thanks, but I think I'll stay in the flat.'

'What did Donal say?'

'He's in a terrible state.'

'I don't know what financial arrangements you have

with your mother. She's in charge of all the money, but I'd like to keep it up, whatever it is.'

'I'm actually doing very well. I've worked out a new way of processing the polls, so I'm in demand. But thanks, all the same.'

When he reached home he telephoned St Vincent's Hospital; the nurse on duty told him that Carmel was still stable and could be visited only by members of her immediate family. He could come at seven o'clock. He drove to the supermarket and bought a newspaper and some groceries. He sat in the car park for a while, not wanting to go home. He went in search of flowers and bought another newspaper before driving to the hospital and waiting in the car park until seven o'clock.

The nurse in charge took out her chart and looked at it.

'I don't know why they kept her in Wexford for so long,' she said. 'We should have had her here immediately. We have her under observation.'

'What do you mean?' he asked.

'She has to be checked every few minutes. It could go one way or the other. We'll know in the next couple of days,' she said. 'You're the judge, aren't you?' she added, as though it were an afterthought.

'Yes,' he said. 'Can I go and sit with her?'

'She won't remember anything,' the nurse said.

'I'd like to sit beside her for a while.'

She was quiet; he did not know whether she was asleep or unconscious. Maybe she was drugged. She looked peaceful.

'Carmel, I'm here,' he whispered. 'I'm here, I'm beside you.'

He could see the grey roots of her hair, and the light-coloured skin of her arm reminded him of her when she was younger. He was afraid to touch her, as though one small movement could damage her even more.

CHAPTER TEN

H E drove home from the hospital and waited in the empty house in case the phone rang. He made himself a sandwich and drank a few glasses of brandy. He hoped that he would be able to sleep. He was drawn back all the time to the scene in the cathedral when he was young, his father standing up as though something had shot slowly through him. As the night drew on he did not turn on the light, but waited in the dark.

He could not remember how long he had stayed with his Aunt Kitty during his father's first illness. He remembered waiting for news and listening in case something was said, but he knew that if he asked he would be fobbed off. The wind, he remembered, for the first weeks was bitterly cold and the evenings were dark, and the house always seemed strange and alien. He could not wait to go home.

'I'm going to fail my Inter-cert if I don't study,' he said to his Aunt Kitty.

There was no secondary school nearby, only a technical school. She assured him that they studied English and Irish there as well, and he could do woodwork and mechanical drawing.

'I couldn't go to the technical school. They don't do Latin in the technical school.'

'And what good will Latin be to you?'

'You have to have Latin to get into university.'

He pictured the technical school in Enniscorthy and the boys who went there, many from cottages on the outskirts of the town, others from rows of houses on the town's edges, boys he knew to see but had never spoken to. When they left school most of them would go to England. He did not want to go to the technical school, no matter how different his aunt assured him it was from the technical school in Enniscorthy.

She put a paraffin oil heater into the parlour for him and let him pile his books up on the table.

'You're a great scholar,' she said to him. 'Your mother, Lord have mercy on her, was a great reader. She used to send to Dublin for books. We have a lot of books upstairs, your uncle's father bought them years ago at an auction. You can take any of them you want.'

For a few hours in the day the house was quiet. He went through the books upstairs and carried some down to the parlour. He recognized the names of most of the authors. There was mildew on a few of the books and a damp smell, but no one had opened them for years and the print was still legible. One day when the fumes from the paraffin had made him drowsy and he could study no longer he picked one of them up and began to read the opening page. He was puzzled by it, the unfamiliar was being described in too much detail. But he carried on, until he found a story to follow and learned how to skip the descriptive passages. He became engrossed in the story, the side plots and the cast of characters. Thereafter, he spent more time in the parlour reading the novels than studying his own texts.

When his cousins came home from school he had to do the farm work with them. He hated leaving his warm room and the intricate stories of the novels, but his aunt insisted that he must. He hated putting on Wellington boots and wading through the thick muck of the haggard. His two cousins took it for granted and had a keen interest in prices at the market and the cost of animal feed. They could not believe that he wanted to go to university. They wanted to leave school as soon as possible and make money for themselves.

After tea in the evening he played cards; he taught his three older cousins to play solo. They understood trumps because they had played twenty-five with their father, and soon they knew the rules. They played at the kitchen table, as his aunt had said that only Eamon could use the parlour. The game was constantly interrupted by workmen and cattle dealers. His cousins began to play solo with as much skill and concentration as he did, and his aunt and uncle, after a few desultory attempts to join in the game, left them alone until it was bedtime, and then there was always trouble over how many more games could be played before the final chores of the evening and bed.

When the lambing season came the house changed: the boys could be woken at any time in the night and told to come and help. They did not go to school, but spent the day with the new-born lambs, or cleaning out sheds. Eamon stood shivering in the barn, watching the lambs, weak and slimy in the dim electric light. They were so small and frail, but within a day or two they were strong enough to be left in the fields with the sheep.

The days were getting longer; he noticed the pale light in the evening sky, but there was still no news. His presence was explained in the same way to anyone who came to the house: his Daddy was in hospital up in Dublin and he was here until his Daddy came home. And some other comment would be added like, 'he's after turning this house into a real card school' or 'he's a great scholar' or 'we'll make a farmer out of him yet'.

Jimmy Walsh often dropped into his aunt and uncle's house; he had a cup of tea and talked about prices and neighbours and football matches. He told Eamon that he could come any time to try out the horse which Jimmy kept in a stable.

'There's still great go in her,' Jimmy said as he looked

up at Eamon and narrowed his eyes. 'A bit of fresh air would do you good.'

IT was a long walk to Walsh's; the first afternoon he went there he thought that he had missed the turning. It took him almost an hour to reach the wooden ledge with the three milk churns he had been told about, and half an hour to walk down the lane, being careful to close each gate behind him, as he had been instructed to do. The house, when he came to it, looked desolate and damp. He went to the front door and rapped with his knuckles and then with his fist, but there was no sign of life. A sheepdog appeared and barked at him. When the dog came closer he patted its head. The dog wagged its tail and followed him as he went around to the back of the house. As he turned the corner the kitchen door opened and a girl a few years older than himself appeared. She was wearing an apron.

'Mr Walsh said I was to have a try on the horse,' he said.

'I'm Anne,' she said and clipped her hair back. 'I thought that you'd be younger.'

'I'm Eamon,' he said.

'What age are you?' she asked.

'I'm fourteen.'

'You look older. My uncle said that I was to saddle the horse for you and show you the ropes. He said that you were to have a cup of tea first.'

'Is Mr Walsh your uncle?'

'Yes. I come down here every day and do for him.'

The kitchen was bare and cold. He sat at the table while she made tea.

'Do you have many brothers and sisters?' she asked.

'No. I'm an only child.'

'I have ten,' she said. 'You can't hear yourself talking in the house. It's great down here.'

She put out some soda bread and butter, and sat with her elbows on the table.

'Is your father sick?' she asked.

'He had a turn.'

'And where's your mother?'

'She's dead,' he said and looked down.

'When did she die?'

'She died when I was a baby.'

'So there was just you and your father? What was it like with just the two of you?'

He hesitated. He did not know how to answer, but she continued to look at him without speaking, waiting for him to say something.

'I don't know,' he said. 'It was all right, I suppose.'

'You must miss your father now,' she said as she came back with the teapot and cups.

'Yes, I do,' he said and smiled at her as she watched him from across the table. It was the first time anyone had asked him about his father. He wanted to say something else. She poured the tea.

'I was with him in the cathedral when he had the turn. I was very frightened.'

She took off her apron and wiped her hands with a cloth. They walked out to an outhouse where the saddle was kept on a wide shelf beside the door. She told him to gather it up, and as he turned he noticed her breasts under her woollen pullover. He caught her eye as he averted his glance.

She opened a gate which led into a field full of thistles and closed the gate behind her. She was wearing a pleated tartan skirt. He noticed her waist, how slim she was. He liked the way she walked and her confidence as she spoke.

'You'd want to be careful,' she said, as they approached the horse in the adjoining field. 'You could fall off and break your neck. The last man on this mare had a terrible fall,' she laughed. 'Don't mind me. I'm only joking. You looked so afraid.'

She told him to catch the mare and steady her. She threw the saddle across the mare's back, ordering him all the while to hold her steady. Then she tied the saddle down.

'Watch her now,' she said. 'She'll kick.' He did not know whether she was serious or not.

She put the blinkers on and forced the bit into the horse's mouth.

The saddle seemed much higher than he had imagined. 'How do I get up?' he asked.

'Simple,' she said. 'I'll hold her and you put your hands on the saddle and lift yourself up. Fast now, fast.'

He tried it a few times, but he fell back each time before he could get a chance to sit on the saddle. She grew impatient.

'Hold on to the reins here,' she said, 'and I'll show you.' When she did it she made it seem easy. He handed her the reins again when she got down.

'You're used to it,' he said, and tried again, but still could not jump into the saddle without unsteadying the horse.

'I'll pull you up, the mare's strong enough for both of us,' she said, and once more without any apparent effort she got up into the saddle. He held on to the saddle again with one hand and held her arm with the other.

'Don't pull me down,' she shouted. 'One, two, three, jump.'

This time he made it, and the horse remained steady; it took him a while to scramble around and sit on the back part of the saddle where she had made room for him. She patted the horse and held the reins.

'Hold on to me now,' she said. She gave the horse a kick with both her legs and the animal started to canter forward.

After a while she made the mare slow down, keeping to the edge of the field, going round and round.

'The secret,' she turned to him and said, 'is in your legs. You have to hold it with your legs.'

His penis was hard, and he tried to move back in the saddle so she would not feel it pressed against her, but each time the horse moved forward his body was thrown against hers. He was unsure what to do. He knew that she could feel it against her but she gave no sign. He wanted to put his hands on her breasts, but he felt a need also to get down off the horse without her noticing his reaction. He moved in closer to her, shutting his eyes and forgetting his embarrassment. He was pressed tight against her, as the horse moved slowly around the field. She seemed oblivious to him. He held her tight around the waist. He could feel the comforting heat of her body as he pressed harder against her, he could feel his heart pounding and he caught his breath when he began to ejaculate. He felt a sudden sadness then, an urge to be away from her, an uneasy guilt which he had not known before.

He was glad to play solo again that evening, happy to be in the house with his cousins. He had changed his underpants and left the old pair behind a bush in the orchard to which no one ever went since the trees had all started to die. But as they played that evening he felt distant from the game, his mind kept wandering back to what had occurred earlier in the day.

In the morning when the others had gone to school he approached his aunt in the kitchen.

'Are you busy?' he asked her.

'Why, Eamon? What's wrong with you?'

'I want to go home,' he said. 'I want to be in my own house.'

'There's no one to mind you at home.'

'But when am I going home?'

'I'll be going up to Dublin next week and I'll see your Daddy and we'll settle it.'

'I'll write him a letter that you can take with you.'

'Of course I'll take it up with me, but be careful not to worry him too much. It wouldn't be good for him at all. And, listen, I was writing to your aunts in America and telling them all about you, and they want you to write as well.'

'I wrote to them at Christmas,' he said.

'You should write to them more often. They love hearing news.'

HE went back to Jimmy Walsh's the following week. Once more, Jimmy was away at a mart and Anne was there alone.

'Your hair is different,' he said as they sat in the kitchen. 'What did you do?'

'I knew you were coming,' she said.

'And is that why you did it?' he laughed.

'I don't know what you're laughing at.'

He had been worried about facing her again, afraid that she would mention what had happened between them. But she said nothing and he was relaxed now at the table in the kitchen.

'How's your father?' she asked.

He did not know how to reply, but told her about his conversation with his aunt.

'Has he not written to you?' she asked.

'Yes,' he said, unsure what she meant.

'I don't think you're cut out for the saddle,' she said. 'Maybe we'll just take the horse for a walk.' She went to the shed and got the reins which she brought out to the field. They went through a few fields with the horse in tow, moving slowly, the mare resisting the pull of the rein, until they reached a rutted lane with high ditches on each side.

Eventually they came into an open field which sloped down towards a stream. Anne walked ahead of him, talking to the mare, coaxing her forward. The sky was low with clouds, but the rain kept off.

There were stones in the stream to make crossing easy. Anne let the mare drink and then led her across the stream and tied the reins to a tree, leaving enough slack for the mare to move around. They walked through a cluster of trees, until they came to a bank which was covered in undergrowth. Flies buzzed around them and there was a smell of damp earth.

'The ground is too wet to sit down on,' she said. 'We should have brought a blanket.'

They both stood there; he kept his distance from her, still not sure why she had taken him here, not wanting to presume too much. She said nothing, but moved over towards a tree and rested her head against the bark. He moved towards her casually, pretending to be preoccupied. She smiled at him, and held out her hand. He had been thinking about her body, her breasts, her waist, her hair, but he had not noticed her lips before until he began to kiss her and taste her warm breath. She put her arms around him and opened her mouth wide so he could roll his tongue in against hers.

At home, he discovered that he could make his penis hard by concentrating on her mouth and her nipples which she had let him touch. He learned to masturbate. He brought half a sheet of newspaper upstairs, and while his cousins were asleep he worked at himself while he thought about her lips and her tongue, the lightness of her breasts and the warmth between her legs.

'You're getting very fond of Jimmy Walsh's,' his aunt said one day as they were all sitting around the table having tea.

'Maybe it's the niece he's fond of,' his uncle said. 'She's

the one that's getting the farm. Jimmy's mad about her. She'd be a great catch, Eamon.' He laughed.

'Will you leave the child alone?' his aunt said. 'He'll have time enough for that.'

As the weather grew better he went to the Walshes' as often as he could. Sometimes Anne was busy and he had to wait for her; they took the mare out and she taught him how to canter and gallop, but he did not learn easily. She asked him questions no one else had ever asked him, talked to him naturally as though he were an adult, and always, on each visit, he knew that she wanted to disappear into one of the outbuildings or to the thicket across the stream, just as much as he did.

She began to let him put his hand into her pants and explore between her legs. She gasped when he put his finger in, but he knew that he was not hurting her. He loved the soft wetness down there, and then the tight entry, and he loved making her wince with pleasure. He was nervous the first time when she unbuttoned his trousers. He kissed her on the lips hoping that she would not want to look at him, but she persisted, put her hand into his underpants and held his penis.

He knew that what they did was a sin. As he walked home he knew that if he died, or if he had an accident, or his heart stopped, he would spend all eternity in hell. He would have to go to confession as soon as he could. The local curate, Father Moriarity, often came to his aunt and uncle's house. He was a big, jovial man with a high-pitched laugh. He seemed to enjoy talking to the children. Eamon could not imagine trying to explain to him, even in the darkness of the confessional, what he and Anne had done together. He knew that Father Moriarity would have to keep what he was told a secret and he could not tell his aunt or Jimmy Walsh, but it would still be impossible to tell him. Until now, the state of mortal sin seemed unimaginable; now he was surprised at how easy it was to study, or read, or eat meals without being disturbed by it. Only at night did the real impact of what he had done hit home.

On Sundays he went to communion with the rest of the family, and one Saturday, with his cousins, he went to the parish church for confession with Father Moriarity. Eamon told him that he had forgotten to say his night prayers, and Father Moriarity told him that God would forgive him if he said his penance. Before he said the Latin prayers Father Moriarity asked him if he was praying that his Daddy would be better and he said that he was. He was surprised that Father Moriarity was prepared to let him know that he recognized him. None of the priests in Enniscorthy had ever done that. He was even more certain now that he could not tell Father Moriarity about his sin. He would have to wait until he went home to Enniscorthy.

When the school holidays came, his cousins' presence around the house made his reading difficult. He had to go and work with them on the farm. He became homesick again, as much for his daily routine as for Enniscorthy and his own house and his father. One of his cousins came to Walsh's with him one day to try the mare. Eamon and Anne tried to hide in a shed, but they had only begun to kiss when they heard his cousin shouting their names outside in the yard and they knew it would be impossible and they would have to wait for another day.

One evening after tea, when they were getting ready to go out again and pick potatoes, his aunt told him that his father was at home, but he was still not well, and Eamon could go down soon to see him, but he would have to be very good.

'Can I go tomorrow?' he asked.

'I'll see if your uncle is going into Tullow. If not, maybe someone else will be going in,' she said.

He packed his clothes and his books. He went downstairs and asked his uncle if he was going to Tullow, but his uncle said that he did not know. He asked his aunt again.

'I shouldn't have told you until the morning,' she said.

Only when they had begun to play cards could he settle down and forget his lift to Tullow. That evening his aunt let them play until much later than usual. She said that his cousins could go and see him soon in Enniscorthy and they could play more solo there.

He woke early in the morning. It was daylight outside, but his cousins were still asleep. He felt his penis hard and he thought about putting his hand on Anne's breast, about the silky skin of her stomach and the strong sweet smell which came from the soft wet rose between her legs. He tried not to wake his cousins as he masturbated, his eyes shut tight as he concentrated on her.

When he went downstairs his uncle was sitting at the table drinking tea; his aunt was still in her dressing-gown.

'I don't think there's anyone going in today,' she said.

'Can I try and hitch a lift?' he asked.

'You're anxious to go, aren't you?' his aunt asked. 'Look at you,' she said. 'You'll be shaving soon. And you've shot up. They won't know you in Enniscorthy you've gone so tall. It must be the country air. Don't look so worried. We'll get you into Tullow some way.'

'I've left all the books back upstairs,' he said.

'You can take any of them with you that you like,' she said.

His cousins stood in the yard to say goodbye to him. He knew that he was going home for good. His aunt had put on her best costume. She sat in the front seat while his uncle drove.

HE caught the bus in Tullow. He could see out of the window this time, his journey just a few months before seemed remote in time. He thought about Anne again. He should have said goodbye to her. He began to worry now about the mortal sins on his soul. He would have to go to confession as soon as he could in Enniscorthy.

His Uncle Tom met him when the bus stopped at the bottom of Slaney Street.

'Your father's down in our house,' he said. 'He's waiting for you there.'

It was a warm summer evening and the gulls were squabbling high in the air over the railway bridge as he carried his suitcase towards the Island Road. His mortal sins now seemed more important than they did when he was away, more real and urgent.

His father was sitting in a chair in the back room of the house when Eamon and his uncle came in. He had grown much balder and his hair had become grey at the sides. Eamon stood back and looked at him. His father's eyes seemed swollen and strange.

His father said something, but his voice was distorted. Eamon noticed that part of his face was paralysed. He stood there watching him while his father tried to speak. He listened carefully to see if he could make out what his father was saying. He made another attempt and this time Eamon saw for sure that only half his face could move. His father was still eagerly smiling at him and saying something. Eamon nodded when he had finished as though he understood.

'I'll walk up a bit of the way with you,' his uncle said. 'You can leave one of your bags here and come back for it later.'

There was nobody else in the house. He watched his father standing up and limping across the room. He saw no pain in his face, just effort and concentration. He went over and held his arm and led him out towards the hall.

His father waved him aside impatiently and started slowly to walk without help. Eamon and his Uncle Tom accompanied him down the pathway to the road. When they reached Irish Street they walked on each side of him. It was hard to walk so slowly. People came to the doors and watched them, greeting them and eyeing his father with curiosity.

'You're a decent man,' one woman said to his father over a half-door. 'You're in all our prayers.'

ON Saturday evening Eamon joined the long queue for confession in the cathedral. He moved nearer the confessional each time a space became vacant. He watched each figure going into the box and he tried to prepare himself for the darkness in there, and the hatch being pulled back and the hushed voice. The priest was old, and he did not know him or any of his family, so it would be easier, but he felt his throat dry as he knelt in the box waiting. When the priest asked him his sins he could say nothing.

'What are your sins?' he asked. He sounded as though he might not wait too long. Eamon told the priest about Anne and what they had done.

'Did you ejaculate seed?' the priest asked.

'Yes, father.' He told the priest how he had masturbated and how many times.

'Is that everything?' the priest sighed as he asked.

'No, father.'

'What else is there, my child?' Eamon told him about making a bad confession and going to communion every Sunday.

'Did you know what you were doing?'

'Yes, father.'

'And where is your intelligence?' the priest asked.

Then it was over. He was given his penance and the priest said the Latin prayers of forgiveness. He went out of the dark box and into the body of the cathedral where he prayed until his penance was said. He had expected to feel different, lighter, happier once his soul was cleansed and his sins were wiped away. But he did not feel any better;

he felt an even greater shame now and wondered about this. It made him uneasy that God should not be able to lift the burden of guilt from him.

In late June the sky was a clear blue during the day and the sun was hot. Eamon moved a chair out into the back garden for his father, and sat reading while his father slept or lay in the shade with his eyes half shut. If his speech did not improve, the doctor said, he would have to go to Dublin again. He had to practise his speech.

Some sounds were easy; Eamon had come to understand a good deal of what he said. He knew when his father said his name, but one day he listened and wondered if an outsider would make sense of the sounds. He heard only 'A-i-n' and he realized that a stranger would not be able to make it out. His father moved slowly and reacted slowly to things. He began to go to the museum again, but he could not go upstairs, nor could he answer the questions which people asked. Eamon found it difficult to talk to him. He tried not to begin a conversation because he knew that it would result in his father stumbling over words and making sounds which he would not be able to understand.

He rode his bicycle to Cush a few days, called in on the Cullens and had a swim before riding back. But he worried about leaving his father alone in the house. He tried to stay near him. Mrs Doyle came every day to cook for them, and clean the house. She could not understand anything that he said.

'What's he saying?' she'd ask Eamon, as though his father was a child.

On a showery day in August his Aunt Margaret and his Uncle Tom were sitting in the back room. They listened to his father's slow, laborious ascent to the toilet.

'He'll be much better when he's back in school,' Aunt Margaret said. Eamon said nothing.

'He's getting much better, isn't he, Eamon? You'd notice it, living here.'

'Is he going back to teach?' he asked.

'Brother Delaney says that it's fine. I'd say the boys will be very glad to have him back.'

They heard him flushing the toilet, and his hobbled step. He smiled at them when he came in, and Eamon promised himself that he would help his father with his speech therapy every day. He had a new terror now: the terror of going back to school. He had not thought that his father would try to teach again. He had wondered about money and how they would live. When his father spoke now, he listened as though he were a classroom and he knew that they would not have his patience. He willed his father to get better, he worked on his therapy with him, trying to get him to say words more clearly, shout them out, pronounce each syllable. But he knew that there would not be enough time; school would resume within a few weeks and his fear of the first class and his father coming into the room stayed with him as something terrible, beyond contemplation.

CHAPTER ELEVEN

EACH morning in the months after Carmel's stroke he drove her into Wexford for her physiotherapy. He had two hours free to wander in the town while they worked on her voice and her bad leg and arm in the hospital. He usually left the car in the car park of the Talbot Hotel and wandered along the boardwalk looking at the old buildings along the run-down quay and the wide water of the silted harbour. Some days the mussel boats were in: they looked like relics, museum pieces, old tubs with winches and cranes added. The smell as he passed was sharp and putrid. He liked the smell and he remembered to tell Carmel about it, knowing how she would react; she squirmed and turned up her nose and smiled and said that she was glad she was in the hospital and not having to smell the mussels.

It was late autumn. Soon he would have to go back to the court, unless he could arrange a further month's holidays, but the courts, as usual, were busy and it was hard. He had spoken to the President of the court about how well Carmel was doing in Wexford and how much easier it would be if she could continue her treatment down here.

It was good for him too; he wondered once more as he walked towards the bridge if he should not retire now. Back in the city he would miss the steel-grey sky, he would miss idly looking at a group of cormorants on a rock in the harbour, he would miss doing nothing much all day. He crossed the cool span of the bridge and stood watching the band of creamy light on the horizon and the stately spires of the town. He walked on towards the sloblands, feeling happy that he knew no one in Wexford, that he could walk around here without having to stop to talk to people he encountered.

It was strange, he thought, how quickly he and Carmel had become accustomed to their new lives; her slow recovery now seemed part of the everyday. He turned and walked back in the direction of the town. It was brightening up now. He wondered if he should try to keep swimming every day, even though the days were often cold. He thought that he should go down to the strand in the afternoon and see how cold the water was. He walked up one of the side streets towards the main street and then up towards White's Hotel. He sat in the lounge and took *The Irish Times* from his pocket.

He looked through the newspaper. Since Carmel's stroke they had had the telephone connected at Cush and had bought a television for the house. The most important item of news for them now was the television schedule for the evening. It was the first thing he looked at in the paper. After that he checked through the news and the opinions, but he found it difficult to read many pieces from beginning to end. He looked at his watch: another hour before she finished. He drank up his coffee and paid. Maybe in future, he thought, he should take his bathing-togs and have a swim in the hotel pool. It would make the time less heavy.

He walked along the main street until he came to the book shop. He hardly ever bought anything more than an English newspaper in the shop but they knew him now as a regular customer. He wandered around, browsing, picking up a book and looking at it for a while and putting it back again. The classics were in a section together, all of them in black-spined paperback, the Dickens novels and novels by George Eliot and Jane Austen. He decided to buy a few of them to see if he could read them now; maybe

Carmel could read them too. He picked them out with the intention of putting some of them back, but he found himself at the cash register with seven or eight paperback novels and an English newspaper. He paid for them and left. He walked as far as the old barracks, stopping to buy some fruit at a shop, and turned down towards the car park. He could easily have done the rest of the shopping in his waiting time, but he knew that Carmel needed to feel that she was involved in the life of the house, even though the consultant had told him she would only ever be able to do light housework.

As he walked along he noticed a three-storey house covered in slate; he examined the narrow street leading down to the silted-up harbour, and he wondered at how it looked like nowhere else in the world. Wexford on a mid-week morning in September, the light-filled sky over the harbour, the blue-black of the slate, the grey buildings all around.

At times Carmel's slow recovery reminded him of his father in the years after his operation. His father's slow limp and impaired voice, and the pretence that, despite the damage which had been done to his system, he was well. He dreaded his father telling a story in the classroom. He would start off so confidently, but some of the words would be mere blurs. There was a story he always told about the gravedigger's son who could not get his father's job as he could not read or write. All the students knew it, knew how the son had gone to America and struck oil and become one of the wealthiest men in the United States. Eamon remembered his father before he was ill using an American accent for the part of the story about the day when the gravedigger's son had to sign a contract there and then, but had to confess that he couldn't sign as he couldn't write his name.

'Here you are one of the richest men in America and you

can't sign your name. Where would you be if you could read and write?' he was asked.

'A gravedigger in Ireland,' was the reply.

But there was a day when his father got stuck in the story, when nothing came from him except vague sounds, and his whole face seemed drawn and twisted, but he still wouldn't stop, even when some of the students began to laugh and others looked away, uncomfortable and embarrassed. He stood there, as he always did, looking at each face in the class, acting out the story. Eamon wanted to shout out to him to stop, please stop, could he not understand that the sounds he was making made no sense? He watched as his father turned away, before the story was finished, and went to the window and stood with his back to them looking out. The boys in the class began to talk among themselves as though the teacher was not there.

He waited outside the hospital until she came out. He did not try to help her into the car. She needed to feel that she was becoming more capable. When she came out of hospital first, she and Niamh had gone into the city and bought new clothes for her and new make-up. She was careful how she looked. A few times in Wexford he had to wait another hour for her while she went to get her hair done, but he understood her need. It was what had made her survive.

'I'm walking better, aren't I?' she asked. 'There's a woman in there, and she was much worse than I was, and she was just saying that keeping your chin up is the main thing.'

Her speech was slurred, but as the days went by he found her easier to understand. He believed that sometimes she said things that would require no response, thus leaving him free to pretend that he understood. But he felt that she was recovering. Her sister drove down to Cush a few afternoons a week and he left them to talk or to go for a drive in her sister's car. All her life Carmel had loved people calling, and each time her sister left he thought that she was better. He wondered if they were right to stay at Cush, now that the weather was getting cooler and the place seemed more windswept and remote.

Carmel liked the television and enjoyed the fire lit in the evening. Eamon fetched the coal and the blocks from the small, damp shed at the side of the house. She placed the coals carefully on the fire with tongs, using all of her energy and concentration. He peeled the potatoes, but she prepared the other vegetables and salads, sitting at a table in the living room with a basin of water in front of her. She made brown bread, even though she found it hard to knead the dough; it took time, and she worked at it, patient and determined.

'Did I rave a lot when I was in Vincent's, or did I sleep?'

'You tried to talk to me, but the nurse said it wasn't good for you.'

'What did I say?'

'I couldn't make it out.'

'I wonder what it was.'

She prayed during the day. He would find her sitting in an armchair with her eyes closed and her lips moving. She talked about God's will to him, but she knew that he did not believe.

'God knows,' she said, 'that you're doing your best in your own way. Everybody can only do so much.'

They stopped in the village on the way home from Wexford and she got out of the car, laboriously turning so she could stand on her good leg, and went into the butcher's. He sat in the car waiting for her, realizing that each time she went into a shop, or into the hospital, he expected a face to come out and tell him that she had taken another turn.

They had lunch at the table beside the window. He put a record on, some quiet music, and they ate without speaking. The day was brightening and the sun was strong through the glass. He told her about the paperbacks he had bought, which he had left in the car.

'We should read more,' she said, 'instead of watching television.'

A wind had blown up outside, which cleared the sky of clouds. He told her that he would take his togs and towel down to the strand to see if the water was warm enough for swimming, although he doubted it.

'Be careful down there, you could be swept out on a day like this.' She was making a real effort with her speech, working on each vowel sound.

'I probably won't go in for a swim,' he said. 'I'll probably just go for a walk.'

He cleared the dishes from the table and put them in the sink. Her sister was coming that afternoon to clean up the house and do some washing. Carmel remained at the table, looking out. She asked him to change the record before he left. She still was not able to handle the record player.

THE lane was muddy with the previous week's rain. He had to walk on the verge to avoid the mud, and even then he was afraid of slipping. It was cold as well as windy and he knew now that taking his towel and togs had been a mistake. He put the togs into his jacket pocket and the towel around his shoulders. When he came to the turn in the lane he looked over the cliff: the sea was rough, each wave as it broke released huge choppy sheets of foam. It was the beginning of the winter sea. He walked down to the strand.

He wondered if the tide was turning. He picked up a flat stone and tried to skim it along the water but it was too rough. He searched for another flat stone but he could not find one. As he walked along he listened to the sound of the stones knocking against each other on the shore each time a wave swept in over them. It was a harder sound now, more brittle and hollow than on calmer days in the summer.

As he went towards Ballyconnigar he watched the waves twenty yards out pouring over each other as though boiling. He began picking up stones and throwing them into the rushing water and listening to the shrill sounds of the gulls heading out to sea. He was enjoying the day, regretting that he had not come down earlier, but knowing that he could not leave Carmel too long by herself.

He wondered what would happen if he swam out now into the sea, how strong the currents were and how hard it might be to fight against the receding tide. The cliffs along here had taken a battering, he noticed. Huge boulders made of hard mud and stone were lying on the strand. Small clumps of clay and a tight film of sand were being blown down the cliff-face as well, even now, as he walked along.

When he came to Keating's he saw that the sheds had fallen down the cliff. This must have happened, he thought, during the previous week. The last time he was here they had been in place, but now the red galvanized material was hanging down over the edge, and bits of the walls were lying on the shore where they would not last long. Two sides of the old shed had been left standing, waiting to be toppled over in a night of strong wind. He realized that this was the first building to go since Mike's house.

He turned back. The wind was still strong and a light drizzle was starting up. He put the towel over his head. The sea was the colour of slate under the grey sky. He walked as fast as he could against the wind. The drizzle turned to rain as he moved along, and then eased off again, but he knew that it would be a wet evening, and was glad of the fire at home and the television. If he were in Dublin now, he thought, he would be getting ready to brave the traffic and set off home from the courts.

He made his way up the gap, holding on to weeds and

clumps of grass to keep his balance. It was raining hard, and he thought that he would have to have a hot shower when he got in. When he turned into the lane he stopped for a second, startled as he saw Carmel coming towards him with a coat over her head, moving much too fast, her limp heavy and pronounced.

'It's all right,' he shouted. 'I'm coming.'

As he drew nearer he could see that she was crying, her face distorted as she tried to shout something to him. She stopped and put the raincoat around her shoulders, letting her hair get wet. He could see that she was still crying.

'What's wrong?' he asked when he reached her, but she did not reply. They turned and walked together towards the house, his arm around her. She was almost choking with tears, desperately clinging on to him.

'You're all right, love,' he said. 'You'll be fine when we get inside.' She tried to speak again, but began to cry even harder. As they reached the gate, the rain started to pour down. He searched in his pocket for the key. Once inside, he felt the house was strangely cold and uncomforting.

As soon as they stood together in the living room he knew that she had soiled herself. After her sister left, she told him slowly between gasps of tears, she had gone down to look for him, even though it was raining, and just before he came around the corner, when she was thinking of turning back she had lost control over her bowels. She started to cry again and he had to hold her.

They went into the bathroom where he let the hot water run in the bath. He emptied a bucket in the kitchen and rinsed it out. When he came back into the bathroom Carmel was standing facing away from him, resting her arms against the wall. He put Parozone into the bucket and filled it up with hot water. He held her as she continued to sniffle.

'You'll be all right,' he said.

He took off her coat and hung it on the back of the door.

He knelt down and took off her shoes. He tried not to smell, tried instead to concentrate on taking down her tights and her pants. He went into the kitchen with her pants and her tights and put them into the black plastic rubbish bag beside the door.

The bathroom was now filling up with steam. He put Radox in the bath in an effort to kill the smell. He felt the water to make sure it was not too hot for her. She was still standing, leaning against the wall. He opened the buttons at the back of her dress, and she slipped out of it.

'You can leave me now,' she said. 'I'll be okay.'

'No, I'll stay,' he said.

He helped her out of her slip and then opened her brassière at the back so that she was completely naked. Her breasts hung white and heavy. He helped her into the bath which was now filled up with suds. He took his watch off and then his jacket and shirt, and he switched on the heater.

'Lie down and relax,' he said. 'I'm going into the bedroom to put on the electric blanket for you.'

When he came back to the bathroom the smell was still there. He did everything he could to resist a sudden urge to get sick. He closed his eyes and tried to breathe through his nose. He took a bar of soap from the wash-basin and put it under the water, letting it soften as he rubbed it along her body. He made her turn on her side and he ran it down her back and between her buttocks. He rubbed her with a cloth and with his hand until he was sure that she was clean. She was quiet now, with her eyes closed. He soaped her legs, and ran the cloth along her belly and under her breasts. The water was dirty, and he pulled the plug out to let it drain. He turned the switch to the shower and tested the water again. Carmel was still lying with her eyes closed. He ran the shower down her body, making her turn as the water drained off her and running the soap down her back and between her buttocks again and then washing it off.

He went to the hotpress and got several large towels. He put a chair for her beside the bath. There were still flecks of faeces on the floor and on her shoes, but the smell had gone. He put her dress and slip into the bucket and began to dry her. She held her hands over her breasts and shivered. He went to the bedroom and fetched her night-dress and her dressing-gown.

'We'll move the television into the bedroom and watch the news,' he said.

He turned the heater on in the bedroom. When he came back she was sitting on the chair with her elbows on her knees and her head in her hands.

'Do you want me to leave you alone?' he asked. 'Maybe I should make tea.'

She said nothing and did not move. He wondered if he should telephone her sister or the hospital.

'Are you sick?' he asked.

She said nothing. He went into the bedroom and came back with slippers for her. She stood up and let him help her put on her nightdress. He had put on his own dressing-gown and he stood there holding her, but she would not speak and soon by her shaking he knew that she was crying again.

She made no sound. They went into the bedroom together and lay down on the bed. After a while she turned away from him as though she wanted to sleep. He turned the bedside lamp on and switched off the main light. The room was becoming warm. He went out to get the pile of books he had bought. He did not know which one he would read. She was quiet now, but she was not asleep, her eyes were wide open. He thought that she was about to have another stroke, and he wondered if he should put her into the car now and take her to Wexford, or at least get a doctor. He put his hand on her waist and asked her what he should do.

'I'm all right. I'm going to sleep now,' she said.

He covered her with blankets and lay on the bed beside her, flicking through the pages of one of the novels, trying to remember if he had read it before. She turned in the bed and faced him.

'I feel I don't know you at all,' she said. Her speech was slurred, even more than usual, but he had no difficulty understanding what she said.

'You've always been so distant, so far away from everybody. It is so hard to know you, you let me see so little of you. I watch you sometimes and wonder if you will ever let any of us know you.'

'I'm trying to help you all day,' he said.

'You don't love me.' She put her arms around him. 'You don't love any of us.'

'Carmel, I do, I do love you.'

'Years ago I tried to tell you about my father and my mother and how much they fought and argued when I was a child, and how much he drank, and no matter what he did how much we preferred him to her, and how handsome I thought he was. Eamon, are you listening to me? Already you are thinking about something else.'

'That's not fair,' he said.

'Eamon, please pay attention to me now. We talked about this years ago, I don't know if you remember. I still feel that we are not close to each other. I am sorry that I am boring you.'

'You're not boring me,' he said.

'You sound bored. It is one of the things that you have learned to do over the years.'

'I'm still worried about you. Should we ring the doctor?'

'Maybe I'm the one who's cold. Maybe I made you like that. Can you understand me? Maybe we looked for each other and found a match, each of us.'

'Why are you talking like this?' he asked her.

'I have had this conversation in my mind so many times over the past few months. But when I imagined it, I saw you speaking too, but you won't.'

'It's too sudden, and I'm not sure you're well.'

'We have all night to talk,' she said.

'You sound so strange,' he said.

'I used to love that, how reserved you were, but I know now that it was wrong of me to want you like that. And I have long given up arguing with you. Everything I think I keep to myself now. I want this to change. I want you to listen to me.'

Half the time her voice was perfect, but then it became slurred again, but she spoke slowly, making sure that he caught each word. She lay back in the bed and covered her face with her hands.

'I went down to tell you all of this earlier. I'm sorry that you had to clean up after me like that.'

'Do you want anything?' he asked.

She smiled and shook her head. 'We have to talk,' she said.

'I'll think about what you said.'

He took his book out into the living room and turned on the lamp. Slowly he set about lighting the fire. It was dark and blustery outside, but the rain had stopped. He went out to the shed to get coal. The night was pitch dark: with no moon or stars. Back inside, he sat at the window and looked out at Tuskar and the fierce beam of light which came at intervals. He watched for it, it was much slower than a heartbeat or the ticking of a clock. It came in its own time, unfolding its light clear and full against the darkness which was everywhere outside.

CHAPTER TWELVE

THE table in the back room was covered in posters, leaflets and envelopes. 'I've done all the M's,' Eamon said to his father. 'I've a pain in my arm.'

'Are there many left?' his father asked.

'There's a day's work,' he said.

The election work made his father tired and sometimes he became irritable. In school, if the boys in the class could not understand him he became angry for a moment, and then tried to calm himself and slow down. He had stopped teaching Irish; it was too hard for him to pronounce the words. He taught Commerce and Geography. But even after two years there were times when he spoke and no one, not even Eamon, could understand what he was saying.

Eamon found something to do or someone to talk to in the classroom at lunchtime and the end of the day's class. He did not want to walk home with his father. It was hard to make conversation. He felt embarrassed when he misjudged how far ahead his father had gone and found himself catching up with him, and having to walk along beside him.

One day he passed the open door of the front room and saw his father sitting on the old sofa with his head in his hands. He thought at first that his father was praying, but the longer he stayed watching the more he was sure that it was something else. He stood there until his father became aware of his presence, looking up with a start. His face seemed drawn and full of pain. And then his father smiled at him and he smiled back before going upstairs.

Now, the coalition government had fallen and his father

had become involved, as usual, in the election campaign and the battle to have Fianna Fáil back in power. For as long as anyone could remember, his father had made a speech at the final rally in the Market Square, but this time he would not be able, his voice was not clear enough. Some of the men who spent their day in the unused shop which had become party headquarters in the town said that Eamon should make the speech, but his Uncle Tom said that he was too young and they needed someone with more experience.

'How can you get experience, Tom Redmond, if you don't start?' a man in the headquarters said. 'He's a real Redmond, this fellow,' he said, pointing at Eamon. Eamon looked over at his father, who was busy consulting a list of voters and paid no attention to the conversation.

There were still two weeks to go in the campaign. All the party workers congregated in the headquarters for the first meeting to discuss the election. His father was in the chair and began by saying that the discussion was open to everybody. Most of the speakers were old party members, men in greatcoats excited at the prospect of returning to power. Each one wanted to have his say now. There were also a few women there, who did most of the organizing and who knew which houses had already been canvassed and which families had problems. There were a few girls at the meeting as well, daughters of party members.

One man was insisting that painting the roads was the best way to win votes.

'You can go from house to house, and you can put what you like in the post, and you can hold a monster meeting out in the barley field, but you put white paint across the road, and that's the thing will waken the people up.'

Everyone listened carefully as the man, who had been an important figure in the War of Independence, spoke, but as he continued, one girl, whom Eamon did not know, whispered something to her companion, and they both giggled. Several people turned around to look at them, but they had now started to laugh out loud.

Eamon stopped listening to the speaker; he waited for further outbursts of tittering and laughter. He looked behind him disapprovingly, but when one of the girls caught his eye she laughed even more. He felt now that they were laughing at him as much as at the man who was speaking. He thought that his father should stop the meeting and call them to order. He wondered who they were.

'This has always been,' the next speaker said, 'a party of young people. It was founded by people with energy and strong convictions and a love of Ireland, and we want to make sure that the young people of this country stay with us now, and I'd like the young people here tonight to go on the canvass, put their names down now, and find out what the problems are on the doorsteps. I also propose that young Redmond makes a speech at the final rally. I met one of the Christian Brothers who says that he's a great speaker. We need young blood in the party.'

The two girls laughed even louder as they ran across the room and out of the door into the street. They continued to laugh and talk when they got outside. No one passed any comment on them.

Eamon waited for his father. It was late. There had been many suggestions about how things should be done; now people were talking quietly among themselves. He noticed that the two girls had come back, and one of them was busily going through the electoral register with one of the older women.

'There's no one in that house,' he heard her saying. 'Mark that down and the Brogans in Number Nineteen are Fine Gael to a man, dyed in the wool on both sides. Whoever goes in there is just to leave a leaflet in.'

She seemed to know the town better than most of them;

he was surprised at how seriously people were treating her instructions.

'And don't send any of Aidan's supporters canvassing in the Shannon, like you did the last time. They were nearly run out of it,' she laughed. He wondered who she was and how she could remember the previous election so clearly. He had worked on the last election but he did not remember her.

'She's Carmel O'Brien, Vinny O'Brien's daughter,' one of the men told him. 'She's in the office over in Buttle's. She's just left school.'

He stood back and watched his father explain a point to someone, but he could see that the man had difficulty understanding what his father was saying. Carmel O'Brien came over to him.

'They want us to go canvassing up in Vinegar Hill Villas tomorrow night. Will you come?' She had the electoral register in her hand.

'I have a lot of envelopes still to do,' he said. 'I'll have to speak to my father about it.'

'Could you do that immediately?' she asked. Her manner was direct. 'I need this sorted out tonight.'

He noticed as she turned away how tall she was and slender, well formed. He wondered if it was right that they should go together to canvass. Maybe it would be better if each of them went with someone older, who had more experience of elections.

His father was doubtful as well, but the man who had spoken about young people was standing nearby and he said that Eamon and Carmel should definitely canvass the new houses in Vinegar Hill Villas. They would be canvassed again anyway, he said, in the few days immediately before the election.

'Do you want to speak at the final rally?' his father asked him on the way home.

'Not if de Valera is to be there. I'd be afraid,' he said.

'Don't mention that to anybody,' his father said. 'It's meant to be a secret.'

THE next night he went canvassing with Carmel. They walked up the Shannon together and then turned into the new estate.

'There's no jobs here,' one woman told them. 'There's nothing for us at all, except the cattle boat to England. We only see them at Christmas and maybe in the summer.'

'If you vote for Mr de Valera now,' Carmel told her, 'we'll get a factory in this town.'

Eamon asked her if she believed it was right to promise things to people.

'Well, there'll be no factory anyway if they vote for Fine Gael, that's one thing for sure.'

Back in the party headquarters she went through the register with one of the older women.

'Now, someone should go and see them again because they're wavering,' she said. 'Thank God for Noël Browne, he's the one that's going to win Fianna Fáil this election.'

'Well, a lot of people out my way say they'd be Fianna Fáil all the way if Noël Browne was in the party. He's rid the country of TB.'

'And Fianna Fáil will follow on his good work – that's what I tell them,' Carmel said. 'But we're the party that respects the Church.' She sounded as though she did not believe what she was saying, as though she was trying out slogans on them, and Eamon moved away when she began talking about the man who proposed painting the roads.

'Did you ever hear worse?' she asked. 'Daubing paint across the roads! It'll be there for years.'

Eamon grew nervous as the days approached for the final rally.

'If de Valera comes,' the local candidate said in a hushed voice to his father and himself, 'he'll talk about Wexford's

glory and 1798 and they'll all cheer. But we're looking for
votes and somebody had better talk pounds, shillings and
pence from the platform.'

The only time, Eamon's father said, that their local
candidate had ever spoken in the Dáil was to ask them to
open the window. It was, his father laughed, the man's
maiden speech and it was widely reported. But he was a
decent man, his father added, and worked hard for the
town. He would help anyone out. He, too, thought that
Eamon should make a speech. Eamon's Uncle Tom still
believed that he was too young.

'He looks older than he is,' the candidate said. 'If you're
against him making the speech, why don't you make it?'
Uncle Tom said that he did not have enough experience at
public speaking.

'Lemass is going to talk first,' the candidate said, 'and
he's going to introduce me, and then Dev's going to walk
across from the hotel and that's when the band will play.
But we need someone before Lemass, someone local to get
the crowd going. Will you do it, young Redmond, will
you?'

'If my father thinks I should.'

'I'm all for it,' his father said.

It was settled then. He took two days off school to work
on his speech. He practised it on his own at first, and then
he went down to his Aunt Margaret who listened to it in
full.

'Oh that's grand, Eamon, that'll bring the votes in. Go
hard on Noël Browne now. Wait until your father and your
Uncle Tom hear it. It's great to see de Valera coming to
the town again. After the Civil War it was very bitter here.
There were others, men your grandfather and Tom had
fought beside and trusted, and all they wanted was an easy
peace. An easy peace and a good job. Once they got power
they wouldn't give it up, they were worse than the British.
They shot their own, and after the war a lot of our side

went to America and never came back. They gave up hope, and if it hadn't been for de Valera and a few others we'd never have got back in. There were people in this town who wouldn't speak to you, or even look at you. But that all changed when Fianna Fáil won the first election. I remember, Eamon, the first time de Valera came after he won, he was led into the square by fifty men on white horses and they were lighting tar barrels all over the Market Square. That was a great day here. That was a day to remember.'

Later, when his father and his Uncle Tom came back from the party headquarters in the town he acted out his speech for them, but he noticed when he was halfway through that they were both quietly laughing. They tried to stop when he looked up but his Uncle Tom had to leave the room.

'That's a great way to treat him now,' his Aunt Margaret said to his father, but his father was still shaking with laughter and he left the room as well.

'Don't mind them now, Eamon, don't mind them.'

He told her about the two girls laughing at the meeting.

'The election makes them all nervous,' she said. 'But don't mind them.'

When his uncle came back he apologized for laughing.

'I just thought of some of the hecklers in the square. They could stop you in your tracks. There'll be a lot of hecklers. You'd want to watch them, Eamon,' he said and began to laugh again.

On the morning of the rally he went to Courtney's barbers in Weafer Street and had his hair cut.

'I hear you're preaching tonight, sausage,' Paddy Courtney said to him. 'We'll all be down to listen to you. People'll be asking about de Valera: who's the long fellow beside young Redmond?'

'No school today?' a man in the queue for a shave said to him.

'Did you not hear the news?' Paddy Courtney stopped and addressed the group of men sitting on the bench waiting their turn. 'Sausage here is going to open this evening's deliberations. The Croppy Boy here is going to address his native town in the first national language.'

'I'd say that there'll be fellows waiting for him in the square. The whole town'll be out tonight, Fianna Fáil, Fine Gael and Labour,' a man on the bench said.

'And the other shower,' said the barber.

'The mother and his child,' one of the men sniggered.

Eamon wore his good suit, a white shirt and a green tie. He went first to the party headquarters.

'Have you it off by heart?' a man asked him. He did not reply. He walked across to Bennett's Hotel. De Valera had arrived and was upstairs. Later, he would be going on to a rally in Wexford. A former minister whom Eamon recognized as Sean Lemass and his group were having sandwiches in the lounge. Eamon was introduced to Lemass and shook his hand.

'I knew your grandfather,' Lemass said. He turned to the group. 'He's one of the Redmonds,' he said. 'You're Michael's son, isn't that right?'

'He's making a speech tonight,' someone said.

'So he should,' Lemass said. 'We're going to need every vote we get.'

As the time drew near they walked up through the town, and when they reached the platform in front of the council building the Market Square was filling up with groups of men talking in serious tones to each other. There were chairs at the back of the platform; a microphone had been set up at the front. Several men were now testing the microphone.

'The trick is,' Lemass said to him, 'look at every face. Don't look down. If you're nervous pick one man in the crowd and address yourself to him. They're all looking at you and you should look back at them.'

Eamon nodded; he was nervous now.

The groups of men were getting larger. There was a big group outside Stamp's public house and another around the monument to Father Murphy and 1798. As yet there were no women in the square.

'Watch,' a man said to him. 'The minute it starts the place'll fill up. There's fellows in from Bree and Ballindaggin and all around the Milehouse for this.'

It was half past seven now, and de Valera had to be in Wexford for a monster rally at nine o'clock, or a quarter past nine at the latest.

'Crowd or no crowd,' Lemass said, 'we have to start.'

Eamon's father and the local chairman and several of the group who had been with Lemass went up on the platform and sat down. They left room for Lemass in the centre, and a space for the candidate beside him. Eamon wondered if they had forgotten about him and he felt a sudden hope that they would decide not to let him speak. It was like the queue for confession, this terrible waiting.

Eventually, the chairman of the local branch of the party went to the platform. It was dark and becoming cold. Eamon noticed that the square was slowly filling up; people were coming in from Cathedral Street and Weafer Street.

'This is a great day for the town of Enniscorthy,' the chairman said. There was a buzz in the microphone which grew into a piercing whistle as he spoke. He stood back while an electrician came on to the stage and began to fiddle with it, and then he tested it again.

'Can you hear me now?' he asked. His voice blared around the Market Square, but no one replied. Again, a whistling, piercing sound came from the microphone.

'Don't go so close to it,' the electrician shouted at him.

'Can you hear me now?' the chairman asked again, standing back from the microphone. His voice echoed in the square. He turned to the electrician and told him to warn each speaker to keep his distance from the microphone.

'This is a great day for the town of Enniscorthy,' the chairman began again. 'Not far away, and soon to appear, is one of the greatest statesmen in the world today, a figure revered both here and abroad. Our past and future Taoiseach.' The crowd was paying no attention; between each phrase the murmuring of voices could be heard. Eamon looked carefully at the text of his speech, although he knew it now word for word. Men were standing on the steps of the monument and people were watching from the windows of the houses, from Byrne's and Godfrey's and the Munster and Leinster Bank.

'Vote Fianna Fáil!' the chairman shouted. 'Vote de Valera!'

There was a small cheer.

'And now,' he said, 'it is an honour for me, as chairman of this Enniscorthy *cumann* of Fianna Fáil, to introduce a young man who hails from one of the Republican families of this town, whose grandfather was at the forefront of the struggle for national freedom and sovereignty and whose father fought in the War of Independence alongside many of the great figures of modern Irish history. He's going to address you now, so could I have silence, please, and your full attention, and there's room at the front here for anyone who can't see, and could I have a welcome please for young Eamon Redmond.'

He walked up the steps to the platform and looked around at the faces in the dark square. Most people were still talking among themselves. He stood at the microphone and took his time. He held the script in his hands.

'In Fianna Fáil,' he began, 'we're looking for your Number One vote. We're not, like other parties, looking for your transfers: left-over votes for left-over parties. This is not the party of transfers. We'll leave it to other people to transfer.'

'Ah, fuck off, Redmond, you little squirt,' a voice shouted from near the Father Murphy monument.

The crowd laughed.

'This is not the party that took a shilling off the old-age pension. We'll leave that to others, the others we are now going to drive from power, because Fianna Fáil is the party of this country, rich and poor, young and old.'

A cheer came up, but there was still murmuring and laughter from around the monument.

'We know, our history tells us, about the persecution of religion in this country. We know of the time when the priests had to flee from house to house. We respect our priests for that, and we don't fly in their faces now, like some others do. We don't start telling the bishops what to do, because we know our history. We know how much this country suffered under foreign rule, and there are others, and we'll put names on them, there are others like Noël Browne and Seán MacBride, who want to bring us back under foreign domination. They want to bring Communism into this country and hunt the priests from house to house, like the English before them.'

A loud cheer came up from the edges of the square and from the party loyals in front of the platform.

'Ireland, under Fianna Fáil,' he went on, 'will respect the clergy of this country. But we will do more than that.' He stopped and looked around the square. 'We were the first to build hospitals in this country, and we were criticized for doing that. But we will build more hospitals and we will stop the curse of emigration which has brought this country to ruin under the coalition government—'

'Fuck off, Redmond, you're only a squirt,' a voice shouted from the monument.

'It's people like you,' Eamon pointed at the area around the monument, 'with your foul word brought here by the English, who don't appreciate that we kept this country out of the war. And you wouldn't understand that this country is in danger from outside influences, but most people in this square and in this town and in this country know that, the decent people of Ireland can make up their own minds whether they want you and your likes running this country or whether Ireland will be led by a figure as internationally renowned as Eamon de Valera.'

He stood back now and looked at the crowd. Most people were staring up at the platform, some were applauding and a few were cheering. Lemass stood up from his seat and shook his hand.

'You're a great speaker,' he said.

He took a seat on the platform while the candidate and Lemass spoke, but he was too excited to listen to them. He noticed the tension building up as each slogan was shouted out, he heard the cheers and whistling and applause. A heckler shouted over and over at Lemass about TB. 'What are you going to do about TB? What did you ever do to rid the country of TB?' No one listened to the heckler; people were waiting for de Valera to appear. It was now a quarter past eight, and Lemass's voice was growing louder and more passionate. He had been alerted to the news that de Valera was in Murphy Flood's hotel.

'He's coming now,' a party worker at the front shouted.

Lemass began to speak about the party leader and his stature in the world. Eamon watched the way being cleared at the side of the platform and de Valera being led along and helped up the steps. Suddenly, Lemass brought his speech to an abrupt end and the band began to play 'A Nation Once Again'.

'People of Enniscorthy,' Lemass shouted into the microphone, 'I present Eamon de Valera.' Lemass shook de Valera's hand and gently brought him towards the microphone. Eamon wondered how blind he was; one of the men in the hotel had said that he would soon have to undergo another eye operation.

De Valera stood on the platform without speaking. There

was still cheering coming from the crowd and he raised his hand for silence. As he did so, a man shouted, 'Up Dev!' and the crowd burst into further cheering. He stopped and waited until there was complete silence in the square. He held the silence, still saying nothing, and then he started.

'I stand in one of the sacred towns of this island. I am proud to be in one of those places which has ever kept the flame of nationhood alight, even in darkest times. Throughout our history, we have asserted our right as a people to be free, and nowhere more so than on Vinegar Hill overlooking this town in seventeen and ninety eight. In this great square, steeped in history and lore, stands the monument by Oliver Sheppard to the bravery of the Croppy Boy and the leadership of Father Murphy in those far-off years. But they are not forgotten, and we are still inspired by those great deeds and those great heroes. We, too, have known difficult times, and in recent days this country has been ruled by unnecessary controversy while our best young people emigrate, take the boat to England and America. We are the national party and we will tackle the real problems facing this country; we will not make controversy where there is no need. Our party is stable and we will not break into factions and go against the will of the people and the will of God . . . so vote Fianna Fáil next week for stable government and the good of Ireland.'

When he had finished the band started again, this time with 'The Boys of Wexford'. Eamon stood back as de Valera was helped from the platform. The crowd had already begun to disperse. One of the men with Lemass asked him if he wanted to be introduced to de Valera. He nodded and was brought down to where de Valera was surrounded by well-wishers and supporters. When he was introduced, de Valera spoke to him in Irish about the importance of the language in the life of the country. Soon, de Valera was brought back to Murphy Flood's where there was a car waiting to take him to Wexford. Eamon

noticed Lemass's friend, the man who had introduced him
to de Valera, talking to his father. Before he left for
Wexford in the car with Lemass he came over to Eamon
and shook his hand again.

'I was talking to your father. He says you're going to
University College Dublin if you get the results. He says
that you're a great scholar. I was saying to him that you
should do the bar. There's a great need now for Fianna
Fáil barristers. We could do with fellows of your calibre.
But I said I'd call up to your father on the way back so I
have your address.' He shook Eamon's hand again and
walked briskly towards the waiting car.

Eamon went with his father to his grandmother's house.
They sat in the front room with his Uncle Tom. Both men
had bottles of stout to celebrate de Valera's visit, Eamon
had a glass of lemonade. His Aunt Margaret came and put
a plate of fancy biscuits on the table.

'Did you hear the man introducing me?' Eamon asked
them. 'He said that you fought in the War of Independence.' He looked at his father.

'I didn't do much,' his father said.

'Your Uncle Patrick and your grandfather were more
involved,' his Uncle Tom said.

'What did you do?' Eamon asked his father.

'I caught the train to Dublin a few times,' his father said
and shrugged as though he wanted to say no more.

'You couldn't just burn a house, you see,' Uncle Tom
said. 'You'd have to get permission from Cathal Brugha in
Dublin. You'd have to present him with all the facts; any
of the houses that entertained the Black and Tans, had the
officers for dinners and parties, they'd be on the list. Your
father'd go up, he was young enough and he pretended to
spend the day in the National Library, but he'd slip out to
see Brugha, or one of Brugha's men, and then permission
would come back and then we'd do the job.'

'Burn the house?' Eamon asked.

'We gutted a good few of them all right,' his uncle sipped his drink. 'Wilton, old Captain Skrine, the Proctors on the Bunclody Road, Castleboro. I have a book upstairs I took from Castleboro the night we went out there. They had a great library. It's a pity I didn't have more time. I still have it upstairs. It has a note inside saying "*Ex Libris Lord Carew*". What's it called? *Cranford* by Mrs Gaskell. I must look for it. I'm sure it's up there somewhere.'

'Were they all Protestants?' Eamon asked.

'They were,' his uncle said. 'And they were all up to their neck in the British Army who were on the rampage here, and the British Legion and the King and the Queen. It's all gone now. At least we got rid of that, whatever else we did.'

THE following Sunday afternoon Lemass's friend drove up to the house in a Morris Oxford. He left another man waiting in the passenger seat. Eamon answered the door and ushered him into the front room before going into the back room to whisper to his father who had come. The man said that he didn't want tea or a drink. He had to make calls before he went back to Dublin, do official party business for the election.

He explained that Eamon could go to UCD and do an Arts degree as his father had done, but in his second year he could study to be a barrister as well.

'There'd be help available if you needed it,' he said.

'We'll be able to take care of that,' his father said.

'There would be a lot of work for him once he was qualified. But let me know anyway. Mr de Valera, incidentally, heard the speech. He thought it was very good.'

When the man had gone Eamon tried to imagine de Valera listening to his speech, but he could not. He wondered if it were true. De Valera had seemed so remote.

'What age is de Valera?' he asked his father later that evening.

His father thought for a while. 'He'll be seventy next year,' he said.

EAMON returned to school on Monday, but he still went down to party headquarters every evening. He tried to talk to Carmel O'Brien as much as he could.

'That was a great speech,' she said. 'It's a pity you didn't talk like that when we went canvassing.'

'You knew all of the people,' he said.

'But I can't talk in public as well as you.'

On the night before the vote they went canvassing again. This time he spoke on the doorsteps as well. It was easier and he felt happy with her. He liked the way she seemed to sympathize with people and talk to them naturally. At the end of the evening they walked back to the head-quarters.

'Do you know something?' she said to him. 'You're the most careful person I've ever come across. I've met you every day for three weeks and I know nothing about you. You could only talk about the election. Do you never think about anything else?'

He looked at her, much taken aback.

'I thought that we got on very well,' he said.

'I don't know what you're thinking. You're miles away,' she replied.

He tried to laugh but he felt uneasy at being spoken to like that. No one had ever used that tone with him before. When he met her at the count, where she was helping her father with the tally, he kept away from her at first, but it was hard not to notice her.

'We've increased our vote in Ballyhogue, isn't that a good one?' She squeezed his waist and laughed. 'It was your speech that did it. But we're down in Monageer.'

He sat in the back seat of the car with her on the way home. He was nervous and excited beside her. Eventually, he took her hand and held it. Her skin was soft; he thought about her body, her breasts, her legs and her long neck. He edged her close to him and kissed her on the side of the face and then she turned towards him and let him kiss her on the mouth.

PART THREE

CHAPTER THIRTEEN

E AMON REDMOND stood at the window looking
down at the river which was deep brown after days of
rain. He watched the colour, the mixture of mud and
water, and the small currents and pockets of movement
within the flow. It was the last day of term; later, he was
due to sit in the Special Criminal Court. He brought a
chair over to the window so that he could read the morning
newspaper by clear daylight. He listened to the sound of
gulls over the hum of traffic.

In the evening he planned to drive alone to Cush, unless,
for some reason, the court needed to sit another day.
Maybe he was wrong to go down alone so soon; it would
be hard. He would try to cook for himself, keep the place
tidy. He closed his eyes.

He was tired because he had drunk some wine and a few
brandies in the Stephen's Green Club the previous evening,
at the invitation of an historian whom he had known for
some years, who was doing research now on the response
of the Irish government to the violence in Northern Ireland.
The historian was looking for leads, and he wanted certain
things confirmed: that meetings had taken place, that
individuals had been involved, that differences of opinion
had occurred.

Eamon had told the historian very little. He had written a report for the government, which he presented early
in 1972, on the ways in which the government should
respond to a concerted campaign by the IRA. He had also
written a number of interim reports over the previous two

years, one of which recommended non-jury courts for IRA cases.

Many of his submissions, as he explained to the historian, dealt with technical matters he had been asked to investigate, such as the relationship between the army and the police in border areas, the safety of electrical installations and water supply, the security of the radio and television stations. With a small team of civil servants he had reported on these matters, and he was prepared to talk to the historian about them, while making clear that he could not show him the actual documents. They were now, he imagined, out of date, but some of the information in them was still current and confidential.

There were two chapters in his report which the historian was only vaguely aware of; no one, beyond those who were entitled to see the report, had ever read these chapters. He had been told several times that they had been influential and had helped to shape government policy on security throughout the 1970s.

He had written an analysis of Irish nationalist feeling for the government. He had warned never to allow public opinion to become inflamed in the Republic by events within its own borders. The north, he argued, must be presented as a different society, a place apart. The dangers, he wrote, would come from the creation of causes and martyrs, which would stir up latent nationalist feeling in the South. Thus, there must be no trouble within the prisons of the Republic, no riots or hunger strikes or bad publicity. Also, he wrote, the courts and the police must be seen to be beyond reproach, even in an emergency. He suggested a special three-judge appeal court to examine cases in which there was a lingering doubt. He proposed that the Minister for Justice should have the right to refer cases to this court. He was still sure that this was a necessity in the Republic, but it had never been done.

He knew that this chapter of the report would seem too

cold and calculating so many years later when the emergency was over. He suggested as they sat at the table that there was nothing of any interest in all of this, and yet, for security reasons, it could not be released. His companion did not know that there was also another chapter in the report which outlined, without comment, how foreign governments had dealt with terrorism and how certain measures had succeeded and others failed. At the time, when he worked on the report, Eamon was sure that internment in the Republic would fail, would inflame both nationalist and liberal feelings and would not improve security. He had tried to show how repression had not worked elsewhere. He had been briefed in detail by British and French security experts who had worked in Israel and Algeria. He did not want this to come to light, felt that it would be misunderstood and knew that the historian would seize on this should he become aware of it.

He had also included a section on how the courts, in particular the Supreme Court, could become a difficulty for any administration trying to combat terrorism. But this had been seen by only the Taoiseach and the Minister for Justice. In the mid-1970s the Taoiseach's department had assured him that his memo on this matter had been destroyed and was no longer on file.

The historian was a clever man, watchful and worldly. He would bide his time, picking up bits and pieces from such dinners and social encounters. He had published very little, and Eamon wondered if his work on government policy in relation to terrorism would ever appear.

After dinner they sat at a side table: there was no more to be said about the report, they had exhausted the possibilities. The waiter came with brandies as they began to talk about their backgrounds, Eamon about Enniscorthy and his family's involvement in 1916 and the War of Independence, the historian about his father's memories of the burning of Cork city.

'Was your father in the Civil War?' the historian asked him.

'He must have been. I know one uncle was on hunger strike, but, to be honest, I'm not sure. It was never talked about. Nineteen sixteen was mentioned all the time, and the Tan War as well, but not the Civil War. I know that my father was aware who did some of the killings in Enniscorthy, a man told him once in a pub, but he swore that he would never tell anyone. And he told me years ago about how they took over the Protestant church in Enniscorthy during the Civil War, and they made mock sermons during the night, but when the shooting started one man shouted out, "Watch the ricoshits, lads!" and they all thought this was funny. He told me the story as though he was there, but I never asked him. If you asked him he would grow silent. It was a very bitter time for them.'

'They were a strange generation,' the historian said.

The two men had a few more drinks as they talked about the past. Eamon remembered the story about Cathal Brugha and his father's going to Dublin to get permission to have the Big Houses burned. But he said nothing about it. He listened to a story about Michael Collins, nodding and encouraging the historian to go on, all the time thinking back to that evening in his grandmother's house when he first heard the story. He kept listening, more and more sure that he should not mention the story about his father and Cathal Brugha, that he should consign it to the past, to silence, as his father had done with the names of the men who did the killings in Enniscorthy. He smiled as the historian came to the end of his story, and stood up, saying it was time to go.

HE sat at the window in the chamber in the Four Courts the following morning. His report was history now; all the lessons had been learned; the state had been protected and would survive. He looked again at the river, the sunlight on the brown water.

His tipstaff came to say that the Gardaí were waiting for
him at the side entrance to the court. He did not enjoy
being driven to the Special Court under armed protection,
but even though there had been no attempted breakout
from Green Street in some years, it was felt that vigilance
must be maintained. He walked down to the unmarked,
but clearly recognizable, police car and sat in the front
seat. He had learned not to speak to the Guards; some of
them had given evidence in his court over the years and,
no doubt, would do so again, and he felt it was better if he
did not know them. The two Guards in the back seat were
detectives and carried machine guns. The driver started
the car and drove out past the Land Registry towards the
Bridewell, and then along North King Street where army
sentries had posted themselves at the junction with Green
Street.

He was the senior judge on the three-man court. He
knew one of the other judges and liked him; the third man,
a recently appointed Circuit Court judge, had been a senior
counsel specializing in insurance cases. All three now
donned their gowns and wigs as they waited for the court
to begin.

As soon as they began to listen to the evidence it became
clear that it was not a simple case. Eamon put his head in
his hands and re-read the statements in front of him. Three
men, two from Monaghan and one from Armagh, were
charged with membership of the IRA, of possession of
firearms, of shooting at a Garda in the course of his duty,
of attempted murder, of resisting arrest. It seemed when
he checked through the Garda statements that there was
real evidence against only one of the accused in the
shooting charge. He wondered why the charges against the
other two had not been dropped. He checked again, as he
continued to listen to the oral evidence. He noticed, with
satisfaction, that his younger colleague was looking as well.

The defence counsel was already questioning the Guard

who had pursued and arrested the three men. He decided
to interrupt the cross-examination.

'Mr Roche,' he said to the counsel, 'I am taking it that
all three of your clients are pleading not guilty to the
firearms offences, is that correct?'

'Yes, my lord.'

'Mr Miller,' he turned to the counsel for the prosecution,
'I take it that you will be producing evidence against all
three.'

'Yes, my lord.'

'All three?'

'Yes, my lord.'

'You can proceed then,' he said. It seemed to him that
they would have to drop charges against two of the accused
very quickly if they did not want to waste most of the day.
He presumed that his two colleagues understood the reason
for his interruption, and he was pleased when he noticed
one of the junior counsel on the prosecution side leaving
the court, probably to seek an instruction on whether they
should drop the charges against two of the accused.

He looked through his notes again, but it was clear that
all three were not armed, and it was clear that the Gardaí
had not established a case against all three through seeing
them using the guns or checking fingerprints afterwards.
He would not accept a charge of attempted murder without
precise evidence. The prosecuting counsel was getting
nowhere in his cross-examination. He wondered, as he
listened to the counsel, if there was an effort being made to
change the way in which the Special Criminal Court dealt
with attempted murder, and the evidence necessary to
prove it. If so, he would stop it immediately. The counsel
was now questioning the main Garda witness. He interrupted again.

'Garda Power,' he asked, 'did you see all three men
armed? I am taking it that only one gun was fired. Did you
see all three men handle that one gun?'

'Only one was armed, your honour.'

'No, listen again. Which of them fired the gun?'

'I saw Fingleton taking a shot at my colleague.'

'And the other two? Did they shoot?'

'No, your honour.'

'Mr Miller,' he turned again to the counsel, who was flicking through his notes, 'will you be producing evidence that the second and third accused are guilty of attempted murder?'

'I am trying to establish that, my lord.'

'I know what you're trying to establish. What I wish to know is what evidence you will use to establish it.'

'I will establish it in my examination of witnesses, my lord.'

'We will attend to you with great patience.' He looked sharply at the counsel.

He knew that the counsel was bluffing, waiting for instructions on whether to drop the charges. He knew that since the main witness had not actually seen two of the defendants shooting, and only one gun was fired, then they could not be found guilty of attempted murder. The prosecution should drop the charges very soon, he thought, because the longer they continued with them the more they would damage the case.

As soon as the court re-convened after lunch the counsel for the prosecution stood up to say that they were dropping the firearms charges against the second and third accused.

'Mr Miller,' Eamon stopped him before he had finished, 'am I to take it that you have been wasting the time of this court?'

'No, my lord.'

'I asked you this morning what evidence you had. It was clear this morning that you had no evidence, at least to me and my colleagues. Was it not clear to you and your colleagues?'

'No, my lord.'

'I see. Proceed with the case, and do so in the full knowledge that this court's patience with you is very short.'

He watched the first accused as he was cross-examined. He was a small man, in his late thirties. He did not look like a man with strong political convictions. And his evidence, too, had that guarded, puzzled quality as though he had been brought in from the street, as though he had never been involved in the IRA in his life.

Counsel for the defence was now claiming that the three men were arrested north of the border, and that their arrest was illegal. Argument continued over this for a while, but was not convincing. There was no doubt but that shots were fired, and that the man identified by the Garda had fired them. His fingerprints, indeed, were on the gun which had been fired. But was this attempted murder? This was the decision the three judges would have to make.

The defence was making very little headway, and had counsel pleaded guilty to lesser charges it might have been easier. By half past three it seemed as though the case could be decided very quickly. The second and third could be found guilty of IRA membership and the first with intent to endanger life. He would give the first six years, and the others two. His colleagues, he thought, might want to give harsher sentences. He did not think that they would take long to decide.

When the hearing was finished they retired to the room behind the court. There was a fresh pot of tea and some cups and saucers on the table in the room.

They sat down and began to discuss the case.

'We must take the first accused, Fingleton, and the other two separately, as they face separate charges. Do we believe that Fingleton is guilty of possession with intent rather than attempted murder?'

'Correct,' said the older man.

'Is he guilty of all the lesser charges?' Eamon asked.

They both assented.

'Are the other two guilty of IRA membership?'

Once more, they both said yes.

'Could you suggest sentencing?' he turned to them both.

'Six and four,' the district justice said.

'Seven and four,' the younger man said, 'with other sentences to run concurrently.'

'You can take that as read,' he said to them both. 'I'm in favour of six and four as well. Can we agree on that?'

After the sentencing they waited in the back room as the prisoners were put in the van to be driven to Portlaoise prison. Usually, there were protesters, or well-wishers, or cameras outside the court, and it was important for the judges not to appear until the tumult in the street had died down. The judges did not speak until the younger man asked the other two if they were going on holidays now that the law term had ended. Neither of them seemed anxious to reply and both, when they spoke, did not go into detail.

THE Garda car drove him back to the Four Courts; there were several phone messages for him, but none was important. He went to the window and looked out at the traffic on the quays, which was heavier now than it had been in the morning, and would not ease off until five or six o'clock. He could not decide whether to leave now or wait. He had packed nothing, but that would be easy; some clothes and books, some food from the fridge. He stood at the window, letting the time go by, wondering what to do.

Carmel had died in the winter. He still found the two or three hours before sleep very difficult, and he did not know if they would be easier in Cush, or much harder. He would have to go there to know and he had not been there since she died. He could imagine himself in the morning, waking in the early light, listening to the radio, making tea and letting it draw on the table in the living room, scrambling eggs and making toast. The morning seemed easy. But the coming down of the summer's night and the few hours of darkness before sleep; he was not sure that he would be ready for it.

In the weeks after Carmel's death it was easier, there were people in the house and when they left him alone there was a silence and a solitude which he needed. He could go back over everything: how tired and distant and only half aware of his presence she was in the last weeks in hospital. He had presumed that this was caused by the drugs they were using. He let himself believe that she was getting better until he came face to face with the consultant in the corridor.

'How do you think things are going?' he asked.

'I'm afraid she's sinking,' he said. 'There's very little we can do for her.'

He sat by her side, going out into the corridor only when the nurses asked him to, but otherwise waiting there with her, talking to her when he felt that she understood and leaving the children alone with her when he thought that they needed to say goodbye to her. Her sisters came and prayed beside the bed and his Aunt Margaret phoned to say that she was praying all the time. He did not pray, nor did the children, but he liked the rhythms of the prayers and he hoped that the sound comforted her. He held her hand when he knew that she would not last the night, and he hoped that his hand comforted her as well. He whispered to her, said her name, and went outside and stared through the heavy glass at the murky yellow lights of the road, and realized what this meant, and was struck by the terrible knowledge that she was going to go.

THEY travelled in a black limousine behind the hearse to Enniscorthy where she was buried. Her sisters started the Rosary in the car, but he stopped them and suggested that each person should pray silently. He knew that they resented this, but he did not want Donal and Niamh to be disturbed. Niamh held his hand at the grave and Donal stayed close to him. Her first night in the ground was unbearable for him to contemplate. She was still whole, complete, her body intact. She might have easily lasted a few more days and be still alive in the world.

They went back to Dublin after the funeral. All three of them felt apart from the rest – city people. They did not speak in the car, but there was no tension between them. Eamon felt that they were trying to support him and help him. The car dropped them in Ranelagh. They both came into the house with him. Donal lit a fire and Niamh put a stew, which a neighbour had made, into the microwave. She set the table.

He felt a bond with his children for the first time in his life, and they both said that they would come to Cush during the holidays and stay with him. Niamh's son, Michael, was more than a year old. He made strange very easily, Niamh said, so it was difficult to get minders for him.

'He knows me from last year,' Eamon said to her.

'I don't think he saw much of you,' she replied.

He tried to check back from bank statements how much money Carmel had given Niamh over the previous year, but he was not sure that his calculations were correct. It seemed much less than he imagined. She told him that she no longer needed the money, but was grateful when he offered to help her to buy a house.

HE stood at the window of his room in the Four Courts, dreaming, remembering things, waiting for time to pass, watching the currents in the river. He turned and put some books into a briefcase, and looked around to make sure that everything important was locked away. Then he took his keys and left, locking the door behind him. The building was almost empty; he greeted one of the cleaning women as he passed, and she recognized him and smiled. He saw no one else as he walked through the Four Courts to the car park.

CHAPTER FOURTEEN

H E remembered being called out of the Law Library
one afternoon and finding his father and his uncle
standing in the Round Hall. He had never thought of them
as countrymen, but now, in this building which was strange
for them, they seemed hesitant and shy, out of place. It
was hard to explain to them that even though he had a
case coming up he would not be speaking, as the senior
counsels would be the only ones to address the court. In
fact, he would probably be running in and out to get books
for them. He was about to say that his role in the case
would be merely that of a messenger boy, but he was afraid
that they would misunderstand. They were beginning to
look around them as though they had a stake in the Four
Courts and in him, an important figure in the system.

A great number of the other barristers were from Fine
Gael families. Although he worked with them, and knew
many of them from university, he did not feel familiar
enough with them to introduce his father and uncle. It
would be considered wrong at this time of the day in the
Round Hall to introduce visiting relatives to a senior
counsel.

His father and uncle looked both eager and out of place.
They had already spoken to several of the porters in search
of him and had established that one of the older porters
was from North Wexford, and this made them feel more at
home, although they did not know the man or his family.

The porter knew Eamon as one of the busiest junior
counsels in the Four Courts. After the Fianna Fáil victory

in 1957 he had regular work for the state, and became an experienced prosecutor. Several senior counsel and solicitors used him whenever he was available, but most of his work came from the state. He was making enough money now to have a car and a flat in Hume Street, near St Stephen's Green. He continued to be involved with Fianna Fáil, working as a speech writer and campaign organizer in the 1959 presidential election and in the general elections of 1961.

As he sat behind his senior colleagues in the court, he was aware of the two men at the back of the court watching him. He would have little to do, and most of his argument would be technical anyway. One of his colleagues was in Fianna Fáil as well, but he was not sure that he could ask him to come and meet his father and uncle when the case was finished. He hoped that they would not feel insulted, or let down by his not introducing them to his colleagues. He found it hard to concentrate as the case went on.

Afterwards, he walked up the quays with them, but by the time they reached the Ormond Hotel his father was too tired to go any farther. He seemed old and worn down by his bad leg and impaired voice. Eamon had left the car at home, since he enjoyed the walk to the courts in the morning. As they sat in the lounge of the hotel and ordered tea, he wondered how his father would get to Westland Row for the train. He felt that they would insist on not taking a taxi.

'That was only a minor case today,' he said.

'You'd need a good murder case,' his uncle said. 'I'd say the courts would fill up then all right. There used to be some great murder cases.'

'They give you one piece of advice when you start on a murder case,' Eamon said, and noticed the two men listening to him as though he were an expert.

'Never look at the accused, even if you're questioning

him. Never even glance at him; that's what they all tell you.'

'Why's that?' his uncle asked. They were listening with great attention.

'Because if they hang him, you don't want to have any picture of him in your mind, you don't want to be able to remember his face. That's what they say, anyway.'

Later, when they had gone, the story he had told them about hanging stayed with him. He had prosecuted only two murder cases, in one of which the man was hanged. At the time, he went to Enniscorthy every weekend and spent Saturday afternoon and evening with Carmel, going for a walk down the Prom with her if the weather was fine enough, sometimes crossing the railway tracks to the Ringwood. He did not talk about work much, nor about Dublin, but this time it was the week before a man was due to be hanged. He knew the man's name but he tried not to let it into his mind. Some people were expecting the Pope to appeal to the government for clemency. He remembered that it was a fine evening and they were walking on the cement path past the hand-ball alley and the river was calm like soft glass. She was talking about the murder case, and hoping that the man would be reprieved.

'I was involved in that case,' he said.

'And you couldn't get him off?'

'No, I was on the other side.'

'What side?'

'The prosecution side.'

'You mean that you were on the side which wanted the man hanged?'

'I was doing my job,' he said.

She stopped and looked down the river towards the sprawling red-brick mental hospital.

'I remember a good many years ago a man was going to

be hanged. It was going to happen at nine o'clock in the morning. My mother made us all say a prayer at nine o'clock exactly, the moment we thought they would hang him. I'll never forget it. And how will you feel if they hang him?'

'I'll feel the same as everybody else.'

'Surely you'll feel worse,' she said.

'How would you feel if someone belonging to you had been murdered by him and raped as well?'

'I wouldn't want them to hang him.'

They walked to where the promenade ended and turned without going up on the railway track.

'I do a lot of prosecution work now,' he said. 'I'm just starting.'

'Are you getting the work from Fianna Fáil?' she asked.

'I get the work through the courts like everyone else,' he said.

He walked back to her house with her. At the top of Friary Hill she asked him if he believed that the man would hang, and he said he did.

'Isn't that terrible?' she said. 'Isn't that terrible?'

'What are you doing later on?' he asked her when they reached the door of the house.

'I think I'll stay in tonight,' she said.

HE drove back to Dublin the next day without seeing her. He thought of leaving a note but he could not think what to say. The day before the hanging he stood around the Law Library with a few colleagues as they listened to the barrister who had worked for the defence. He had seen the condemned man that morning.

'He still doesn't believe it. He asked me how long he'd have to serve if they commuted it. I didn't know what to say. He thinks the Pope is going to make a last-minute appeal for clemency. I should have let the solicitor go on his own.'

Eamon listened to the evening news on the radio. There was a vigil outside Mountjoy jail; people were going to say the Rosary all night. There were calls to the President to commute the sentence on the advice of the government, but the news in the Law Library was that there would be no change, the Cabinet had made up its mind. There were good reasons, he was told, for letting it go ahead.

In the morning, he listened to the eight o'clock news. There was still a crowd outside the jail. He knew that Carmel would be listening to the radio, and once she heard the morning news, she would know that there was no chance of the sentence being commuted. He went out and walked in St Stephen's Green. He did not want to hear the nine o'clock news.

He did not go to Enniscorthy for a few weekends; he had an important case for which he needed to do detailed and meticulous study. He wrote Carmel a note, saying he would be home soon, but he received no reply. When he drove to Enniscorthy he knew that it would not be easy to talk to her again without discussing the hanging. She did not forget about things easily. He sat with his father in the front room, looking nervously out the window, all the time commenting on the neighbours.

'Are you going out tonight?' his father asked.

'I probably will,' he said.

He had a bath and put on a clean shirt and a tie. His father was listening to the radio in the back room as he went out. It was a fine evening. As he passed he looked at each house in John Street and Court Street, each door painted a different colour, some windows clean and shiny with lace curtains, others with grime at the edges, in need of paint. Some of the houses in Court Street were bigger than the rest, with larger windows and potted plants in brass bowls on the windowsills inside. One house had no lace curtains, you could see right in: the new three-piece suite, the thick grey and red carpet, the lamps and the ornaments on the mantelpiece. Everybody looked in as they passed; the room was always perfectly neat, a showcase. The family had made money in England.

When he knocked on the door of Carmel's house he could hear voices inside, but they quietened as Carmel's sister came to the door.

'Is Carmel here?' he asked.

'No,' she said. 'I don't know where she is. She went out earlier on. I don't know when she'll be back.' It sounded like a speech she had learned off by heart and when he looked at her, she looked away.

'You don't know where I'd find her?' he asked.

'No,' she said, and sounded even less convincing this time. 'I don't know where she went.'

He knew she was in the house and he stood at the door wondering what he should do.

'Tell her I'll be at eleven o'clock Mass tomorrow,' he said.

'I'll tell her that,' her sister said.

He sat at the back of the cathedral the following morning but he did not see her, and he waited in his seat, watching out for her, as the crowd slowly left the church. He waited there until most of the congregation had gone out. He wondered as he genuflected if she would be in the grounds of the church, but he knew that she had not turned up. He walked home along the Back Road and turned down the Tanyard Lane into Court Street. He was tempted to knock on the door of her house and ask for her; even when he had passed he considered turning back, but in the end he continued walking along John Street towards home to eat with his father.

He did not see her until later that summer when he was staying for a few days with his father and the Cullens at Cush. It was a warm, mild Sunday. He had been at late Mass with his father, after which they had gone for a drink to Mrs Davis's pub, now run by her nephew. As he started

the car in the village he noticed a group of girls going by
on bicycles and spotted Carmel among them. They turned
left at the bridge in Blackwater. He drove past them, and
glanced in the mirror as they got off the bicycles to walk up
the steep hill which led to Ballyconnigar.

In the afternoon he had a swim. When he had dried
himself he changed into his trousers and shirt, leaving
his shoes and pullover with his towel and togs near a
marl boulder, and walked along the strand towards
Ballyconnigar.

He could see a group of girls sitting on the grass bank
across the river as soon as he turned the corner. He was
walking in his bare feet in the shallows, and had to roll up
the bottoms of his trousers to cross the river. There was a
number of groups sitting on rugs in the fields in front of
Keating's house, or farther along the strand, but he was
sure that Carmel's group was on the bank. When he came
level with them he stood still and looked up towards her
with his hand on his forehead shading his eyes. He knew
that they all saw him, he began to move up the strand,
slowly approaching them, but stopping halfway to roll
down the bottoms of his trousers. When he stood up he
could see that Carmel was making her way slowly towards
him, wearing a summer dress. He watched her approach.

'I saw you in Blackwater,' he said. 'I thought that you
might be over here.'

'Are you in Cush?' she asked.

'Yes, I'm staying in Cullen's with my father.'

Neither of them spoke, until it became awkward.

'I should go back up,' she said. 'We'll probably go back
soon. You forget how many hills there are until you come
down on your bicycle.' She smiled.

'I could drive you in later on,' he said. 'We could tie the
bicycle on to the boot.'

'No,' she said. 'I should go back with them. We came all
the way down together.'

'I'm sure they wouldn't mind,' he said.

'No, I'd rather not,' she said.

'That's very disappointing,' he said. He could see that she was anxious to go back to her friends. 'Are you sure?' he asked.

'Yes,' she said. 'I'd really prefer to take the road home with the others.'

'I'll see you sometime, then,' he said, and turned back towards home. He wondered what she would say to the others, but was sure that she would not say much. When he had walked a certain length, he sat down in the shadow of the cliff and looked out at the sea. He did not think that he would see her for a long time. He was unsure if she did not wish to see him because of the hanging, or if there was some other reason why she did not want him.

HE was surprised when a few months after his father's and uncle's visit to the Four Courts there was a message for him in the Law Library to phone Carmel O'Brien giving the number of her office in Enniscorthy. As he waited for the receptionist to put him through, he wondered why she would phone him and he felt interested and excited at the prospect of speaking to her.

'It's Eamon Redmond,' he said when he got through to her. 'I got a message to phone you.'

'Yes, your Aunt Margaret asked me would I phone you and leave a message. They couldn't reach you, and they knew I'd be in the office.'

'What's the trouble?' he asked.

'Your father's in Brownswood. He took a turn yesterday, but your Aunt Margaret said that he's improved today.'

'I'll be down as soon as I can. Will you pass on that message please? I'm in the middle of a case but I'll see what I can do to get away,' he said.

'I'll pass it on. Your Aunt Margaret said that she'd ring me before five,' she said.

'Is it serious?' he asked.

'No, they told me to tell you that it wasn't serious, but they just wanted you to know.'

He could not leave the case and had to wait until the weekend before going home. He spoke to his Aunt Margaret several times, and she assured him that his father was being kept in hospital merely for tests and observation. When he finally arrived in Enniscorthy he felt uncomfortable as he opened the door of the empty house with his key, and then walked from room to room as though he had just returned from a long time away. He knew that he would have to come back here alone when he had seen his father, and spend the night here.

He drove to the hospital and looked into several rooms, searching for his father. It was visiting time and visitors sitting around the beds glanced up at him expectantly and then looked away. Eventually, he found his father in the corner bed of a small ward. They had marked his throat with a bright red paint; he seemed weak as he smiled up at Eamon.

'It's lovely and bright here,' Eamon said.

His father nodded, his eyes alert.

'Do you want anything? I didn't know what to bring down with me.' His father pointed to the bedside table to show that he had everything he wanted.

Eamon sat down in the chair beside the bed and they talked until visiting time was over. He told his father that he would be back the next day; his father's head did not leave the pillow. He smiled, and Eamon remembered what the smile reminded him of: his father in his wedding picture and the solid, kindly, contented expression he wore then.

He drove along the Wexford Road towards the town. He would call on his aunt and uncle and then go home. He dreaded the empty house. He wondered if he could call on Carmel; she had seemed friendly on the telephone. He was puzzled still by his aunt's asking her to telephone him and wondered if it were a ploy to encourage him to contact her again. He decided to try. When he left his aunt and uncle's house he drove to Court Street and parked his car outside her house. As he knocked on the door and waited for an answer several people passed and greeted him, and he knew that his visit would become the subject of gossip in the street. Her mother and her sister came to the door together.

'She's out,' her mother said. 'She went out to do a message. How's your father?'

'He's well enough. He's in good form,' he said. 'Will she be back?'

'She's only gone out for a while,' her sister said. 'I'd say if you call back in half an hour she'll be here.'

She was there when he called back. She asked him if he wanted to come in, but he wanted to talk to her on her own.

'Can I see you tomorrow night?' he asked.

'All right.'

'What time would suit you?'

'Say half past eight? I'll be ready then. Were you in Brownswood?' Carmel asked.

'I was. He seems weak enough. I'll know more tomorrow.'

He wondered as he sat by the fire at home if he should tell her that the state was going to abolish hanging. He had advised Charlie Haughey, the Minister for Justice, on the proposed legislation. He had, in fact, drafted a bill for him, and gone with him to a private meeting with representatives of the Gardaí, who had to be consulted about any new legislation. Eamon had come up with the suggestion that the murder of a Garda should remain a capital offence. Otherwise, he knew that there would be strong opposition to the legislation from the Gardaí. He liked Haughey, admired his pragmatism and his clear mind. Both men had agreed that, despite the clause about the murder of a Garda remaining a capital offence, it was unlikely that there would be any more hangings. As he turned off the lights downstairs and got ready to go to bed, Eamon decided not to tell Carmel about the meeting and the proposed reform. He had become involved because Haughey asked him, not because he wanted to placate her.

CARMEL had been to the hairdresser's and put on good clothes. Eamon was nervous in the car with her. He asked her where she would like to go. She said that she wanted to get away from the town.

'Your Aunt Margaret says that you're going to be a senior counsel,' she said.

'In a few months,' he said.

He drove along the cement road to Wexford; she talked about her job and her family. It was good, she said, to go out on a Saturday night, as her father was drinking heavily.

'Saturday night is his big night,' she said. 'From about four o'clock you can feel the tension as my mother watches him to see if he's going out. Drink makes him quiet. He's hardly able to walk when he comes in after the pubs close. He never says anything. He sits down and looks at the ground, and then my mother starts to give out to him. He never says anything much, but she attacks whatever he says, and goes on and on at him. Some of the things she has said to him I couldn't repeat to you.'

They went to the Talbot Hotel in Wexford and sat in the lounge having a drink before dinner.

'Do you fancy us seeing a bit more of each other so?' he asked.

'If you're around, I'd love to see you,' she said.

He asked her no other questions, but saw her again the following weekend. On Saturday nights she began to stay in his father's house until late to avoid the trouble at home. She came to the hospital with him a few times to see his father, but there was still no sign of him getting any better.

One Saturday night when he was about to walk her to her own house they stood in the hall. He turned and kissed her and caught a sense of her body, the life in her, and he wanted to ask her to stay with him. As he held her, without moving, he could feel his penis stiffening against her. She opened her mouth and he could feel her small wet tongue against his.

'You won't be involved in any more hanging cases, sure you won't?' she asked as they walked down John Street.

'Are you serious then, about us?' he asked.

'Are you?' she asked.

'Yes,' he said.

ONE Friday evening he found his father asleep in the bed. He sat down and watched him, trying not to disturb him. But after a time he went over to the window, and then out to the toilet. When he came back again, he examined the chart at the bottom of his father's bed, reading the comments for each day: poor, weak, very poor. He moved away as quickly as he could and sat by the bed again.

A while later, his Aunt Margaret and Uncle Tom arrived; he knew by their attitude that his father was not getting better. He saw his uncle talking to one of the doctors in the corridor. His uncle looked worried. He turned and went to sit by his father's bed once more. His aunt was kneeling by the bed, saying the Rosary. In the corridor again, he saw the doctor coming towards him, but he turned back towards the ward, pretending that he had forgotten something. Later, he telephoned the senior counsel in a pending case, and explained that he would have to be excused.

He noticed everything changing: they did not seem to be treating his father for anything except pain, they put a screen around the bed and restricted visitors to his immediate family. He told Carmel nothing, but realized that she knew, that everybody knew, not just in the hospital but

in the town. But still he did not ask, and still no one told
him.

His Aunt Kitty came from Tullow; he watched her
leaving her chair beside the bed and going into the corridor
to cry. She returned and knelt with a nun who had been in
school with his mother and they said the Rosary. They put
a pair of special beads which had been blessed by the Pope
into his father's hands. Eamon knelt with them, but did
not pray. He waited with his Aunt Kitty and the nun until
it was late. He saw them whispering when they had finished
the Rosary, and then they went out into the corridor while
the doctor and two nurses attended to his father. He did
not speak to them, but went to the toilet to wash his face.

When he came back his aunt was crying in the corridor
as she spoke to the doctor. They watched him as he
approached. The nun came up to him and held his hand.

'Eamon, *a stór*, we're going to lose him. Your poor
mother will be waiting for him with all her prayers. He's
after getting pneumonia and he won't last. He won't last
the night. We're going to send word to your uncles and
aunts. He needs all our prayers now, Eamon, for his
journey.'

His eyes filled up with tears as he went to the window.

'He didn't know up to now,' his aunt said to the doctor
in a voice loud enough for him to hear. 'None of us could
tell him.'

'Is he going to die?' he asked the doctor.

'He's not in any pain,' the doctor said, 'but I don't think
he'll last the night.'

He turned away crying, and moved farther down the
corridor away from them.

'Eamon, you'll have to be brave,' the nun came and held
him.

AFTER the funeral he went to his aunt and uncle's house.
Neighbours called and shook his hand and spoke a few

words to him, some of them staying for a cup of tea or a drink. Carmel's mother told him to sleep the night in their house if he wanted to, she had made up a bed for him. When he saw Carmel, he asked her to stay behind with him. They went into the kitchen, but more neighbours called and he had to go and accept their condolences. When it grew late he drove through the town with her, and stopped the car outside her house.

'Do you want to come in?' she asked. 'There's a bed for you. You heard what my mother said.'

'No, I'll go home, or I might go back down to the other house.'

They sat in the car without saying anything. The street was empty.

'What about tomorrow?' he asked. 'Can I see you after work?'

'That's fine,' she said.

'I'll park the car in the Railway Square, so no one will notice me. I've spoken to enough people. Could you come around there?'

'That's fine,' she said again. 'I'll see you tomorrow.'

CHAPTER FIFTEEN

H E could no longer sleep in the house. Too much of its atmosphere brought back her memory and he could not bear it. He made a bed for himself in the car and spent the day away from the house, walking, desperately trying to make himself tired so that he could sleep. Now as he walked along the strand he saw a black shape bobbing in the sea. He left his rucksack down on the sand and looked again, but a wave had risen and blocked his view. When he saw it now it looked like a man's head, a diver's head perhaps. It seemed so inert in the water, floating without moving and disappearing each time the water swelled and folded.

It was a seal. And it was much closer to the shore than he had ever witnessed in all the years. When he was a child, the appearance of a seal would be greeted with wonder by the people on the strand in Cush. He had a vivid memory of a day in the past, a mild summer's day, and someone, a woman, standing and pointing and telling all of them who were lying down taking the sun to look, there was a seal, look how close he is. And they all stood up to watch.

Eamon was too old then to be lifted but someone hunched down and pointed out to sea and he had searched the waves and had seen nothing while the adult – who could it have been? he was sure that it was not his father – had become impatient with him for not seeing. And then he saw it out there, a small, black shape in the water: the seal's head. The seal had come in to look at them. He's harmless, someone said. Even then, he had felt unsure about this blubbery animal in the water, and for the next few days he felt uncomfortable swimming.

HE left the house late in the morning and walked down to the cliff. It was a warm, sunny day, but there was also a strong wind which whistled in his ears as he turned in the lane towards the gap in the cliff just beyond Mike's house. He paid no attention to the house as he passed. It was only when he turned to descend the cliff that a figure caught his eye. Mike was sitting in an old wooden chair beside the chimneypiece where his living room used to be. He had glasses on and was reading a newspaper. If the front wall of his house had not been missing it would have looked like an ordinary, domestic scene, but now it was strange, almost comic. Eamon did not know if Mike was aware of his presence or not. Maybe he did not want to be greeted. It would be hard to know what to say. Eamon stood there for a moment longer, giving his cousin every chance to look up from the newspaper, but Mike did not move. Eamon walked down the cliff away from him.

He could not wait to tell Carmel what he had seen. He thought about when he would see her next as he took a few steps down, and then he realized, as a slow pain went through him, that she was dead, that he would not have a chance to tell her about the scene he had witnessed. This made him understand, more than ever, that he could not face her not being with him, that he had spent the time since she died avoiding the fact of her death. He went down to the strand and sat in the shade. The wind was still strong and blew sand at him. He thought about it: the interval just now when he had believed that she was alive, that she was back in the house, in the garden maybe, or in the porch, reading the paper, or a novel, and he would come back in from his walk or his swim and he would tell her the news. Mike has taken to sitting in the shell of his house, with its walls open to the four winds reading the paper. But, slowly, painfully, it sank in that there would be nobody when he went back to the house.

Two days later he was still thinking about that small episode, his lapse into believing that she was still alive, and as he walked along he tried to think about her dead, he repeated to himself that he would not see her again, that he was alone now, and she was alone too in her grave, her flesh slowly rotting until she would be unrecognizable, bones and a few remnants of hair. Carmel is dead, he whispered as he walked. Carmel is dead.

He sat down on the sand. It was early and the sun was still low over the soft horizon. His back was sore from the previous day's walking, but his feet were well rested. He thought that in future he would not carry the rucksack which was too heavy for his back. He wondered how he would carry the togs and towel, the raincoat and the pullover, and he let his mind wander over arrangements for the next day's walk. He closed his eyes.

When he stood up he noticed a tractor coming from Ballyvalden or further north, moving slowly along the shore. He walked towards Ballyconnigar, thinking that soon he would have to stand aside while the tractor rolled past. He saw the scene already, visualized himself saluting the driver and the driver waving back. He wondered if the driver would be wearing a cap.

He stood at the beach below Keating's house and inspected the damage which the previous winter and spring – there had been bad storms in the spring – had wrought. The County Council had put more huge boulders just below the cliff in an effort to ward off the sea. He remembered when there was a road on this side of the house and a field beyond the road. He remembered the cars edging around the road in the years when the field had disappeared and the drop was sheer down to the strand. One of those Sundays in summer: a clear blue sky and a sharp sun glinting off the windscreens of Morris Minors and Morris Austins as they turned gingerly, cautiously into the car park. The sound of the big radio in Keating's kitchen, blaring out reports of hurling matches and the fate of the Wexford team.

The tractor passed him as he stood there. He turned and waved, smelling the thick smoke from the exhaust pipe which rose from the body of the engine. The driver waved back and slowed down to cross the river where it spread out into shallows as it neared the sea. Some years before, with money from Europe, they had built a stone slipway for the small fishing boats, but they had not understood how vulnerable the land here was to change, how the sand levels shifted each year. Now he could see the exposed foundations of the slipway. It no longer reached the sea. It was an eyesore, he thought, and soon it would be completely useless.

Keating's house still hung on at the edge of the cliff. The whitewash was bright and glaring, and the building itself seemed firm and strong. Soon it would go, but they had been predicting this for years. He recalled someone showing him once how it would not be finally threatened from the side but from behind, where the hill had been. But this prediction had turned out not to be true.

He sat on the wall, watching a herd of cows gathering against the fence in a field across the river. The air was full of flies and he had to move his hand up and down in front of his face to ward them off. There were a few caravans in the field which led to the strand and in the adjoining field which was used all year as a caravan park. There was also a modern tent pitched close to the river with a station wagon beside it. But there was no one to be seen.

He stood up and walked back to the strand, making his way slowly south. Earlier, when he set out, the air had been still, there was almost no wind, but now a thin film of sand was being blown northward along the strand. He could feel the wind in his face, but it was pleasant and warm as he walked along. He tried to move with an even step.

There were gulls and a few other solitary sea birds lurking over the waves. The sea was calm. He was hungry already, even though he had eaten a boiled egg and some toast before he left the house, but he decided to go for another hour or so without opening the sandwiches. He felt sweaty and tired but decided to have his first swim of the day later, when he had walked farther along the strand. Since he began to spend each day walking he had learned how to divide up the time.

He was almost at Curracloe now and looked back along the strand. The day was becoming hazy and the sand being blown along the shore lessened visibility. There was nowhere sheltered he could sit to eat the sandwiches he had packed. He walked up the strand towards the dunes where there was more shelter. His back was beginning to pain him and he was glad to take off the rucksack. He sat down and removed his canvas shoes. His feet were hot and there was a small blister on his heel. The skin around it was red and raw. He took out the towel and put it behind his head as he lay stretched out.

He looked up at the pale sky, feeling sleepy but knowing that he must not sleep. He would have to keep going. He sat up and opened the flask, poured the hot tea into the cup and unwrapped the sandwiches and ate without thinking, staring down towards the sea, which was washed of all colour now, just vague hints of blue and green against white and grey.

He threw away the last drops of tea and re-wrapped the sandwiches which were left, then packed everything, including the canvas shoes, into the rucksack and stood up again. He rolled up the bottom of his trousers and walked along in his bare feet, but the blister was too painful so he had to sit down on the sand, open the rucksack again, put on a pair of socks and his canvas shoes.

He set off walking once more. He carried no watch or clock so he had no idea how long he had been on the strand, but guessed that it was one o'clock or two o'clock and that he had been walking for two or three hours. He passed a few people, but there was no one lying on the sand or going into the sea to swim; the wind was too strong. The sand was softer nearer the sea; he walked where it was wet. At low tide, he knew, you could pick cockles here, but the tide was well in and the strand grew narrower as he walked along. In a few miles it would disappear altogether. Then he would take to the road.

After a mile or so the sun became stronger, although there was still a haze over the sea. The wind had died down. He sat again and fished into his rucksack to find his togs. He took out his towel as well and slowly took off his clothes and put his togs on. The blister on his foot was bigger now. He tried to burst it but it was too hard. He stood up and tested the water. It was not too cold. He limbered up, arching his back to see if he could get rid of the pain at the base of his neck which spread down his back every time he moved his head. But the pain was still there. He turned and walked slowly into the sea, ignoring the waves and wading without hesitation once the water was up to his waist. Without stopping, he dived in and swam out, lifting his head only to take in air, trying to exercise his arms to relax the muscles in his neck.

He set himself goals: to swim out twenty strokes and back in again, and over to the side and back again, and over to the other side and back again once more. Growing tired he rested his head on the water and floated. He closed his eyes, unsure now whether he was floating in towards the shore or out towards the horizon, but on opening them he found that he had let himself float a good distance northwards and swam back until he was close to where he had left his rucksack.

When he had dried himself he moved away from the shore, farther up the strand. He dressed and lay down, too tired to put off sleep. He placed the towel under his head and closed his eyes.

On waking he knew he had been in a deep sleep. He was cold and reached into the rucksack and took out his pullover. His legs were stiff. He wished that there was a bed close by with clean white sheets that he could crawl into, but there was still a long day ahead. If he went back now, he knew he would sleep and then wake in the night, and he could not bear that prospect. For the first few days in Cush he had been unable to spend time inside the house but instead had sat in the garden or gone into the village. He had begun to sleep in the car but when he woke after an hour or two – as he usually did – he felt a terrible blackness.

He had nowhere to go. The court was on holidays and the house in Dublin was too big and empty. Soon he would have to go back there, he could not carry on like this day after day, this interminable walking from the morning until darkness fell, this trudging along, forcing himself to keep going. There was nothing else he could do here, he could not read, or listen to music, or sit in the garden. He hated going into the house. At least now at the end of the day, on arriving home at nightfall, he could sleep the whole night long. He was occupied walking; it kept him going. As he lay there in the afternoon haze on the empty strand beyond Curracloe he knew that he could not turn back, that he would have to go forward for another hour or two, before making his way home.

The sky had become clear by the time he started back. He walked up a long lane, past a few white-washed farmhouses and along a well-worn track across a field, before hitting a by-road which led to the main road from

Wexford to Curracloe. He took off his canvas shoes and put on the stronger leather shoes which he carried in his rucksack. The blister on his heel had become more painful and he felt a pain, too, in the back of his legs each time he took a step. Walking was more difficult on the road. Each step became an ordeal, but he knew that he still had miles to go.

The weather had settled, and the late afternoon sun was strong. He tried to concentrate on patches of white in the sky, small impermanent wisps of vapour he had been taught to imagine the soul would look like when you died. He believed in nothing now, no soul, no cloudy spirit offered him consolation. He believed that death was absolute, the body died and became dust.

He was tempted to stop and have a drink in the village pub, but he knew that alcohol made him broody and morose, even one drink turned his mind towards self-pity. Also, he was afraid to go in to have an orange juice or a glass of water because he did not want to stop now, he knew how hard it would be to begin walking again. He turned from the village back down towards the strand. It was important, he knew, not to think about how near or how far he was from his destination. Everywhere was far. He walked: took step after step and allowed himself to think only about the ground he had already walked along.

When he reached the Strand Hotel at the top of the hill he could see the sea and the pale line which the horizon made. He felt a sudden surge of warmth as he walked through the marsh towards the sand dunes. His back still ached and his heel pained him at each step and the pain in the muscles of the back of his leg persisted, but he felt intensely alive as he passed the shop and walked along the old wooden rampart which led over the dunes to the strand.

He recognized the exhilaration: it came each day unless there was rain. It came, he thought, from walking a long distance and then turning towards the light, or witnessing a sudden brightness in the sky. He walked faster now, breathing in the rich sea air. He sat down and took out his sandwiches and flask again, but kept his eye on the sea as much as possible. It was so still now, grey-blue and glassy. The sun behind him was warm. He was content, he ate what was left in the wrapping paper and finished the tea. He put the flask and the paper back in the rucksack and changed into his canvas shoes.

He guessed by the light that it was seven or eight o'clock: the sun was going down and there was an edge to each colour and shape, a darkening, an increased distinction and definition. He imagined himself and Carmel in Wexford for the day, standing in the vegetable shop, looking at the sugar peas, wondering how long they would keep. And then walking beside her down Main Street until they came to the butcher shop she liked. And lamb, she turned to him, would they have lamb? Or would he prefer pork? The pork was always good here, and the stuffing. Eventually she made up her mind, and they both watched as the leg of lamb was weighed and then wrapped and paid for. 'I have potatoes,' she said to him. 'I need to get mint sauce and we need to get wine. We should get a few bottles to have.'

They stood in the off-licence looking at the wine. She smiled at the assistant and then went over and examined the labels, squinting her eyes slightly.

'What do you think?' she asked.

'I prefer red,' he said.

'Yes, we'll get a few red and maybe two white, but I'd like to get one good bottle for tonight to go with the lamb, the peas and the new potatoes. Something special.'

They looked through the selection of red wines. He tried to help her, knowing, however, that in the end she would make up her mind without his help. Still, she liked him to be there and to comment.

As he walked back towards Ballyconnigar in the fading light he imagined Carmel and himself picking out the

bottles of wine and carrying them to the counter. He saw
her changing the good bottle for an even more expensive
wine and saying to him that they did not often spend
money on wine, but this evening, this evening they would
have a special dinner.

'No reason, no special reason,' she said.

She was dead. Carmel is dead, he whispered to himself,
but still he imagined them wandering in Wexford. He saw
himself opening the driver's door and pulling up the lock
on the passenger door for Carmel to get in. But there was
no one there; there was no point in pulling up the lock.
And when he thought of this as he walked slowly north-
wards his eyes filled up with tears.

This always happened at the end of the day when he
neared home, the exhaustion and the wondering what he
would do when he climbed up the cliff at Mike's house,
when he turned in the lane and saw the corner field full of
white clover and walked straight ahead in the lane full of
midges; what would he do?

He was walking along slowly as the lighthouse started
up, its beam faint. There was a dew falling and it was
becoming cold. He knew that he could not face the house.
He was hungry and wanted a bath and a shave, but he
knew that he could not bear to enter the house where they
had lived.

As he walked up the cliff he noticed that it was much
easier than usual; he was becoming fit. He glanced at
Mike's house to see if his cousin had returned or had left
his chair behind, but there was no sign of him. There was
a red stretch in the western sky; soon, that, too, would
disappear and night would come down. He was tired; he
knew how simple it would be to shut his eyes and fall into
a deep sleep, despite the hunger he felt. But he knew too
that if he was hungry now, he would wake in the night and
he was desperate not to face an hour lying in the dark
waiting for the grey light of dawn to appear over the sea.

He left the rucksack against the door of the house and went to the car. He had filled the leg-space between the back seat and the front seat with cushions and pillows, but ignored these now and put the key into the ignition and turned the car around. He opened the gate to the lane, got back into the car and drove towards Blackwater. He tried to drive slowly. He knew that he was tired.

He drove down to Etchingham's in the village and left the car outside. There were a few men in the pub who looked up when he came in; there was a family group, who looked like holiday-makers, in the corner. Closing the door, he walked into the grocery which was also a bar. There was no one behind the counter. He sat up on a stool and waited. When the barman came he asked for a small whiskey from the bar and a loaf of bread, some butter and a tin of tuna from the grocery. The barman served him the whiskey first with a jug of water. After a while he came back with the groceries in a white plastic bag.

When the drink was finished, he went back to the car. He knew that he would have to go into the house to get a knife and a tin opener, and he wanted to have a shower. He thought that if he did not switch on the light, if he searched the kitchen in the darkness and used the bathroom without any light, it would be easier.

He turned on the car radio and listened to a song he vaguely recognized; he tried to keep his mind on the driving. He had to stop and move in towards the ditch when another car approached. He saluted the driver, without knowing who it was.

He drove the car in through the gates to the front of the house, switched off the lights and sat there for a while, staring at the lighthouse. The beam was fainter than usual as the moon was bright, the sky cloudless. He got out of the car and looked up at the stars, fumbling in his pocket for the keys. The sky was inky blue. He turned, walked towards the front door and went inside. There was a stale smell, and the rank smell of damp was there too. He left the front door open and made his way to the bathroom.

He knew there was no hot water, but still felt he needed a shower. He turned on the cold tap and put his hand under the spray of water to test it. It was lukewarm from the day's heat. He took off his clothes, searching in the darkness for the soap and shampoo.

When he had finished he dried himself and went towards the bedroom looking for a change of clothes. Here there was another smell, a mixture of mothballs and lavender and perfume. He wanted to get out of the room as soon as possible, close the door behind him, leave the room locked in its smells. He rummaged in a chest of drawers and found some socks and underpants and a shirt he had brought from Dublin. He put them on and went back to the bathroom to get his shoes. His blister was throbbing and he was desperate to get to sleep. He searched in the kitchen for a tin-opener but was unable to find one in the dark. He did not try for very long; instead, he went out to the car and fixed up the back seat so that he would be comfortable. He closed the door and curled up but he was too hot. He opened the windows and the sun-roof and took off his shirt and trousers. He fell asleep.

It was past dawn when he woke. He was thirsty and still tired. He lay without moving. He could not face another day's walking. And yet the thought of staying around the house and garden all day seemed impossible. But he could not go on: he already had a few days' growth of beard. There had to be some end to this. He closed his eyes and curled up again, but realized he would not get back to sleep.

He had left the door of the house open. The day was grey, the sky low, threatening rain. He went into the living room and sat at the window before going into the kitchen to get a glass of water. The sink was full of dirty dishes and there was a green mould on some of the plates. He drank glass after glass of water.

He went into the bathroom and found his shaving gear. His face had become thin and brown and the grey stubble made him look old, like someone in a hospital. He wet his face and spread the shaving cream on his beard. It took time to shave; the bristles had become strong and tough.

Later, he went into the bedroom, which had become untidy, like the rest of the house, and drew the curtains and lay down on the bed. He thought that he might sleep again now. He went out to the car and retrieved the pillows from the back seat. Having closed the front door of the house, he took off his clothes in the bedroom and lay between the clean sheets of the bed. He was conscious that he had begun once more to let himself believe that she was alive, that she would come in at any moment with a breakfast tray, or the newspaper, or to fetch something. He began to imagine how they would talk, letting his mind range over the details, her dress, the smell she had left in the bed, her voice. He smiled to himself at the thought of her and then he covered himself with the quilt and fell into a deep sleep.

CHAPTER SIXTEEN

THE days remained grey and overcast with light showers of rain coming at intervals. He swam in the sea when he could and tried to keep the house tidy. He sat in the porch and if the sun came out he moved into the garden. A few days he went walking, wandering north-wards as far as Morriscastle and then back along the road.

He had brought with him a number of recent books on the law. He now kept these and a notepad on the living-room table and spent much time reading them, going over old cases and the implications of recent legislation. Two of the books dealt with the law of the European Community, about which he knew little. He had left that to his younger colleagues. But now he felt it was an area he might take up to keep his mind occupied in the long winter which was to come.

For much of the time, however, he still thought of Carmel, of days they had spent together in the past. Odd moments became vivid in his mind, clothes she wore, expressions on her face, snatches of conversation.

One day when they were married for less than a year and still living in his old flat in Hume Street, she had telephoned him at the Law Library. She was pregnant, he remembered, five or six months pregnant. He recalled coming back from a case and seeing the message and being concerned. Normally, she never telephoned him at the court. He was worried and he phoned her as soon as he got the message.

'I bumped into your Uncle Tom and Aunt Margaret on Dawson Street. They are in Dublin for a few days staying in a guest house in George's Street and they weren't going to contact us because they thought that we'd be too busy. So I invited them out either this evening or tomorrow.'

'Are you all right?' he asked.

'I'm fine,' she said.

'What about tonight then? Why don't we take them to dinner at the Russell Hotel?'

'I'll ring the guest house so. Will you come home first?'

'Yes, I'll see you soon.'

It was early June, the weather was soft and warm as he walked from the courts up to St Stephen's Green. The case he was working on was long and laborious, but he had done most of the preparation in the spring, reading through all the documents, checking and cross-checking precedents and potential lines of attack in the spare room at the desk which Carmel had set up for him. He was a senior counsel now and most of his work was for the state. Over the past few years he had begun to turn down briefs which did not interest him or which he did not have time to do. He had begun to represent the state in any of the constitutional cases which arose in the High Court and the Supreme Court. Unofficially, he had been offered a seat on the bench in the High Court when a vacancy arose in the autumn. He had not yet asked Carmel what she thought; it would mean a loss of income, and among his colleagues the view would be taken that he was too young to become a judge. He would be ten years younger than any of his colleagues.

He walked along Wicklow Street and then turned into Grafton Street. He would need to think about accepting the offer to become a High Court judge. If he waited, there could be a change of government, and he would not be offered a seat on the bench again until Fianna Fáil returned to power. But maybe it was too easy to make the move. He went into the Eblana Bookshop and browsed for a while, looked at the new books on the table, but bought nothing and went out into the street.

He did not want to go back to the flat. At first he did not know why, but as he walked through the Green he realized that he did not relish a night in Dublin with his aunt and uncle. He looked forward to seeing them, but he knew he would not be able to meet them without thinking about his father and about being a child in their house. They would treat him as they did when he was a child, they would smile at him and approve of him as they did when he came to their house with his father. He was happier with his law books and his days in court, away from all that had happened, or in the flat with Carmel, making plans to buy a house, knowing that their first baby would come soon, knowing that they could go to bed later and make love.

He sat down on a seat in the Green. He had his briefcase with him. He took *The Irish Times* out and began to read the news on the front page. The Green was quiet except for the hush of traffic in the distance and the rustle of leaves in the light wind. If someone came and sat on the bench with him he would leave, he knew, but people passed by without paying him any attention. Eventually, he folded the newspaper and put it back into his briefcase.

CARMEL was in the small kitchen when he came up the stairs.

'I rang them,' she said. 'I think that they're delighted we're taking them out.'

'They come to Dublin twice a year. I saw them when they came up a few years ago,' he said.

'I booked a table in the Russell for eight o'clock,' she said.

He had a bath and changed his clothes. He stood at the window looking down into the empty street as Carmel sat sewing a button on to a blouse. The closer the time came to go to the hotel and meet his aunt and uncle for dinner, the less comfortable he became.

'How do you feel?' he asked Carmel.

'I feel fine,' she said. 'I'm looking forward to going out.'

'Do you want a drink?'

'Now?'

'Yes, a gin and tonic or something,' he said.

'No, I won't,' she said. 'You have one.'

He went into the kitchen, poured a measure of gin into a glass and added tonic and ice.

'Are you in court in the morning?' she asked.

'Yes, I am.'

'We mustn't stay out too late then.'

They walked into Stephen's Green and along the paths to the artificial lake. They were in good time and could afford to walk slowly.

'Did you tell them that you were pregnant?' he asked.

'No, and I don't think they noticed.'

They waited in the bar of the hotel. When Aunt Margaret and Uncle Tom came in they seemed shy, looking around the bar as they spoke, and uncertain about whether they would have a drink or not. They mentioned several times that they hoped they were not disturbing Eamon and Carmel or putting them out in any way.

Eamon often came here with colleagues and clients. He knew the head waiter and was pleased now to be led to a table with his aunt and uncle.

'We haven't been in here for years,' Aunt Margaret said when they had settled at the table. The restaurant was half full, but as they were looking at the menu people came and sat at the tables around them. They talked about home and the price Eamon could expect for his father's house which he was about to sell.

'You'll get a good price for it,' his uncle said. 'There are plenty of people coming back from England.'

His aunt told them about two sisters who had come back

from America after fifty years. They had never been home in all that time and came down the Island Road in search of people who would remember them. Hardly anyone remembered them, she said, all their family had left as well, there was no one belonging to them living in the town, but she remembered them well, remembered them leaving as soon as the Great War was over, as soon as you could leave. They had never married, she said, but worked for a rich family and were getting ready to retire. They were talking, she said, about retiring to Enniscorthy, but she didn't suppose that they would, since they knew nobody.

The main courses came and as they were eating Carmel said in a low voice to Aunt Margaret: 'Don't look now, but over there beside the window to the left, there's Charlie Haughey. I don't know who it is that's with him, but maybe Eamon will know.'

Aunt Margaret continued eating as though she had not heard and then stealthily turned her eyes over to the window and took in the scene.

'You can look now, Tom,' she said. 'It's all right.'

Eamon and his Uncle Tom looked at the same time.

'He often eats in here. A lot of the young ministers and Fianna Fáil men come in here,' Eamon said.

'So I've heard. But it's great seeing him all the same,' his uncle said.

'We've something to tell them when we go home,' his Aunt Margaret said. 'Who's that with him?'

Eamon looked over.

'I don't recognize him,' he said.

'Your father would have loved this,' his aunt said.

As they ordered dessert Eamon caught Haughey's eyes. He saw him nodding to his companion and then rising and walking over to their table. Eamon stood up. The waiter waited to take his order.

'I'll have the trifle,' he said as Haughey slapped him on the back and made him sit down.

'Mr Redmond,' he said, and then looked at the others, greeting them with a brief nod, before Eamon introduced them.

'This,' he said, 'is the Minister for Finance. My uncle has been in Fianna Fáil in Enniscorthy all his life,' he said, turning to Haughey.

'You're up for a brief stay? Well, this is a good hotel,' Haughey said.

'Oh, we're not staying here,' Aunt Margaret said. Haughey looked at her sharply, his clear blue eyes holding her gaze.

'Will we hold the two seats in Wexford?' he asked Uncle Tom.

'It'll be hard without Dr Ryan, but we'll do it.'

'It would be good to select someone from the constituency, someone with a hurling background,' Haughey said.

'It'll be someone local. I can guarantee you that.'

'Otherwise we could run this man here,' Haughey said, putting his hand on Eamon's shoulder. 'But we've other things in mind for him.' He smiled and then became serious again.

'Wexford is a great county,' he said.

'Will you come down yourself during the campaign?' Uncle Tom asked.

'All the ministers are very busy,' Aunt Margaret said. 'It's hard for them to go everywhere.'

'I'll do my best,' Haughey said. 'It's very good to meet you, anyway. And enjoy your meal.' He addressed this to Carmel and gave her a small bow before walking away.

No one spoke for a while as the waiter came with their desserts.

'I didn't know you knew him,' Aunt Margaret said.

'I drafted some stuff for him when he was Minister for

Justice. He's very able. He has a great way of getting things done,' Eamon said.

'He's a great man,' his uncle said.

'What do you think of him, Carmel?' Aunt Margaret asked.

'He has a way of looking at you as though he knows something about you,' she said.

'You're right about that,' Aunt Margaret said. 'I nearly died when I told him we weren't staying here and he looked at me. I didn't want him to think we were staying here and then find out that we weren't.'

When he had finished his cup of coffee Eamon went to the toilet. Haughey's table was empty. As he opened the toilet door, Haughey was coming out. Haughey gave him a mock punch in the chest and grinned.

'You're for the bench,' Haughey said.

Eamon said nothing but held his stare.

'Will you take it if you're offered it?' Haughey asked.

'I will,' Eamon said.

'I'll see you soon,' Haughey said. 'It's good to meet you again.'

THEY had more coffee and then Eamon and his uncle had brandies. Eamon paid the bill despite the protests of his aunt and uncle. It was almost eleven o'clock when they walked out of the dining room. They stood in the hall, Eamon and Carmel insisting on walking with them to George's Street, Uncle Tom and Aunt Margaret adamant that they could walk alone.

As they spoke Eamon glanced into the bar and his Aunt Margaret turned and looked as well. Haughey was still in the hotel, standing in the bar with a glass in his hand, talking to a man who had his back to them. Beside him, on his left, was another minister.

'Are they here every night like this?' Aunt Margaret asked him.

'I don't know. I don't imagine so,' he said. He watched his aunt examine his face carefully as though she doubted what he was saying.

THEY walked slowly back along Stephen's Green, standing to watch as a demolition squad worked on one of the red-brick Victorian buildings near the corner with Earlsfort Terrace.

'I hope they're not going to put up one of those terrible glass contraptions,' Carmel said.

In the flat they sat together on the old sofa and held hands.

'That was a nice evening,' Carmel said, 'I hope they enjoyed it. Your Aunt Margaret is very alert.'

He went to the window as a car started up in the street and then made tea while Carmel sat with her feet up. There was no sound from the street, not even when he opened the long window of the living room. They sipped the tea without saying anything.

'Can you feel the child moving?' she asked and caught his hand, holding it to her tummy. He could feel some vague motion, something alive. He took his hand away.

'Don't you like touching it?' she asked. 'Does it make you uncomfortable?'

'No, it doesn't. I just can't believe it,' he said.

They went into the bedroom together. Carmel had already turned on the lamp beside the bed and drawn the curtains. They undressed slowly without speaking. When he turned she was naked, her breasts heavy over the round bulge of her belly. He went over to her and held her. He could feel the blood throbbing in the veins of her neck. He held her against him, kept his hands on the soft, fine skin of her back.

They moved over to the bed and pulled back the blankets and lay down without covering themselves. He played with her tongue, closed his eyes and kissed her as softly as he could. But he still did not touch her breasts or her belly. She ran her hand down his chest as they lay on their sides facing each other, and then put her hand on his groin and his thighs. He could feel his breath coming faster and when he put his ear against her neck he could feel her blood throbbing.

Her breasts were firm as he put his hands under them and held them. He knelt up and kissed her nipples and then lowered himself in the bed and put his face against her belly. He fondled the taut skin and pressed his fingers against the hardness. He closed his eyes and began to run his tongue along her roundness, aware now of the warm, sweet smell of her vagina. She caught her breath when he put his finger into her. He sat up and held her in his arms. She kissed him. His penis was hard and when she spread her legs out he knelt in front of her and slowly guided his penis into her while she held him by the shoulders. At first he thought that he was going to ejaculate immediately, but he relaxed his body and waited. He could feel her tightness around him and he shivered as though he was elsewhere, not in a room with her but in another world. He found her lips again and her warm tongue. He was worried about pushing in too hard, but she seemed to want him to come into her as far as he could.

When he had ejaculated he lay beside her, his hand on her back, holding her against him. He smiled. Her temples were damp with sweat. She pulled a sheet over them.

'I feel very close to you sometimes,' she said.

'It's good being together, isn't it?' he said.

'Sometimes you become very distant,' she said. Her voice was low. She held him closer now.

'Sometimes I'm not sure that you want me here at all,' she continued.

He had not been listening to her carefully; he had been thinking about something else. But now he noticed a tone he had never heard before.

'I don't know what you mean,' he said.

'You seem so far away,' she said.

'All the time?' he asked.

'No, just sometimes. I feel . . .' she stopped. 'I don't know how to say it.'

They remained in each other's arms with the sheet over them. Carmel sat up and pulled a blanket over the sheet.

'I'm getting cold,' she said.

He said nothing.

'Are you not happy here?' he asked.

'I find you very distant sometimes. Cold maybe.'

'Cold?'

'Sometimes when I feel very warmly about you. Maybe I've been looking forward to seeing you all day and I want to hug you when you come in, I find you don't want that, I feel that you resent me coming close to you.'

'That's not true,' he said.

'I need to talk to you about it. You've got to help me talk to you. You must know what I'm talking about.'

'Can I think about it? Can we discuss it again?'

'Eamon, it's very hard for me to bring this up. I won't feel comfortable raising it again. I need to know something of how you feel and I need to talk to you.'

'Can we do it again?'

'If you want to.'

'I thought you were happy.'

'I'll be happier when I talk to you about this.'

WHEN he came back from the courts the following day, she had the table set with a special tablecloth they had received as a wedding present. There was a bottle of wine on the table. It struck him that he had some work to do on the case and he would need to spend at least two hours in the spare room going through his notes and the submission he intended to make. Carmel was wearing lipstick and make-up and there was a strange, sweet smell in the room he had never noticed before.

He kissed her and dropped his briefcase into the spare room.

'What's the smell?' he asked.

'Perfume.'

'And what's the occasion?' he smiled.

She did not reply, but went into the kitchen.

'Dinner will be ready soon. Do you want a drink?'

'I've got some work to do,' he said. 'Will we be having dinner immediately?'

She came out of the kitchen and looked at him. She was wearing an apron.

'Do you have much work to do?'

'It'll take me a while.'

'Dinner will be ready in about half an hour.'

'Will you call me then when it's ready.'

He went into the room and took out his papers. The case was becoming more difficult as the days went by, the judges more receptive to the plaintiff and more interested in the American precedents than in the precedents from the House of Lords. He would need to be very careful or the state could lose the case, indeed he felt in the attitude of the judges that the state had lost already. He would be interested to read their arguments.

He began to go through the papers; he took down a casebook of American law and checked through the index. He was still in his suit from the courts. He wondered why he had not changed. And then he realized that he did not want to eat with Carmel, that their conversation from the previous night had unsettled him. He stood up and looked around the small room, moved across to the door and opened it. Carmel was sitting on the sofa near the window. At first she did not notice him. She seemed preoccupied, drawn. She looked over and saw him.

'I'm sorry,' he said. 'I can do the work just as easily in

the morning. I was dreading talking to you about how we're getting on.'

'Yes, I know,' she said. 'I was wondering what I was going to have to do.' She smiled.

He sat down, then, and had a drink. He told her about the case and she nodded, listening attentively.

'It's really hard for me to talk,' he said.

'Wait until we've eaten.'

She had made a special casserole with new potatoes, the first of the year's crop. She opened a bottle of wine.

'They say that pregnant women are not meant to drink,' she said. 'But I'm just going to have one glass.'

A few times when the wine had run low in his glass she filled it up again. He felt close to her, as though they had conspired in something together.

'I feel sometimes that you are very distant from me,' she said. She made it sound like an ordinary remark.

'I know what you're talking about,' he said. 'Just now, in the room, I was doing that. It's taking me a while to get used to you.' He sipped his wine.

'You know, when either of your parents are mentioned you become strange. I don't know if you know that but your whole body changes. I feel there's a sort of pain in you, I feel it even now that I've mentioned your father and mother.'

'My mother died when I was a baby.'

'How do you feel about that?'

He was silent, sipped his wine; then he looked out of the window and back to Carmel who was still watching him.

'She is just someone who wasn't there.'

'And your father?'

'We managed together, I suppose. It must have been hard for him.'

'And for you?'

'It's hard to talk about it. It made me very self-sufficient. I can look after myself.'

Again, he was silent, and stood up to remove the dishes from the table. When he came back he sat down on the sofa beside her.

'I learned never to need anything from anybody. I suppose that's true. Do you find that difficult?'

'No, I want to know how you feel about it.'

'I have never asked anyone for anything. I think I feel that if I did I would be turned down.'

'By me?'

'I don't believe that anyone has ever wanted me,' he said and turned away. There were tears in his eyes.

She held his hand; they sat on the sofa without moving. She made coffee and when they had drunk it she suggested that they go out into the street for a walk. It was a bright, sunny evening as they walked around the Green and then down Kildare Street and over into Molesworth Street. They went into the downstairs bar of the Royal Hibernian Hotel. There were one or two people at the bar but the tables were empty. They sat down and had a drink. They whispered at first, but then they realized that voices did not carry in the bar and spoke in normal tones.

He told her about the house and his father; his grand-father's death followed by his Uncle Stephen's. He told her about his father's illness and his time with his aunt in the farm near Tullow. He left out the bit about the girl, but he told her about his father's voice and his waiting in the classroom for his father to hobble in, knowing that they were waiting, a few of them at the back, to shout up 'Sir, we can't understand you' as soon as his father spoke.

She knew some of it. She remembered his father's illness and she had heard about the death of his grandfather and his uncle from her mother. But she listened to him as though it was new to her, and he watched her as he spoke for a sign that this was boring her, that this was information which she did not need to know.

'He would come into the classroom. I could understand

him and if you listened you could follow what he was saying. He was a brilliant teacher. And he worked out ways of saying as little as possible. But still there was the dread as he came in the door of the classroom, and there was the phrase he couldn't get right, and he would catch my eye sometimes and it would be really hard not to look away.'

Night was coming down when they walked along Dawson Street. He felt drained; he wanted to sleep. He would have to get up early in the morning to look at the case. When they arrived home they went into the bedroom and lay on the bed in all their clothes, holding each other, not saying anything.

CHAPTER SEVENTEEN

ONE day when he was coming back from a long walk he turned in the lane to find a Garda car outside his house. There were two Guards in the car, but they did not notice him until he was close up. Both of them got out of the car. One of them was bare-headed; the other had his cap pushed back on his head. He did not recognize either of them.

'We're the Guards from Blackwater,' one of them said. 'We were told to give you a message. We couldn't find you all day. You must have been out.'

'What's the message?'

'Your daughter wants you to ring her.'

'Have you been here long?' he asked them.

'We were told to wait until you came home.'

'I'll ring her then. Did she say it was urgent?'

'Oh, I think it's urgent all right,' one of the Guards said.

'I'll ring her this minute then. Thanks,' he said.

When he rang there was no reply. He waited for a while, then wondered if he could go back down to the strand and have a swim since the sun had come out, but he felt that he should not leave the house again until he had made contact with her. He did not know why she could want him to ring her. He made himself a sandwich and a cup of tea and looked through the newspaper which he had bought in the village that morning as soon as the shop opened.

He dialled again but there was still no answer. He did not know Donal's number, but he got it from directory enquiries. Donal answered on the first ring.

'Niamh sent two Guards here with an urgent message for me to ring her. Do you have an idea why?'

'Yes,' Donal said. 'She's been trying to ring you for days and has got no answer. She's been really worried about you.'

'I'm fine. Will you ring her and tell her I'm fine.'

'Will you be there this evening? I'd say she wants to talk to you herself.'

'Yes, I'll be here.'

IT was becoming easier to sleep in the big old bed which he had shared with Carmel. And he was making an effort to keep the house clean. But he still wanted to be out of the house for most of the day, walking on the strand or on the road. When it was too rainy to walk he read his law books, keeping careful notes on cases he would need to look up when he went back to Dublin.

He watched the evening news on the television and when it was over he went out into the kitchen where he started to stack the plates to wash them. When the phone rang he knew it was Niamh.

'I'm sorry about the Guards. I was going to come down myself,' she said. 'Or Donal was going to drive down.'

'I've been out a lot,' he said.

'I was going to take two weeks down in Cush. I don't think you should be on your own like that. I can take the computer down with me and get some work done if I can find a babysitter.'

'Niamh, I'm all right. I don't need a babysitter,' he said and laughed.

'No, I meant for Michael.'

'I understood what you meant.'

'Are you all right?' she asked.

'I'm managing,' he said.

'Donal is going to drive me down on Sunday. Is that all right?' she asked.

'I don't want to be looked after,' he said.

'Do you want us not to come?' she asked.

'No, come if you want, you'd be welcome, but I'm not a patient. I was worried about you. Are you all right?'

'Yes, I'm fine. Can we come early on Sunday morning then?'

'Niamh, will you ring Aunt Margaret and call on her when you're here. I just can't face going into the town. I'd be afraid I'd meet someone who'd want to talk to me all about your mother. People are very nice and well-meaning but it's very hard to talk.'

'Do you want her to come down on Sunday as well?' she asked. When he did not respond she said: 'Maybe that's not a good idea. But I'll ring her anyway before I come.'

He put the phone down and waited, toying with the idea of ringing Donal and asking him to tell Niamh that he would prefer if she did not come. Niamh would disturb his slow routine. He was becoming used to this: the solitude, the long walks, the law books. He did not know what it would be like to have someone else with him.

He began by cleaning up the house, making sure that nothing was out of place. He found this difficult and boring, but he took long breaks with his books and then went back again, dusting and sweeping.

The area around the back of his neck and the top of his spine had become tense. If he put his chin down on to his chest a pain ran down his back. When he touched the base of his neck he could feel the hard tension. He went to the window and looked out feeling the pain moving through his shoulders. For a split second he thought of asking Carmel to deal with the situation, presuming that she was nearby. He thought about her.

The night when he had washed her in the bath and lay on the bed beside her came back to him now. He had avoided thinking about it. He remembered that it was a warm, close night like this with moths blundering against the windowpane. He remembered her voice, her voice telling him that he had never listened to her when she tried to tell him about her parents. He had gone over everything, every talk they had in all the years and he could recall nothing. He thought that she loved her parents, he remembered her talking about them in the months after they died. He could not remember her telling him that they fought in the house, nor that her father drank too much. As he sat there now in the night he asked her to forgive him if he had done anything wrong, he told her that he had tried to remember everything, but nothing came back to him, no time when he could have listened to her and comforted her about what had happened during her life at home. He simply could not remember.

HE got up early on Sunday morning and drove into the village to get the papers. None of the English papers had come. He sat in the car, looking through the Irish ones before deciding to drive into Wexford to get the other papers. He had not been in Wexford since Carmel died. No one would stop him on the street there or know anything about him and on a Sunday morning it would be quiet.

The roads were busy with people coming and going to Mass, the women wearing bright clothes. He turned on the radio and listened to a Gregorian chant broadcast live from a church. He turned it up. As he drove the weather grew more blustery, with sudden bursts of sunlight followed by short showers of rain.

When he saw the spires of Wexford he became unsure: why was he coming back here? He still had in his mind the image of her walking with him through the streets of the town, both of them content, having bought enough food to do them for a week, and some wine. He saw it again, the car parked on the quays in Wexford, the flat light on the water and the huge sky, the box of groceries already in the boot, him opening his own door carefully to avoid the sweep of an oncoming car and then sitting in the driver's seat and pulling up the knob on the passenger's door to find that there was nobody there, then getting out of the car and looking all around, tracing back their movements to find that she had never been with him that day, that her body was under the ground. It had been buried fresh and perfect, like a flower which had been picked, and slowly it would rot and decompose until there was nothing.

He drove across the bridge and parked on the quays. He walked up one of the side streets into the main street until he found a newsagent, but they had no English papers either. They told him to walk to the very end of the street, near the barracks. It was quiet in the town. Soon, he knew, crowds would spill out from the three churches where Masses were in progress. He thought of sneaking in, standing at the back. That moment when you took communion on your tongue and then the slow walk back to your seat, avoiding all eyes, the kneeling down with your head in your hands, the deep, concentrated prayer, the movement all around in the gaunt, arched building as people walked up the centre and side aisles and back down again, and the sense of each person wrapped up in prayer. He wished he could do it now, wait for one of the later Masses and take communion again, having been away from it for so long.

He found a newsagent with the English Sunday newspapers and took the papers with him to the lobby of the Talbot Hotel where he ordered a pot of tea and sat reading as people came and went. He read some of the foreign affairs articles and a few interviews. He flicked through the magazines. He thought of having lunch in the hotel but he realized he had to go back to Cush to receive his daughter. He would come back, he thought, during the week, if things became difficult at home.

He walked along the quays to the car, wondering if he could find music on the car radio for the journey home. He thought that he should get a cassette player in the car. There was no traffic on the quays when he started up the engine. He turned and drove back across the bridge.

WHEN he reached the house in Cush he knew that he had stayed away too long; Donal's car was parked in the lane and there seemed to be people in the back seat. He pulled up behind it. Donal and his girlfriend were in the front of the car; Niamh and her son were in the back. Donal got out of the car.

'Have you been here long?' Eamon asked.

'We didn't know what to do. We were going to break in.'

'There's always a key under the stone beside the door,' he said.

By now the others had got out of the car as well. Niamh was carrying the child.

'Well, come in. I went into Wexford to get the papers. I didn't think that you would come so early.'

When he opened the door of the house he caught a smell of damp air and stale cooked food. It seemed stronger than before, and the house, too, seemed shabby. He was conscious of Donal and Niamh looking around as though it were their property.

'It could do with a lick of paint,' Donal said. There were flies circling the lampshade in the living room; and the room seemed darker than usual and oddly untidy.

'It'll be over the cliff before we know where we are,' Eamon said. 'One bad winter and it could all go.'

'Oh there's still a field between us and the cliff,' Donal said.

Niamh and Cathy went out to the car to get Niamh's computer and her cases. They left the child down on the living-room floor. As Donal and his father spoke the child began to scream, his face becoming red. Donal went to pick him up, but he screamed even louder and tried to hit Donal. He seemed inconsolable as his mother came in and took him in her arms. She carried him out into the garden where he continued to cry. Eamon watched them from the window as the child pointed towards himself and Donal and screamed.

'You're all right now,' Niamh said as she rocked him in her arms.

'We brought some food down with us, cold stuff,' Donal said.

'That's good,' he said. 'But it's early yet. I'm going into the bedroom to read the papers. Maybe you'll give me a shout when it comes to lunchtime.'

He closed the door behind him and carried a chair across to the window. Niamh was outside rocking the child, who had become placid and preoccupied now as he rested his head on her shoulder. Eamon flicked through the newspapers again, found the foreign section of the *Observer* and began to read an article. He was uncomfortable in the straight-backed chair and soon he went and lay on the bed, resting on his side, and continued to read. When he had finished he lay back, his head on the pillow, and closed his eyes. The muscles in the neck were still painful.

The light from the window kept him awake, and he did not feel that he could go over and draw the curtains. They would think that he was sick. He heard his grandson crying again and other voices in the living room.

When he went out he found that all three of them were cleaning. Niamh was dusting, while Cathy and Donal worked in the kitchen. All the windows had been opened wide. The child was walking around wearing just a nappy, a bottle half full of milk held firmly in his mouth. Niamh took the chairs and put each one upside down on the table so that she could sweep the floor. She had already put the rugs out on the gravel in front of the porch. Eamon thought of going into the garden, but the sky was low and dark. He turned to warn Niamh, who paid him no attention as she began to clean the windows, that the rugs would get wet if it rained, when he noticed the child looking at him. He looked down and smiled. The child still had the bottle in his mouth, he stared at his grandfather, remaining quiet. Suddenly, he began to scream again, running towards Niamh as though he was about to be attacked. She lifted him.

'Don't worry. You're all right,' she said.

The child continued to cry, even when she carried him into the garden. Eamon wondered what he should do now: he could not sit down at the table since the chairs were resting there upside down. He could not go into the kitchen as Donal and Cathy were there. He could hear the clattering of plates and cutlery and he wondered what they were doing. He could not go into the garden as the child was there in his mother's arms, still crying. He stood there doing nothing, looking out of the window.

He was hungry now, and he would have enjoyed eating his lunch alone. He wondered when they were going to eat and decided to go back into the bedroom and wait for them to call him. He sat beside the window again. He searched the room for a book but could find nothing that he wanted to read.

AFTER lunch the sky became brighter. Cathy was in the kitchen making coffee with a new machine which they had brought with them from Dublin. Niamh was in her room changing the child's nappy. Eamon stood up from the table.

'I think I'll go for a walk while the day is still clear,' he said.

'Are you not going to have coffee?' Donal asked.

'No, I'll take my walk now.'

'We'll be going back early,' Donal said.

'I'll maybe not see you then.' He looked at Donal evenly.

'We'll wait until you come back, if you like.'

Cathy came into the room with the shining new coffee pot. Eamon had his raincoat on and an umbrella in his hand.

'Are you not going to have coffee?' she asked. It sounded like an accusation. He did not reply. There was silence in the room as they both looked at him.

'Are you sure you won't have some?' she asked again.

'I take a walk every day at this time,' he said.

He walked down the lane to the cliff. The eastern sky looked like rain, but he went down to the strand anyway. He did not want to go back to the house. There was a wind blowing from the north which whistled in his ears and made walking difficult. The clouds were inky-black over the sea.

HE woke early to the sound of the wind whistling around the house. When he opened the curtains he discovered that the sky was blue and the light clear and sharp. But the wind was up and it would be hard to find shelter outside. He went quietly down to the kitchen and had a glass of water. As he passed Niamh's door he could hear her talking to the baby and laughing as Michael tried to shout out some words. He was going to ask her if she wanted tea, but worried in case the child began to cry on seeing him.

He drove into the village to get some groceries and the morning newspaper.

'They were all down yesterday,' Jim Bolger said to him.

'Were they in here?' he asked.

'No, I saw them going up the hill. Have they all gone back?'

'No, Niamh and the baby are still here.'

'You'll have plenty of noise then,' Jim Bolger laughed.

The child was sitting on the rug on the living-room floor when he came back. He was playing with bricks. Niamh was in the kitchen.

'Have you had breakfast?' she asked him.

'No,' he said. 'I haven't even shaved.'

He went and sat at the table, paying no attention to the child, afraid that if he tried to lift him or talk to him he would cry. He spread out the paper and began to look through the news pages. The wind was still strong outside. After breakfast he would search the garden for a sheltered spot to put his deckchair. He looked behind and saw that the baby was creeping towards him, but as he caught the child's eye, the boy began to scream as though he had been hit. Niamh came running from the kitchen.

'What happened?' she asked.

'He just looked at me and started to squeal,' he said.

'He's acting strange. It must be very unsettling for him,' she said. 'Mrs Murphy is going to take him every afternoon, so I can do some work.'

'He'll be even more unsettled up there.'

'He's used to women.'

'A small recently-born feminist,' he said and grinned. Niamh did not smile.

AFTER a few days watching Niamh with her son he took the view that she carried him around too much. He said nothing, but avoided the child as much as possible, and suggested to Niamh that they wait until the child went to bed before having dinner in the evening. He went back to his law books, setting up a table in the bedroom, as Niamh had set up a computer in her room, and he became absorbed once more in the intricacies of European law.

He noticed on the fourth morning that Michael had nothing to do: he had been put down on the floor while Niamh had a shower. She asked Eamon to keep an eye on him. The child crawled towards the door, checking to see if he was being followed. Eamon let him go. It was a fine, dry day. He carried out the toy bricks which were on the table and put them on the gravel in front of the house, pretending that he was paying no attention to the child. He acted absent-minded and distracted, making sure not to catch the child's eye. He went back and sat at the window, keeping the child in view, making sure that he did not start eating the gravel. The child played with the bricks for a while and then sat doing nothing.

Eamon went into the kitchen and filled a basin with water. He found a few plastic cups in a press above the sink and put these into the water. He carried the basin out to where Michael was sitting and put it down in front of him without looking at him. He stood back and watched as Michael eyed the water suspiciously and then looked around him to see if there was anyone other than his grandfather watching. The child looked at the water again and then took up a brick and threw it into the water. He put his hand in and fished it out, and then threw it in again, this time with greater force. He was concentrating on the water, so that Eamon could watch him without worrying about the child looking up and seeing him and starting to cry. Michael now put his hand into the water and splashed, ignoring the plastic cups. The sun came out between the clouds; Eamon carried a chair from the living room into the garden, but the child did not notice him, he had become so absorbed in the water.

Niamh came out and stood at the door.

'Did you give him the water?'

'Yes, he had nothing to play with.'

'He is usually afraid of water. He hates having a bath.'

'He's happy enough there.'

'Yes, he does look happy.'

Michael had begun to laugh and squeal as he emptied the water on to the ground with the plastic cups. He protested as Niamh held him to take off his jumpsuit. He refused to wear the white hat she had brought out for him, so she took it back inside and left him there with the water. He played a little longer with the plastic cups, then stood up and tried to empty the basin but fell back and sat down again, trying to turn the basin over from a sitting position. When a tractor passed along the lane he looked up and tried to crawl towards the gate. Then he tried to stand, but the gravel was too hard on his feet. Eamon went over quickly, picked him up and brought him to the gate just as the tractor was going by. He pointed at it, and tried to say 'tractor'; he laughed and clapped his hands at the noise and the smoke, as the tractor went away from them up the lane. As soon as it had gone Eamon put him down again beside the water.

The following day, while Niamh was having her breakfast at the table by the window, Michael followed his grandfather into the kitchen and pointed at the basin. Eamon filled the basin up with water and put it on the kitchen floor, as the day was too dull to go outside.

They watched as the child splashed the water with his two hands.

'How did you get the idea for water?' Niamh asked.

'Your mother used to do it all the time. Do you not remember? You and Donal were put sitting out in the garden with a basin of water. You used to play with it for hours. I remembered it the other day.'

'I don't remember it at all,' she said. 'I must have been too young.'

SHE worked after dinner most evenings; he saw very little of her, he still walked for hours during the day. He had lunch alone in Wexford a few times. In the evenings he read, watched television and had a few glasses of brandy to help him sleep. Once the child was asleep, or out of the house, Niamh's presence was calm, unobtrusive. He noticed that she seemed to dress carefully every day, as though she was working in a city office. When the weather was warm enough she went for a swim in the early afternoon, but the autumn was slowly encroaching, and the nights were becoming cold.

Michael was still fascinated by the water, and came to associate his grandfather with the red basin. One night when he woke and was carried into the living room, he looked at his grandfather and pointed to the kitchen. He wanted his basin of water and cried when he was told that it was too late.

Every night before going to bed Eamon and Niamh had a cup of tea together. At times he found her strangely like her mother in the way she spoke and responded. Sometimes when she smiled she looked exactly like Carmel, even though her face was a different shape and her colouring was different.

'I see there's a For Sale sign at Julia Dempsey's,' she said one evening.

'It's only a few fields,' he replied, 'and the house. But the house is in a terrible state. I don't know who could buy it.'

They said nothing for a while.

'Was Julia Dempsey born in that house?' Niamh broke the silence. He looked up and thought for a moment.

'No. Her aunt and uncle lived there and she came to stay with them and they left it to her.'

'She had a great collection of caps,' Niamh said. 'I never saw her without a cap.' She poured more tea.

'There was a funny thing about her,' Eamon said. 'She always believed that her uncle had money hidden away somewhere.'

'And did he?' Niamh asked. Her way of responding was so like Carmel's that Eamon hesitated.

'She never gave up the idea that it was somewhere,' he went on. 'She told your mother that she'd often wake in the middle of the night and think of a new place where it might be hidden.'

'And she never found anything?' she asked.

'No.' He shook his head. 'I don't think there ever was any money. But all her life she was convinced that her fortunes would change if she could only find it.'

Niamh looked at him, smiled, and nodded her head.

'I never knew that about her,' she said. She was interested in the story and attentive in exactly the same way as Carmel.

A FEW days of Indian summer came to Cush, the temperature higher than it had been all summer. Eamon found it hard to sleep in the heat and woke at first light, feeling tired and worn, with the pain in his back and the base of his neck which became acute when he bowed his head. He tried to do exercises with his arms to loosen the muscles, but it was not enough, and he decided he would have to swim much more to ease the pain.

At half past eight he drove into the village to get the paper. When he came back the sun was already strong over the sea. Michael was sitting up in his high chair being fed, banging his spoon against the plate and laughing. Eamon patted him on the head with the newspaper and he blinked his eyes as though afraid, and then Eamon did it again and he laughed, wanting more.

'I'd love to spend the morning down on the strand,' Niamh said. 'How do you think he'd react to the sea?'

'Have you not tried him?'

'He can just play on the sand. Maybe you would carry his basin down?'

After breakfast they set out for the strand. Michael still refused to wear a hat, and when Niamh tried once more to put it on him he threw it on the ground. They carried a rug and some cushions, a flask of tea and some biscuits and a bottle of milk, in case Michael grew hungry. They also brought towels and togs.

When they came to the turn in the lane they looked over the cliff at the short strand and the sea stretching out for miles, like bright frosted glass, smooth in the strange heat of the September sun. Eamon carried their things while Niamh carried Michael part of the way and then let him down to walk when he insisted. On the strand she tried to put his hat on him again, but he refused.

As he unfolded the rug on the strand and changed into his togs, Eamon wondered which of his children had refused to wear a hat in the sun, or was it he himself. His father, he remembered, wore a straw hat. He saw it once blowing off as his father sat at a table, and paper blowing as well in a sudden gust of wind. He could not remember where this was: he went through each corner of the garden in Cush in his mind, unchanged since the days when the Cullens lived there, but he could not see his father sitting at a table and the wind coming suddenly and blowing his hat off. Where had it happened?

Niamh interrupted his attempt to recall.

'Michael wants you to get him a basin of sea-water,' she said. She had taken the child's clothes off and was rubbing him with sun-tan lotion.

He walked down to the sea with the basin and filled it. The water was warm, much warmer than he had expected. He played with Michael while Niamh went in for a swim. She did not spend long getting used to the water. Her movements were swift and decisive. Michael became absorbed in the sea-water and the sand until he turned over the basin and covered himself with water. Eamon lifted him and held him in his arms. He got a towel and dried him. Suddenly he turned when he heard Niamh's voice shouting to them. She was urging them to come into the water.

'Your mama wants you to go into the water,' he said to

Michael. 'What do you think?' The child rubbed his eyes and squirmed and then smiled. He put his arms around Eamon's neck.

Eamon knew that the water would be a shock for Michael. He stood at the edge for a while, drinking in the sun and watching Niamh as she swam away from them. Then he began to wade out, talking quietly to his grandson to soothe him. He jumped at each wave until Michael began to watch for waves and laugh as each one approached. Eamon held his grandson under the arms and lifted him high so the sun was on his back, and then he lowered him into the water until his legs were wet, holding him firmly all the time. He ducked him down into the water and out again, but it was too much for him. He was frightened. Eamon began to carry him slowly in towards the shore.